Katherine Towler

ISLAND LIGHT

Other books by Katherine Towler

Snow Island

Evening Ferry

Katherine Towler

ISLAND LIGHT

MACADAM CAGE

MacAdam/Cage
155 Sansome Street, Suite 550
San Francisco, CA 94104
www.macadamcage.com

Library of Congress Cataloging-in-Publication Data

Towler, Katherine
 Island light / by Katherine Towler.
    p. cm.
 ISBN 978-1-59692-188-7
 1. Middle-aged women—Fiction. 2. Inheritance and succession—Fiction.
 3. Aunts—Death—Fiction. 4. New England—Fiction. 5. Islands—Fiction.
 6. Domestic fiction. I. Title.
 PS3620.O94I85 2009
 813'.6—dc22
                              2009028908

10 9 8 7 6 5 4 3 2 1

Printed in the United States of America.

Book and jacket design by Dorothy Carico Smith.

For Marie and Leela, the best sisters and friends

PART ONE
October

Chapter One

The island was held in the grip of a silence so pervasive, Ruth felt as though she were leaning into it, a door that would not give. She stood with the bicycle balanced between her legs at the edge of a narrow dirt road, gazing at two houses sitting side by side like crouched cats, an eerily frozen tableau that might have sprung from the last century. The houses were painted a maroon red with black trim. Shutters latched from the outside over the windows gave the places an abandoned look. They were identical, mirror images of each other, two halves of a whole cleaved neatly down the middle. Ruth lowered the bike's kickstand, attempting in her mind to put the pieces back together, but the houses were duplicates of each other in reverse, an optical illusion that would keep repeating itself.

The quiet that surrounded her was louder than the honking of horns and screaming of sirens beyond her windows in the city. She had expected when she came to the island that she would find the absence of people freeing. For the first day or two, she had wandered through the emptiness with the sense that she had become someone else. The blank space that met her on all sides, like the water that circled the island, a clean slate, brought nothing with it—no pressing thoughts of phone calls she needed to return or where she must be by noon. Her mind spread out, still as the wide sweep of sky; she drank in the silence like someone hungry for air. But before long the quiet became too quiet, her own company more oppressive than that of the most annoying friend, and she suspected that she had made a mistake. She was not ready to spend weeks by herself, though she was too stubborn to admit this to the people watching from afar: her mother (who had repeatedly tried to talk her out of the plan), her sister (who never approved of anything she did), and Liza (who sounded vaguely wounded in their nightly phone calls and went on about how the cats missed her).

This morning Ruth had headed out early, determined to get the better of the empty day before her. Her camera bag secure in the milk crate lashed to the back of the bike, she had ridden across the island to find the twin houses she remembered as being somewhere over on the west side. Now she took the camera from the bag, slung it over her shoulder, and waded into the tall grass. As she approached the houses, she saw that the paint was fresh, applied within the last few years at least. She had imagined boards missing on the porch and ripped screens over the doors, but everything was perfectly in order, as though the places had somehow managed to preserve themselves without human intervention for years on end. She climbed the steps of the house on the right and pressed her face to the glass pane in the front door. It was covered by a yellowed square of newspaper, but through a thin gap she could make out the room inside—an old wicker couch against one wall, a table and chairs, a worn hooked rug. When she pulled away, she noticed the upside down date along the bottom of the newspaper: September 18, 1989, a little more than a year ago.

Her examination of the newspaper was interrupted by the sound of a man clearing his throat. Startled, Ruth turned to find someone standing at the foot of the steps.

"The door's locked," he said.

She moved quickly away, embarrassed at being caught with her face pressed to the door.

He raised his lips in a tight suggestion of a smile that did not extend to his dark eyes. "I didn't mean to scare you."

She inched toward the top step. "I'm sorry. I was just curious."

He remained below her in the grass with his hands shoved flat in the pockets of his blue jeans. "Are you a day tripper?"

She gave him a questioning look.

"A day tripper—on the ferry?"

"No. I'm staying here, on the other side of the island."

The man was tall, with a large head that sat awkwardly on his squat neck and wide shoulders out of proportion to his narrow waist. He did not look like the other men on the island, the ones who gathered by the store when the ferry came in. His face was clean-shaven, his stiff blue jeans new, and he wore his hair short instead of in a ragged ponytail. She took him to be about her age, maybe a little older, but not more than forty.

"I didn't mean to be trespassing," she said. "I thought no one lived here."

"No one does, really. I just look after the places. So what are you doing on the island?"

"I came to see about the inn."

"Oh, you're one of the Gibersons."

She nodded. "Well, my mother was a Giberson."

"You planning to sell that place?"

"Why? Are you interested?"

"No. The roof leaks like a sieve."

Ruth had noticed the dark spots dotting the ceiling upstairs, but had not given them much thought.

"I used to work for your aunt sometimes, do stuff around the place." He nodded toward the camera hanging from her shoulder. "I heard you were a photographer."

What else, Ruth wondered, had he heard.

"People around here aren't too crazy about that sort of thing," he said.

"What sort of thing?"

"Publicity. Anything that draws attention to the island. We don't need this place getting discovered and becoming another Martha's Vineyard."

She stared back at him for a moment before answering. "Have you ever been to Martha's Vineyard?"

"No."

"I have. There's not much chance of that happening here. This place is about a quarter the size of Martha's Vineyard, for one thing."

"People can still come here and buy up land and build big houses."

"I don't think my photographs will make them do that."

"No, probably not. I'm just warning you, if you're going to be going around taking pictures, people might get touchy."

Ruth descended the steps. "Thanks for the tip. I'll try to keep a low profile."

He smiled. "Nobody keeps a low profile on Snow Island."

"Nobody does? Or nobody can?"

"Nobody can. It's the nature of the beast."

"I'll remember that," she said.

Ruth crossed the grass and flipped the bike's kickstand up with her foot. He was still standing there giving her that quizzical look, as though he knew even more about her than he had let on. She set the camera in the bag and climbed onto the bike.

"What's your name?" he called after her.

"Ruth."

"I'm Nick. See you around."

She pushed off, wobbling over the pebbled surface of the road, feeling awkward and self-conscious, but he didn't wait to watch her go. He disappeared around the side of the house. After a moment, she heard a lawnmower starting up. The sound echoed off the hillside and seemed to follow her as she went weaving out to the road.

Ruth pedaled slowly, feeling her feet through the thin soles of her sneakers, and tried to shake off her annoyance. What right did he have to warn her against taking photos? Now, she thought, she was back to wanting to be alone, if interacting with people was going to be like that.

She rode past the schoolhouse with its long windows and bell on a pole out front, like something out of the last century. The lookout tower her mother had manned with her friend Alice during the war had been somewhere along this stretch. Ruth's mother used to tell the stories every summer, how the girls sat there for hours with binoculars, scanning the sky for enemy planes. By the time Ruth started coming to the island as a girl, the lookout tower had been torn down, but she had heard the story so often, she felt that it had happened to her, too.

When she was a child, none of the islanders struck her as odd. Everything about the place had a quirky charm, but the man she had just met at the twin houses made her nervous, and so did the other islanders she had encountered down at the store. She felt that she was missing a beat, unable to figure out how conversations with these people were supposed to work.

When she reached the inn, Ruth hauled her aunt's old one-speed Schwinn up onto the porch. The door handle rattled in her hand, loose enough that one good tug would send it to the ground. Almost everything in the inn seemed to rattle and groan and wheeze—the floorboards, the ancient refrigerator, the water pipes. The smell that met her inside was instantly familiar, a mix of aging wood, sea air, and something vaguely fishy, a combination of old clam shells and dried seaweed. A row of battered straw hats hung from pegs on the wall, the same hats that had been there when she was a child. In the living room, the sofa was covered in upholstery she knew all too well from afternoon naps and summer colds. The red plaid had faded, and the arms were bare and frayed, but the room was unchanged. She had the unnerving sense of stepping into another time.

She left her jacket and camera bag on a wicker chair with half the seat missing and climbed the stairs to the second floor, where she and her sister had not been allowed when Ruth was a girl, except on the rare occasions when they had guests and the rooms downstairs were full. The place had not been run as an inn for a long time even then, not since her grandmother's day. Her mother said it was too chilly on the second floor with the wind seeping through the cracks around the windows, and she didn't want them tracking sand all over and bouncing on the old mattresses, but on afternoons when everyone was at the beach, Ruth would sneak upstairs to imagine herself as one of those long ago visitors who draped damp towels over bedposts and ate pot roast and blueberry cobbler together in the dining room.

Ruth made her way to the room at the end of the corridor and opened the door. Light spilled through a tall, narrow window. The curtains were gone, and the mattress on the single bed was bare, showing its pillow ticking stripes, but in every other way the room was the same. A Currier and Ives reproduction, torn from a calendar in the 1950s, remained tacked to the wall, the yellowed edges flaking. A girl and boy faced each other on a snowy lane, the girl in a long red coat and old-fashioned boots, the boy in a cap with a scarf wound round his neck. She held a snowball in her mittened hands. The caption beneath the boy read, "Throw if you dare." Beneath the girl, "Shall I?" It had not occurred to Ruth when she was a child that this was a strange choice of wall decoration for a place inhabited only in summer.

She slumped onto the bare mattress and examined the ceiling. Huge circles of darkened plaster covered one corner, one black ring contained by another, like markings in a tree stump. She could only guess at what it would cost to replace the roof—five thousand dollars at least, probably more. Ruth studied the peeling paint and the cracked windowpanes, and imagined not water dripping from the stained ceiling but dollar bills. This is what it would take to save the inn: money falling like rain.

Her mother had declared she would not put a cent into the place. Besides, it was not hers, as she had repeatedly pointed out. Ruth and her sister had inherited the inn; in Aunt Betty's final act of spite, she had left her own sister out of the will entirely.

Out in the hallway, Ruth ran her eye over the ceiling. No spots here. Maybe a few buckets in the bedrooms would take care of the problem for now. She left the rest of the doors closed against the drafty air and retrieved her camera from the canvas case downstairs. It was always, she reminded herself, hard to get started. She held back, afraid to plunge into the concentrated work of searching for images. Just as she knew this hesitation in herself, she also knew that the cure for her fear and inertia was to grab the camera and head out the door, though knowing what she needed to do and actually doing it were sometimes two entirely different things.

Ruth slung the strap of the Nikon over her shoulder and went outside. It was still early, the morning light almost ghostly, the way she liked it. She zipped up her jacket and took the path behind the inn toward the lighthouse. The sand gave beneath her feet, shifting when she least expected it. She had forgotten that feeling, like walking in slow motion.

Close to the water, the sand was scored with deep lines like the furrowed skin of a puzzled brow. She removed the lens cap, dropped it in her pocket, and brought the camera to her eye.

Chapter Two

Nick woke, as he did most mornings, to the honking of geese. The grating barks, or shrieks, or whatever you wanted to call them (he could not make up his mind exactly what the honking most suggested) seemed to surround the bed, as if the birds had thronged into the house to deliver the hysterical news that one of the flock was dead. He reached for the extra pillow and pressed it over his head. Stretching his legs to the foot of the bed, he lay there, thinking for a moment that maybe he could drift back into the world of sleep. The hazy comfort of that state was so close, but the pillow muffled the anxious chorus of the geese without silencing it, and he found himself, once again, reviewing the options, shuffling through them like a deck of cards: a gun (impossible because, for one, he could never bring himself to fire it, and because it would cause such an uproar among the island's animal lovers); poison (better but still problematic); somehow rounding the birds up and getting them shipped off the island (the only viable solution, though he couldn't quite picture the deck of the ferry strewn with caged geese and didn't know how he would catch the things).

Tossing the pillow aside, he swung his legs over the edge of the bed, reached for a tee shirt lying on the floor, and pulled it on. Why had the geese chosen him? He had a nice little plot of lawn, it was true, but there were plenty of other stretches of grass on the island. Four months. Four months of waking at dawn with a headache. The geese had wandered off a few times, taking up residence over near the schoolhouse, but they always returned. They seemed to view his place as home. His mother insisted they would leave eventually, being migratory birds, and though he wanted to believe her, he was not so sure. Birds had been doing strange things lately. Ian, the local weather expert, said the odd behavior was due to global warming—an interesting theory, except that the past few winters had been colder than usual.

Nick crossed the bare floor and went to the window. There they were, a carpet of gray and black across the lawn, all thirty-two of them. He did not need to count. Sun was just spilling over the tops of the trees, making the frost-covered blades of grass shine. Down below, the surface of the bay, dark and still, waited for the first light.

In the bathroom, he filled the sink with water and shaved. Even if the geese migrated, he feared they would be back the following year, that his little square of lawn was their territory now. All sorts of bizarre plans came to him, like covering the lawn in wooden stakes so the birds couldn't touch down, or encasing the grass in sheets of black plastic. He couldn't bring himself to try any of these tactics, in the end caving in to the sight of them waddling back and forth. They couldn't help being geese. He just wished they would be geese somewhere else. He toweled his face dry, then reached for a pair of blue jeans hanging over the side of the tub and pulled them on.

Downstairs, he pushed play on the tape deck and shoved his feet into a pair of sneakers lying by the couch. John Lee Hooker's voice came crooning out of the speakers. Nick had seen the old bluesman once in a Boston club in the early seventies. He did not so much sing as moan, his head hung over the guitar, looking for all the world like he might fall asleep at any moment.

In the bread box on the kitchen counter, Nick found half a joint propped in the old peanut butter jar lid that served as an ashtray. He didn't remember smoking the first half. He took a match from a pack lying on the counter and sucked the smoke deep into his lungs. With that sweet taste, something went loose inside him, the honking of the geese sluiced off and flushed away. Hooker's gravelly voice, winding through the room, added to the effect, like wavering light seen through water.

Nick smoked the joint down to the end and, through the window over the sink, scanned the trees at the perimeter of the lawn for the doe that came most mornings. He thought he saw movement in the leaves and squinted, but his gaze could not penetrate the darkness of the woods, and the deer, if she was there, did not show herself. He snuffed out the joint, placed the roach in the lid, and sniffed his fingertips. The smell of pot was etched into them. He couldn't get it out, even after scrubbing them with cleanser. He kept vowing he would use that little silver clip to hold the joint, except he could never find the thing.

He scooped up the keys to the truck and pulled his lined denim jacket from the peg on the wall before stepping outside. He was about to close the door when he heard Hooker still mumbling in the house. He went back and shut off the tape deck. The thermometer attached to the side of the house read 38 degrees. His breath hung in the air when he stepped outside again. The geese squawked, darting toward him and then away in a fluttering mob.

"Get lost," he said.

The geese let out a high-pitched ruckus, but moved away as he crossed the grass. They flapped their wings and hopped about uneasily. He avoided the piles of their leavings and climbed into the truck.

He stared through the windshield at the blurred branches of the trees, lost for a moment. Then he remembered. It was morning, and he was going to work. He backed out of the driveway with gravel spinning beneath the tires. The calm surface of the bay stretched on the other side of the dirt road. No breeze. It wouldn't stay this way for long. In another month, the wind would come howling off the bay and rattle the windows in their frames. In some places, winter meant snow, but on the island, winter meant wind. The sound of it was constant, like a beast circling, trying to get in.

He drove along the water past the large houses of Snow Park that dotted the hillside, their windows shuttered and long porches empty. At the crest of the hill, he turned onto a dirt road just wide enough for a single car. Beyond a row of summer houses, he entered a wooded area, and then the view opened again on a spacious lawn and the twin houses set side by side. He pulled onto the grass and cut the engine.

The small notebook was in the glove compartment where he kept it. Nick flipped through the pages of notes until he reached one that was blank, took a pen from his pocket, and wrote the date and beside it the words, "First frost. Cold and clear." He sat gazing vacantly through the windshield before setting the notebook back in the glove compartment and climbing from the cab of the truck.

He made his way toward the twin houses and went up the porch steps of first one, then the other. The doors were locked, as they always were, and a quick circling round the back revealed nothing out of order. It was doubtful anyone other than that girl from the inn had so much as driven by the houses in the past week, but this, like everything else, made no difference to the job he was given to do, and it was, he reminded himself, a job, one for which he was paid. Not handsomely, but money was money.

Back in the truck, he thought about adding "no girl snooping around" beside his observation about the frost, but this would only alarm George Tibbits, the owner of the twin houses, who pored over the notebook for any signs of trouble. Nick's bland notes about the weather, or the deer and fox he found at the edge of the woods, became a toxic brew of tea leaves for George to read, though this was not his intent. He added the comments to distinguish one day from another for himself, not for George.

Nick started up the engine, blasted the heat, and pulled away. At the end of the dirt road, he turned onto the main road that cut across the center of the island. As he approached the schoolhouse, he searched for Rachel's car, as he always did, but her parking space was empty, the door to the schoolhouse closed. Then he remembered it was Saturday. When he crested the hill, the bay stretched in front of him, the water a diamond blue, as though it had gathered all the color it could before the gray days to come. He passed the lighthouse and the inn, where he saw no sign of Ruth other than a bicycle propped on the porch, and drove on to the dock. The ferry was clearly in sight when he pulled into the parking lot by the store, though still a ways from the island. He went inside and found his parents seated in their easy chairs behind the counter with cups of coffee in hand. He skirted the counter, poured himself a cup, and took a donut from the open box beside the coffee maker. The marijuana made him hungry and blurred the edges of things. It gave the morning a nice little glow.

"You got a delivery coming over?" his father asked.

"They're supposed to be sending the lumber for the Lundborns' kitchen," Nick said. "It better be on the boat, or I can't work."

"You're finished with that deck already, huh?"

"Just about."

"Ralph won't forget you. He'll have the lumber on the ferry."

Nick grasped the styrofoam cup in his hand and blew on the steaming surface of the liquid. "I wouldn't be so sure. How's your back?" he said to his mother.

Alice shifted in the chair. "All right."

"All right or painful?"

"Oh, it aches a little. Nothing bad."

Nick gave her an appraising look. "I don't want to see you carrying boxes of groceries off the ferry." He set the cup down and ate the donut in a few bites, licking the powdered sugar from his fingertips.

Outside, the ferry's horn sounded. Nick followed his parents out to the porch. He spotted the pile of lumber off to one side on the boat's deck. A BMW with Massachusetts plates was parked beside it. The car belonged to Nora Venable, the owner of the old mansion out at the end of the island, he assumed. Today was the day she was due to arrive.

Alice nodded toward the BMW. "Is that her? Mrs. Venable?"

"Must be."

"I didn't think she was ever going to show up."

"Neither did I. I guess she wants to see if there's anything left of the place."

"We could have told her there's not much."

"She didn't ask."

Alice gave him a small smile, as if to say that of course Mrs. Venable wouldn't ask.

"That's a damn pretty car," Brock said.

"What did you expect? A Pinto?" Nick said.

Brock laughed. "Not exactly."

Nick descended the porch steps. He met Eddie Brovelli at the foot of the ferry ramp and wondered, as he always did, why Eddie felt it necessary to wear his policeman's uniform at every hour of the day and night.

"Is that your delivery?" he asked Nick with a jerk of his head toward the lumber.

Nick nodded. "For the job at the Lundborns."

"I'll have to get you out to my place one of these days. Rachel's whining for a new kitchen."

Nick tried not to react, either to the mention of Rachel's name or to the characterization of her as a whiner, which struck him as false and unfair. He had never heard Rachel whine about anything. He wished Eddie would stop talking, but of course he didn't.

"Good thing you've got some indoor work lined up," Eddie went on. "Looks like it's going to turn cold."

Nick downed the rest of his coffee. He crushed the styrofoam cup in one hand, tossed it through the open window of the truck, and climbed inside.

"I mean it about taking a look at our place. Come by sometime when you're out that way, see what you think." Eddie leaned back as he spoke, so that the big bowl of his belly stuck out even farther.

Nick said okay, he'd stop by sometime, though he had no intention of doing so. Eddie told him so long and went to join the knot of islanders in front of the store.

Captain Otis lowered the ramp into place. Nick waited until the BMW drove off the ferry, then backed up the ramp. Otis helped him load the lumber into the bed of the truck. The fresh wood smelled of work, of long days when he would be alone with the ringing sound of the hammer. When the lumber was secured, Nick waved to Caleb up in the wheelhouse and drove off the ferry.

His father was still outside, leaning against the porch railing. He pulled over.

"Looks like it'll stay clear," Brock said.

"Maybe. I'm hoping I can get this porch done in a couple of days."

"How are the geese?"

"Noisy. Dirty. A pain in the ass."

"Watch out for Mary Lou Danks. She's been going over there to feed them when she knows you're not there."

"I told her to stop that."

"I saw her there yesterday when I drove past."

"Jesus, that woman is a menace."

"That and a few other things."

Nick told his father he would see him later and took off, going on up the hill. He went the other way around the island this time, by the dump and the Improvement Center, home of the island library and the gathering place for chicken suppers and square dances. His buzz was wearing off too fast. He shouldn't have had the coffee.

Near the turn for Gooseneck Cove he spotted Rachel Brovelli jogging toward him, her feet lifting lightly and surely off the ground. She wore a pair of tightly fitting leggings and a sweatshirt, and her hair, in a ponytail, bobbed up and down. He came to a stop and rolled down the window.

"Hey," he said.

Her face glowed pink, and little beads of sweat lined her upper lip. She continued jogging in place. "Hey."

"Eddie wants me to stop by and see about re-doing your kitchen. He says you've been whining about it."

"That's news to me. I said I wanted a new dishwasher."

"I don't think Eddie really wants me in your house every day."

"No. I'll see what I can do."

She placed her hand on the window rim, her fingers curling toward him. He resisted the urge to cover her hand with his own.

"It's been a while," she said.

"Yeah, it has."

Rachel glanced behind her, as if to make sure no one could hear them. "Eddie keeps saying he's going over to help Silas with that jeep some night, but he hasn't done it yet."

Nick held her gaze. If he looked at her long enough, maybe he could drink in every inch of her body. "He's probably heading this way. I just left him at the dock."

She nodded and let go of the window rim. "See you."

Her words came out not as a casual goodbye, but as a breathy promise. He glanced in the rear-view mirror. No one was coming in that direction, and the road ahead was clear. He considered for one brief, mad moment seizing her and giving her a probing kiss, but she had already moved away from the truck, her feet bobbing from side to side.

"See you," he said.

He turned his head to watch her go. In the leggings, the firm lines of her hips were visible, swaying ever so slightly as she picked up the pace and broke into a run.

Chapter Three

Nora breathed in the thick scent of pine and felt the soft cushion of the needles beneath her feet. Down below, Isabelle walked slowly up and down the beach with her shoes dangling from one hand. After a moment, she glanced up, squinted into the sun, and raised one hand in a wave. "It's cold," she shouted, before turning away from the water toward the path.

It was right to have come. Nora had felt this immediately, from the moment they boarded the ferry. She watched Isabelle climb the path with the light framing her face.

"It's just the way I remember," Isabelle said when she reached the top of the hill breathing hard.

"Yes. It's amazing."

Isabelle let her shoes drop and sank beside them. Nora sat next to her. They did not speak for some time. Nora ran her fingers over the pine needles, so they fanned out in a rippled spiral over the sandy ground.

"I remember the smell."

"Low tide, that's what you smell," Nora said with a laugh.

"No, it's the pines. Something particular about this place."

They were silent again. Now she understood what Gerald had experienced after they spent the hours of the storm in the boat, anchored in the cove. Though at the time she had appreciated the beauty of the cove, she had no interest in the island and could not see why he did. If Gerald had been present, if he were still living, this would have remained the case. They had never been able to experience anything together. They had canceled each other out, nullified what was best in each other.

Isabelle turned her head. "Should we look at the house?"

Nora took in the thin blue of Isabelle's eyes, brushed the pine needles from her hands, and turned away from the water. She waited while Isabelle pulled on her socks and shoes, and they wound down the path on the other side, away from the cove. The wide, golden space of the marsh stretched before them. In the distance, gulls wheeled over the water off the end of the island. The white points of their wings flashed in the light, dipped, then disappeared. At the foot of the hill, they skirted the marsh and crossed an overgrown field ringed with trees.

"I shouldn't have listened to Gerald's family," Nora said. "We should have buried him here. It's the only place he ever really cared about. But even in death he had to have a good address. They saw to that."

"Did you expect anything else?"

"You know, I think Gerald actually believed he could own the entire island if he wanted. God, what grandiose lives we led. Doesn't it make you sick sometimes?"

As they reached a bend in the path, the house came into view beyond a stone wall. Even at a distance, the place looked huge, the fieldstone walls and turreted towers rising strangely out of the tall grass. Isabelle sucked in her breath and took Nora's hand.

"It isn't even local fieldstone," Nora said. "Do you know what it cost to have all that brought over on a barge? He could have built an ordinary house. I begged him to build an ordinary house, but no, this was going to be it, his secret masterpiece tucked away on his very own island."

Hands still linked, they waded into the thick expanse of dead grass. The house had been divided into two parts connected by a long stone terrace. One side had been finished before Gerald's death, the floors laid and the walls painted. He had sent Nora to choose curtains for the windows and furniture for the rooms. They would live in the finished half of the house, in good weather, while the rest of the place was completed. Word of the accident reached her when she returned to Boston. The train had derailed between Stuttgart and Zurich. Gerald was not among the survivors.

His family made it clear they wanted nothing to do with that crazy house on that godforsaken island. They washed their hands of the place once Gerald was gone. Various friends offered to help, and there were numerous trips to the island and experts called in. Nora had circled the stone structure countless times with an assortment of concerned parties. They viewed the place from every angle and considered what it would take to make the house habitable. After a couple of years of telling herself she had to put the contractors back on the job, for Gerald's sake, she began to ask herself why. She did not want to spend even a weekend in the house, though selling the place was out of the question. No one wanted a half-finished mansion on a poor little island they had never heard of, where few people went. So she had left the house just as it was, and it had sunk bit by bit into ruin. In many ways, the abandoned house seemed the most fitting memorial to Gerald.

Nora had always refused to call the place a mansion and persisted in referring to it as "the house on the island." To the islanders, however, it was undeniably a mansion, the largest structure anyone had ever attempted to build on Snow. According to the reports of caretakers over the years, the islanders believed the place was haunted. They claimed to have seen Gerald wandering around on Pine Hill. Nora knew that Gerald was much too sensible to haunt anyone or anything; even in death, he would have refused to get involved with the occult, viewing it as beneath him.

Isabelle tightened her hold on Nora's hand as they came to the edge of the terrace, her thin fingers pressing into Nora's palm.

"I didn't even try to stop him from building this thing," Nora said. "He never listened to me. He never listened to anyone. Come on—let's see how the cottage looks."

Nora released Isabelle's hand and skirted the porch. The caretaker's cottage sat in a clearing behind the shell of the "big house," as Gerald had called it. A maple tree shaded the plot of lawn, where the fading grass was not as high. Nora took a key from the pocket of her pants and unlocked the door, which swung in to reveal a small porch taken up by two Adirondack chairs pulled together as if in conversation. A second door opened into the house. A musty, sweet smell met them inside. Like the scent of molding hay mixed with honey, it was not unpleasant at first, but then a pungent odor emerged, vaguely sickening.

"Mice," Nora said emphatically.

"Mice?" Isabelle echoed.

"Yes. The smell of mice. Unmistakable."

A pot-bellied wood stove sat in one corner of the room with a gas oven next to it. The sink and refrigerator took up the opposite wall. A couch pushed beneath the windows had lost most of the upholstery from its arms and life from its cushions. The square table occupying the center of the room was covered in an assortment of tools—a hammer, loose nails, screwdrivers—and a stack of paper plates and napkins, a few old coffee mugs stained brown around the rims, the crumpled wrappers from candy bars. A portable tape player was perched in the center of it all, with a pile of cassette tapes beside it. Nora strode through the door, pulled up the window shades, and brushed the palms of her hands against her pants. Wrinkling her nose against the smell, Isabelle followed her tentatively inside.

"Not bad is it?" Nora said.

Isabelle nodded unenthusiastically.

Nora skirted the table and peered through the doorway into the back of the cottage. The small bedrooms were nestled side by side, each containing a double bed and an oversized dresser. Heavy curtains pulled over the windows blocked out the light. The bed in one room was made, covered in an old quilt, with two pillows in flowered pillowcases at the head.

"I thought that man I hired as caretaker wasn't staying here," Nora said. "That bed looks as if it is used."

"Doesn't he have a house on the other side of the island?"

"Yes. Well, this place is better than I remembered." Nora turned and brushed past Isabelle.

"Where's the bathroom?"

"The bathroom? I thought Gerald put plumbing in this place." Nora crossed the main room and stepped onto the porch, where she found the bathroom behind a narrow door. A claw-footed tub took up most of the small room. Curled by the drain, its tiny paws pulled stiffly against its body, was a dead mouse.

"Here it is," she called. Nora leaned over the bathtub and lifted the mouse by the tail. It had not been dead long.

"Excuse me," she said as she came face to face with Isabelle in the doorway.

Isabelle let out a shrill scream and ran out onto the lawn. Nora followed her; with a quick flip of the wrist, she tossed the mouse into the bushes.

"Did you have to do that?" Isabelle asked.

"Did you want me to leave it in the bathtub?"

"You didn't have to dangle it in my face."

Nora took her by the elbow and guided her toward the doorway. "It's a dead mouse, not a lion."

Isabelle remained outside while Nora continued her inspection. Nora had not come with the intention of staying. She meant only to circle the big house as she had all those years earlier, to check on the state of the cottage, and to take the ferry back to the mainland, but now she realized that she might remain, that it was, in fact, precisely what she needed to do. As she surveyed the dusty clutter, it occurred to her that this is why she had put off coming to the island for not just years but decades: because a part of her feared that if she did return, she would stay.

There was a passable set of dishes in the cupboards, a few pots and pans, and some old cans of pork and beans. The place needed a thorough cleaning, but that was not much of a challenge. She turned the faucet at the sink. After a moment of nothing but brown dribble, the water ran in a clear stream. If she had water and electricity, what else did she need?

"What are you doing?" Isabelle called from the doorway, where she stood on the threshold.

Nora had her head in the opened oven door. "Seeing what I'll need to do to make this place livable."

She let the oven door shut with a bang, returned to the sink, and shut off the water.

"Livable?"

"That's what I said."

"Who's going to live here?"

"I am."

Nora squeezed past Isabelle. In a rusted can on the floor, she found a rag which she used to dust the seats of the Adirondack chairs. She sank into one and patted the other. The air carried through the open porch door, rich with the smell of salt water and sunlight, the pines and the open blue of the sky. The clean taste of that air was like a vital sustenance she had been missing for years without realizing it.

Isabelle remained standing and regarded her anxiously.

"Why do you think he put the bathroom here?" Nora said. "Not exactly convenient. What if you have to pee in the middle of the night? Must have been an oversight. One of those hordes of people he hired forgot or something."

"Nora." Isabelle folded her arms over her chest. "What do you mean?"

"Mean?"

"About living here?"

"Just what I said."

"But here?"

"Well, I'm not going to rebuild the big house. I think I'll have what's left of it torn down, and I'll build a normal little house in its place. In the meantime, this will do. Wouldn't Gerald be amused if he knew I was going to build something here? There's a certain justice in it, coming full circle."

Nora leaned back and closed her eyes, determined to ignore the stupefied expression on Isabelle's face. The air lapped at her skin like water. In the distance, she heard a car approaching, followed by the slam of a door. She got to her feet as a tall man came striding around the corner of the house.

"Are you Nick?" Nora asked.

He nodded.

"We finally meet." She extended her hand, and he shook it. He was dressed better and looked younger than she had expected. She had imagined the islanders as a bunch of chronic smokers with grayed skin, all of them in vaguely poor health. Nora gestured toward the chair, where

Isabelle remained seated. "This is my friend, Isabelle Whittet."

Isabelle did not extend her hand, and he did not extend his.

"I hope you've found everything all right," Nick said.

"Yes. Well, what is all right? The mansion is falling into the ground, but that was about what I expected. That's no one's fault but my own. It does look like someone might have been sleeping in one of the bedrooms here in the cottage." Nora arched her eyebrows, giving him a pointed look, and went on without allowing him to respond. "I've decided to stay. Here in the caretaker's house. I'm going back to the mainland tonight and then I'll be back with a few supplies. Do you know anyone who could clean this place for me?"

Nick was clearly surprised, though he made an effort to keep his face composed. "How long are you planning on staying?"

"A month or two, maybe longer. I think I'll have the mansion torn down and build something in its place, but I guess we can't do much on that until spring. Well, maybe the tearing down. Maybe I could get that done this winter. What do you think?"

"Sure, but that's a big job. A job for somebody with the equipment."

"And no one on the island has the equipment?"

"Not really."

"I'll see what I can do over on the mainland. Do you have anyone to recommend?"

"There's Healey. Healey Construction. They do a lot of big jobs."

"What about the cleaning?"

"My mother does cleaning. Alice McGarrell, down at the store. She should be there when you go back on the ferry."

"I'd still like you to work for me," Nora said. "I might need someone to keep an eye on the place when I'm not here, and there may be other things. I'll keep paying you as I have been. Can I hire you on an hourly basis for anything else?"

"Sure."

"Fine, then. I'll call to let you know when I'll be back."

He mumbled a quick thanks and turned to go, like a schoolboy dismissed at the end of class. Nora tried not to smile until he was safely gone, his broad back disappearing beyond the wall of the house.

A gull let out a shrill-pitched shriek as it flew over the roof of the cottage. Nora raised her eyes to follow the path of its flight with the sense that, like the bird, she was headed somewhere at last.

Chapter Four

"I guess they call this place the Priscilla Alden because no one's cleaned it since the 1600s." Nora eyed the sheets disdainfully as she pulled back the bedspread and slid into the double bed beside Isabelle.

Isabelle sat propped against the pillow, a book open on her raised knees and her eyes fixed on the page, though Nora wondered if she was really reading or just using the book as an excuse to ignore her. Nora knew this mood all too well, the sneering silence, the rigid pulling away, as if Isabelle were inwardly flinching every time Nora looked at her.

"The moon's almost full," Nora said. She turned her gaze toward the window. She had tugged on the tattered shade when they entered the hotel room and sent it flying.

"Oh, Really?" Isabelle made the clipped response without raising her eyes from the book, then turned the page deliberately, so the paper rattled ever so slightly.

"Isabelle." Nora ran her hand over the folded top of the sheet. It had a very odd feel, more like cardboard than cloth. "I meant for you to come with me to the island."

"You did? I wouldn't have guessed it."

"Do I have to spell everything out?"

"You were planning this all along, weren't you?"

"No. It just occurred to me. When we got there and I saw...how wonderful it was."

"It didn't occur to you, of course, to ask what I thought."

"I assumed you knew that you were included."

"Included." Isabelle let out a sputter of exasperation. "For Christ's sake, Nora. I can't leave Henry. You know that."

"They take perfectly fine care of him. You could leave for a couple of weeks, a month, and he would never know the difference."

"Nobody knows what makes a difference and what doesn't. That's why I have to be there."

"Fine. Then don't come with me."

Nora stepped from the bed and pulled on her bathrobe. In a moment Isabelle would be crying, the tears sliding noiselessly down her cheeks, her nose slowly turning red. Nora reached for the toothbrush and tube of paste on the dresser and one of the folded towels. She let herself out into the hallway, ignoring Isabelle's pleading eyes. She hated that drowned look.

Nora made her way along the narrow corridor with its dingy walls. An overhead light at either end of the hallway provided dim illumination that only made the walls look grayer. The door to the bathroom was marked with a rusted metal sign, once painted blue, that proclaimed in white letters *Water Closet*. The attempt to give the decaying hotel a European air was not a success.

She reached for the door handle, but it did not give. She remained there in front of the door for a long moment, half-expecting it to open of its own accord, before she heard water running on the other side. She had not imagined there was anyone else staying at the Priscilla Alden Hotel. The lobby had been entirely deserted each time they passed through, the faded carpet and peeling walls looking like the abandoned set for a movie made long ago. A large sign affixed to the front of the hotel proclaimed that H. R. Lamprey Real Estate would be converting the hotel to condominium apartments and selling them. This struck Nora as a formidable undertaking. Barton was a charming little town in its way, with its picturesque main street and houses dating back to the 1700s, but it did not have the flair of towns over the border in Massachusetts.

There was something about Rhode Island. No matter how many condominiums and fancy restaurants came in, the state could not shake a

1950s feel and look. A battered pickup truck would always be the vehicle of choice here. Gerald's family had been appalled by his plans to build a house on Snow for this reason more than any other: it was in that low-class state populated by nothing but Italian Catholics. Their accent was so atrocious, you could barely understand the people when they talked. Newport could not redeem the rest of the state, and besides, he was not building in Newport. If he had chosen anyplace in Massachusetts or Connecticut or on Long Island, his family might have been forgiving, but an unknown island in the center of Narragansett Bay was beyond acknowledging.

Nora leaned against the wall next to the open window at the end of the hallway and felt the cool air on her bare legs. Naturally Isabelle was angry, but then she was often angry. She did not like sudden changes – the unpredictable, the spontaneous gesture. She wanted to know what was going to happen in advance, so she could be prepared. Or rehearsed, you might say, if you were inclined to put a cynical spin on it. Nora supposed that in some fundamental way she loved Isabelle for being steady and calm and loyal. Nora had long ago recognized that she relied on these qualities of Isabelle's far more than she cared to admit. Still, at times like these, she wanted to grab Isabelle by the shoulders and turn her in another direction.

The bathroom door opened with a rattle. An old man with a white stubble of beard on his chin leaned on a cane and stared past her as if he did not see her. His face, puffy and white, had a doughy look. He held a towel between the long fingers of his free hand as if attempting not to touch it.

"Excuse me," she said. "I was just waiting."

He nodded and turned down the hall. He walked unsteadily, his weight on the cane, with the towel fluttering beside his leg. He wore loose-fitting warm-up pants with white stripes down the sides, the sort that everyone wore during the running craze of the 1970s, and a cardigan sweater that flopped at his waist. Nora wondered briefly what in the world he was doing at the Priscilla Alden before she stepped into the bathroom and secured the door behind her.

A large bathtub took up half the room. The curtain circling the tub, pulled back, revealed a rusted shower head that looked like an upturned watering can. The tub was dry. Apparently the old man had not taken a bath. Nora opened the tap and let the hot water run. The steam rose and clung to her face. This was what she needed, to lower herself into the hot water and let it close over her for hours, until her skin was as white and doughy as the skin of that man and her insides were the same—bleached, washed, empty.

She longed, as she always did, for that quick sense of discovery, the feeling that something new waited around the corner, though exactly what this might be she was often hard-pressed to say. Nora realized there was a certain foolishness to a woman having such thoughts at the age of seventy-four. She should be content at last, able to let go of all that restless striving, but here she was, suddenly taken with staying on the island, certain of the brilliance of her plan, while Isabelle sat there brooding about Nora's self-indulgent disregard for everyone but herself. Alienating Isabelle had not been her intention, of course. She did not come up with her inspired ideas—or whims, as Isabelle called them—because she was trying to exclude Isabelle or anyone else. They were an essential piece of who she was, and it was not her fault if no one was willing or able to go along with her.

Nora undressed, hung her nightgown and bathrobe from a hook on the back of the door, and stepped over the side of the tub. The water was so hot it felt cold against her skin, like icy hands pressed the length of her body. She slipped in up to her neck and rested her head against the high back of the tub. Her father was the only one who had ever fully and truly understood her, but he died when she was twenty, and there was no one to take his place, until Isabelle Whittet appeared on the deck of Gerald's boat one bright September morning. Returning to the island now, Nora had been certain that Isabelle knew what this trip meant to her and what it could mean to stay, but then at the last moment, like so many times before, Isabelle pulled back, unable to take the final step with her.

Nora closed her eyes and inhaled deeply. Isabelle would always be ashamed of her. It was inevitable, and not just because of the long secret of their lives, a secret that now seemed quaint and old-fashioned, a relic of another time. Nora knew she should give Isabelle credit. For all her deliberate caution, she had loved Nora on stolen afternoons and weekends that over the years became all the sweeter because they were stolen. Yet what was the sense of it now? Who cared, in this day and age, about a couple of aging lesbians and their clandestine affair? Who could they hurt or shock now? It wasn't just that word *lesbian*, a word Isabelle hated and refused to use, that made her ashamed of Nora. Something even more basic was at work. Isabelle recoiled from the way Nora would go to bed without brushing her teeth sometimes, or her habit of speaking too loudly in public places, or her overly familiar air with strangers.

The water was growing cold. Nora raised her foot, gripped the hot water faucet with her toes, and turned it. After a moment, the water sent ripples of warmth toward her. She would return to the island with cleaning supplies and sheets and towels. She would make that little cabin her own. This much was clear. What Isabelle chose to do was another matter, one Nora could not help.

She ran a hand back and forth in the water, so that the warm currents moved over her stomach and legs. She savored the feel of the water a minute longer, then pushed herself up and stepped out of the tub. The towel had the same cardboard quality as the sheets. She wrapped it around her shoulders and thought of all the bathtubs she had made use of in all the hotels where she had stayed for a night or two. She liked the thought that there were still places for her to discover, still views from bathroom windows she had not seen.

Chapter Five

It was dark by the time Nick left the house and went rattling over the dirt road out to Gooseneck Cove. He gave a quick glance at Rachel's place as he drove past. Eddie's car was gone, but a lamp shone in the kitchen window. Tonight they might be in luck. Beyond the white circle cast by the headlights, fronds of marsh grass moved in the breeze. He reached the cove and searched the still surface of the water. There were no boats anchored for the night, just the lights of the mainland in the distance, winking on the horizon.

Nick parked the truck in the shadow of the pines and took the path into the field. The dead grass brushed his legs, sending up a low rustling that sounded like a smattering of applause. Against a black sky dotted with stars, the stone walls of the mansion took on a menacing look. He scanned the ground for signs that anyone had been there. A couple of weeks earlier, he had found the remains of a fire in the dirt below the terrace. He suspected the oldest of the Hershel and Manning kids, though he had not seen them out this way. He would have spoken to their parents if they were not so sanctimonious, smugly believing that they were going to heaven and he was going to hell. They were probably right. He would no doubt go to hell when the time came, but that was no business of theirs.

Nick skirted the crumbling mansion. He had found candy and gum wrappers, spent matches and cigarette stubs, and the occasional used condom, an offering from the summer kids, but tonight the path was clean. Gerald Venable's stone palace had been reduced to this, the place where the teenagers came to get into trouble and scare each other with ghost stories. Nick was not entirely sure why Nora Venable had hired him as a caretaker, since there was little left to care for, but he did not complain. She paid well and sent the checks on time.

He left the shadow of the mansion and went around to the caretaker's cottage in back. Inside, he flipped on the overhead light and crossed the room to pull the shade over the window. He didn't like the feeling that there might be someone out there watching him through the glass.

In the bedroom, he knelt down and slid the transmitter, receiver, and turntable from under the bed, and then a wooden crate full of records. He carried the things into the main room, one by one, and set them on the table, pushing the tape player aside. It didn't appear that Nora Venable had discovered the equipment beneath the bed or noticed the antenna attached to the roof. If she made good on her plan to return, he would have to come up with another location or shut down the operation entirely.

When he had the transmitter hooked up and everything assembled, he flipped through the albums and pulled out the ones he wanted. The covers were worn and frayed at the edges, the images faded to white in the corners. He ran his fingers over them, the feel of worn cardboard bringing back the years when he spent hours in the used record stores in Boston.

Nick turned on the receiver and the microphone, and took a seat at the table. "Good evening, everyone," he said into the mike, making his voice as deep as possible. "You're listening to WBAY, Jolly Roger radio, the music of the bay. It's cool out there tonight, 37 degrees by my thermometer, with just a touch of wind. I haven't been able to visit with you for a while now, but I hope you all are tuned in tonight. I know I'm not predictable, but then most things aren't predictable, are they? I'll always be your Jolly Roger, pirate of the airwaves. Okay, but you don't tune in to listen to me ramble on. You tune in for the music. Tonight I'm going to do something a little different. No blues, for a change. We're going to go on a journey down memory lane with some tunes off debut albums from

1967, '68, and '69. These are, as they say, seminal works, and they're worth another listen."

He took a record from the sleeve and set it on the turntable. "This first cut is an oddball piece of progressive rock that I can't resist from It's a Beautiful Day. That's the name of the group and the album. They were a band out of San Francisco, only had a couple of records, and this one, their first, came out in 1969." He switched on the turntable and lowered the needle. "'White Bird' is the title of this number."

After a moment of scratchy dead space, the needle settled into the groove. It was a sound whose days were numbered, though he was not a fan of compact discs. The music felt canned and flat. CDs did not have the expansive sound of vinyl. The drama was gone, too, the lovely tension as you lowered the needle to the record and lined up the right cut.

He switched off the microphone, propped his legs on the table, and took a bottle of beer from the pocket of his jacket, listening to the airy opening of "White Bird." He gulped down the beer, thinking how revelatory he had once found this music. The memory would be comical if he did not still find the song slightly hypnotic, if he did not catch himself following along, mouthing the words, "White bird must fly or she will die." Everything was a metaphor for something back then, the smallest details of daily life fraught with hidden meanings. In his upstairs room on hot summer nights, playing the album over and over, he was that white bird trapped in a cage, and beyond the confines of the house, where his parents slept down the hall, beyond the stultifying boundaries of the island, there was a whole country trapped in a cage, rattling the bars, trying to get out. His thinking had been simplistic, like the music, but there was a purity to what he believed then, just as there was a purity to the lilting violins in "White Bird." He didn't want to reject either now, the thinking or the music, though both were so easily parodied.

The song came to an end. Nick reached for the needle and switched on the microphone. "That was It's a Beautiful Day doing 'White Bird' off their 1969 album. Trippy music, we used to call it. So how is everybody tonight? We're headed into that dark time of the year. We need a little music to keep us company. Okay, let's get right back to it. I'm going to

1967 now. I know I said I wasn't playing the blues tonight, but this is an early experiment with blues from a groundbreaking rock band. From Jefferson Airplane's debut album, *Surrealistic Pillow*, here's 'In the Morning.'"

He took another gulp of beer and wondered who might be listening. The antenna, rigged up on the roof with a clear path over the water, carried enough of a signal that on a still night, his show could be picked up over on the mainland, up to ten miles away. He liked to imagine strangers listening in little apartments along the shore, maybe drinking a beer like he was, trying to figure out why they had never heard this station before. He didn't risk being on the air for more than a few hours. Some weeks he only came on air once or twice. If he became more regular than that, someone on the mainland might try to figure out where the illegal broadcast was coming from. It was doubtful the FCC would come around with questions, but Nick didn't want to take too many chances. Eddie Brovelli, and just about everyone else on Snow, knew that Nick was broadcasting somewhere on the island, but they kept it to themselves, taking a secret pride in having their own station. Eddie was not such a bad guy. He was capable of looking the other way, especially when minor offenses, like pot or pirate radio, were involved.

A rattle sounded at the outer door. "Nick," a voice said from the other side. "It's me."

He went and unlocked the door to find Rachel on the porch, leaning her bicycle against the wall. She slipped inside, and he bolted the door, then wrapped his arms around her and kissed her. Beneath the layers of clothing, he felt her breasts pressed to him. Already he could see her naked, those breasts uncovered. She held her hand to the nape of his neck, running her fingers over the ends of his hair, and broke away. "I've been sitting in my house listening to static on that damn radio every night this week," she said.

He smiled. "My mother keeps insisting I come over for dinner."

"It's cold in here."

"You want me to start a fire?"

"No. I don't have long. Eddie's over at Silas's."

"It'll take them till tomorrow morning to get that jeep running."

He pulled her to him again and kissed the tip of her nose as he slid the jacket down her arms. He was about to start on her blouse when he realized the song was ending. He grabbed the needle and turned on the microphone. "That was The Jefferson Airplane for you, 'In the Morning' from *Surrealistic Pillow*," he said into the mike. "We're listening to debut albums from 1967, '68, and '69 tonight. Those were some good years, musically speaking at least. All right, now I'm going to play a whole side for you. On the original vinyl, here's *Cheap Thrills* from Big Brother and the Holding Company. This came out in 1968."

He switched one record for another and set the needle in place. The silent gap of dead air lasted only a couple of seconds. He turned off the microphone, went back to Rachel, and unfastened the buttons down the front of her blouse. She grasped his belt buckle, easing the tongue from the clasp, and pulled at the zipper on his jeans. They shed their clothes quickly, pushing awkwardly at pants and underwear, shoving them to their feet and stepping out of them.

She ran her hands over his back with a light, teasing touch. He slipped his tongue into her mouth and brushed his fingers through the strands of her hair. It had turned almost completely gray, but she wore it long, past her shoulders. He loved her for refusing to cut her hair like all the other women her age. He stepped back, taking in the sure lines of her body. He wanted to linger, but there was no time, and she pulled him to her again, wrapping her legs around him and straddling his waist. He carried her to the bedroom and lowered her to the bed.

They were practiced at this now, knowing what worked, what each of them wanted. They were practiced, too, at timing their lovemaking to the side of an LP. The music was their alibi. Everyone on the island listened for Nick's broadcasts. How could he be stealing off with Rachel when he was on the air?

They drew it out as long as possible, almost reaching the brink and then pulling back. He thought of it as a slow, excruciating dance, building step by step until the sweet intensity became too much to bear, and her head dropped back, her nails digging into his back. A moment later, he followed, letting go inside her, and they fell against the pillow. He lay next to her, stroking her hair, until the last strains of music died out, and the scratchy sound of the needle took its place.

He hurried into the other room, switched on the mike, and lifted the needle. "That was side one of *Cheap Thrills* from Big Brother and the Holding Company with the late, great Janis Joplin. You're listening to Jolly Roger radio, the voice of the bay. I'm cueing up side two of this album for you now, which ends with the live version of 'Ball and Chain' recorded at the Monterey Pop Festival in 1967. You'll notice the crowd is completely silent until the end of this piece. That's because nobody had ever heard of Janis Joplin. After this performance, everybody had. Here they are—Big Brother and the Holding Company with Janis Joplin."

Rachel emerged from the bedroom once he had switched off the mike. "Very suave."

"What?"

"Standing there with your big dick at attention."

"They can't see me."

"It's a good thing."

She reached for her clothes, extracting the bra and panties and blouse from the pile on the floor, and dressed quickly. Nick retrieved his boxer shorts and pulled them on, followed by his jeans. She took his hand and squeezed it, then stepped into her corduroy pants. As she slipped her arms into the sleeves of her jacket, she leaned forward, giving him a series of darting kisses. "Nice seeing you."

"Nice seeing you, too."

He grabbed her, holding her tight for one last kiss. She broke away, unbolted the door, and let herself out. He watched as she wheeled the bike down the porch steps and pushed it over the grass. After a moment, when he could no longer make out the shape of her body moving off in the dark, he closed the door.

The beer was warm, but he downed the rest of it. Janis Joplin crooned and screeched, her voice beyond the range of what seemed humanly possible. This album would never seem dated to him. Joplin had reached artistic heights that stood outside time or style. You could say she paid for this achievement with her life, but maybe that was overstating the case. Maybe she just had a problem with booze and drugs.

Outside, he heard the wind kicking up. It could play havoc with the signal. When it was windy enough, his show didn't reach the other end of the island, but tonight he didn't care if no one was listening. He was playing the music for himself.

Chapter Six

The hamburgers sizzled in the pan. Alice stood at the stove, spatula in hand, staring at the beads of grease that dropped from the edges of the meat. The kitchen window was dark, the pool of black on the other side impenetrable. She seemed to forget each year how early and how completely the dark fell.

Brock rattled the newspaper. "The school department's making noises about the schoolhouse again."

Alice turned her gaze from the stove. "What's it now?"

"The cost per pupil. It's the highest in the state. They're saying they can't justify that kind of expense for ten kids."

Alice pressed the burgers with the spatula to squeeze out more fat. "We didn't used to have these problems. We just hired a schoolteacher. The people on the mainland ignored us. We did our thing, and they did their thing. Everyone was happy."

"Now you've gotta pay a living wage. You've gotta give them health insurance and a pension and all that crap." Brock snorted. "Who's got a pension on this island besides Eddie and Rachel Brovelli?"

"You can't blame them for being smart."

"Smart, my ass. They just know how to work the system."

Alice thought that getting the only jobs on the island, the police chief and school teacher, that came with benefits was a form of being smart. She didn't begrudge them. Besides, she wouldn't want their jobs, and neither would most of the islanders.

She took a can of green beans from the cupboard and opened it with the electric opener, a gift from Brock one Christmas. The limp tendrils fell into the pot. People on the island did not like to be told what to do and when to do it. They did not like to answer to a boss or a committee. That's why she had spent her life running the store, on her own time and in her own way. The profits, and losses, were all hers.

The burgers turned gray in the pan. She flipped them and gave them a few minutes longer. The arguments were the same from one year to the next—the threat of closing the schoolhouse, the high property taxes, the blind eye the Barton town council turned on the island. Some of the islanders, her own son included, had proposed seceding from the mainland.

Alice slid the burgers onto the buns waiting on the plates. The heated green beans took on an even limper quality. She spooned them from the pan and said, "That girl looks so much like her mother."

"What girl?" Brock said as she set the plate in front of him.

"Ruth. The one staying at the inn. I keep thinking I'm seeing Lydia when she walks into the store."

"Lydia never had a crew cut and big, baggy pants like that."

"You know what I mean. She doesn't have a crew cut anyway."

"Close to it."

"Her hair's just short."

Brock turned the ketchup bottle upside down and slapped it with his palm until the ketchup landed in a huge splat on his burger. The ketchup oozed out around the edges of the bun as Brock pressed the burger between his large fingers and took a bite. He chewed noisily for a minute. "When was the last time you heard from Lydia?"

"I don't know. A long time ago."

"She's done with the island, huh?"

"She was done with the island when we graduated from high school."

"She must be pretty steamed about the will."

"If Betty had left the inn to her, she would have sold it or torn it down faster than you could blink. Nick says the place needs a new roof."

"That would be a nice job for him."

"He's already doing that kitchen renovation."

"With this economy, who knows if anyone will be hiring in the spring? He needs all the work he can get."

Alice smiled. Brock had recently become an expert on the economy.

"Well, things ain't getting any better," Brock said.

"No, but the economy on Snow stays pretty much the same, good times or bad."

"Not if the summer people don't have money to spend." Brock dabbed at his mouth with a napkin, removing a large smear of ketchup. "And if house prices keep dropping."

"It's obscene what people are paying for houses."

"Sure, but people who spend money like that for a house have plenty to spend down at the store."

Their forks clacked against the plates. Alice saw no need to point out that the wealthy people who had discovered the island in recent years did not shop much at the store. They wanted the gourmet items she didn't carry.

Brock finished a last mouthful of beans and stretched his legs beneath the table. He remained in his seat while Alice ate what was left on her plate and cleared the dishes.

"That ain't dessert," Brock said as she set a bowl of cut fruit in front of him.

"It's all we've got."

"No ice cream?"

"No ice cream."

"Are you trying to starve me?"

"I'm trying to make you healthy."

He laughed. "I don't know why I should take up being healthy at my age."

"That's precisely why you need to pay attention to these things."

"Hell, our parents went to the grave eating any damn thing they pleased."

"Our parents worked harder than we did. They worked outside every day. They burned off the calories."

"Your mother sat on her can all day at the store."

This, Alice had to admit, was the truth, but her father, a quahogger, was out on his boat from sunrise to well into the afternoon. Brock accepted the bowl of bananas, apples, and melon she served and switched on the radio on the shelf behind the table. Alice listened to the static as she helped herself from the fruit bowl. A couple of stations came in from the mainland, fuzzy and broken up, before he found a clear signal.

"That's him," Brock said.

"You can't get any other stations that end of the dial normally."

"Yeah, that's him. That's the kind of weird stuff he plays."

Brock finished eating the fruit, and she carried the bowls to the sink, which she filled with soapy water. She plunged her hands in as the song ended, and Nick's voice sounded in the room.

"That was The Jefferson Airplane for you, 'In the Morning' from *Surrealistic Pillow*. We're listening to debut albums from 1967, '68, and '69 tonight."

It always surprised Alice to hear Nick's disembodied voice beside her in the kitchen. He sounded the same and not the same, his cadence slower and more melodious, as if when he made his broadcasts, he had all the time in the world. He sounded older, and more certain of himself.

She placed the last piece of silverware in the dish drainer and went to sit beside Brock on the couch. He held the newspaper folded as he gazed at the blank surface of the window. Alice thought of the Sunday services she attended at the Union Church when she was a child. Listening for Nick on the radio was a bit like being at one of those services, when the islanders waited in patient silence for the visiting pastor to begin, careful not to break the mood, as if they were collectively holding their breath. Except that Nick's radio broadcasts were a lot noisier, especially tonight. She wasn't sure she could listen to the dizzying music much longer.

Brock's head fell back and his eyes closed. She took the newspaper from his hand and scanned the headlines. "Bush Issues Ultimatum to Saddam Hussein Over Kuwait Invasion." She started on the first sentence of the article, but stopped, unwilling to read more. Another war. She felt a numb dread at the thought of it. She took the afghan from the back of the couch and draped it over Brock, then shut off the radio.

On the stairs, she paused at the window on the landing. The beam from the lighthouse swung across the glass and moved on, out into the dark. She imagined Nick in his house on the other side of the island, sorting through his record albums and fussing with his sound equipment. Pirate radio, he called it. She preferred "unlicensed." She worried about him, she knew, more than she should. Brock was always saying, "He's a grown man, for God's sake," but grown men, as every mother would attest, were still their children.

In the bedroom, Alice lifted her flannel nightgown from the hook on the back of the door and set it on the bed. As she undressed, she made a mental list of the men on the island. Some of them were young, but not, she hoped, young enough to consider the military. Snow Island did not need to send any more men, or women, off to war. She climbed under the covers and reached for her book on the bed stand. Downstairs, Brock let out a long rattle of a snore.

Chapter Seven

Alice stood inside the door, surveying the caretaker's cottage. She would have to scrub the walls to get the grime from the woodsmoke off them—if it was possible to get it off. She did not think she had ever been inside the cottage before, though she had wandered through the empty rooms of the mansion a few times, on summer nights when she and Brock brought the kids down to Gooseneck Cove for an evening swim, before there was a caretaker watching over the place. Despite the strange and impulsive whim Mrs. Venable had taken to staying at the cottage, she had struck Alice as someone who would be particular about the cleaning. She was probably accustomed to having such things done for her and done right.

Alice brought in the bucket of cleaning supplies and the vacuum she had left on the porch and set to work, dusting and vacuuming first, then filling the bucket with water and taking a sponge to the walls. The soot ran down the wood paneling in snaking lines. With prolonged scrubbing and repeated applications of soap and water, she was able to remove most of the black residue. She was wiping down the walls one last time when she heard the unmistakable purr of Nick's truck outside. It did not rattle and belch like the others on the island.

"You're washing the walls?" he said as he stepped through the door.

"They were pretty bad."

"Don't overdo it."

"I'm not sure it's possible to overdo it for Mrs. Venable."

"She can't be too picky. She's moving into this place. That tells you something."

"I'm not sure what."

Nick scanned the room, as though looking for something he had left there. "She's sending some furniture over on the ferry tomorrow."

"I hope she's paying you well enough."

Nick shrugged. "Is she paying you well enough?"

"I suppose."

Alice went back to wiping the sponge over the wall. Nick took a plastic shopping bag from his back pocket and began scooping the cassette tapes scattered across the table into it. She had wondered if the tapes were his and wondered further why he would want to listen to music here. She had thought he only drove by occasionally to check on the place.

"I found the remains of a fire in the grass over on the far side of the mansion," Nick said. "A couple weeks ago."

"Who would be having a fire out here?"

"The Hershel and Manning kids, the oldest boys."

"I didn't think their parents let them out of the house after dark."

"I'm not sure those kids are the saints their parents make them out to be."

"Are you going to speak to them?"

"It's not exactly a conversation I want to have. Fred Hershel doesn't have much use for me."

"He's like that with everyone."

"Holier than thou?"

Alice wrung the dirty water from the sponge into the bucket. "We never had people like them on the island before."

"You mean religious nuts."

"I don't know that I would call them that."

"I would."

"I just meant people with such strong opinions, people who think they're different from everyone else."

"Right. Religious nuts."

Nick went into the bedroom. She could hear him doing something, though she wasn't sure what. Smoothing sheets, maybe, except she didn't think the beds were made. He emerged and said, "I guess Mrs. Venable will be back in a couple of days. She wants me to get the old furniture out and the new stuff in. You're not straining your back, are you?"

"No. I'm taking little breaks. What about you? You should get Cliff and Ian to help you rip out that kitchen."

"I'd rather work by myself."

She gave him a pointed look. "Moving all that heavy stuff around, hauling refrigerators. You could hurt yourself."

"I do one thing at a time. I'm careful."

"Cliff and Ian could use the work. They aren't busy now."

"They're quahogging again."

"What about the schoolhouse? You could give up that job. You could let somebody else have it."

"I don't want to give up working at the schoolhouse. What's with you? Have you got some mission to find work for all the shiftless men on the island?"

"No, I'm not an employment agency." Alice said these words knowing they were not quite true. Down at the store, she heard everything. If someone was looking for work or just about anything else, she knew.

"Did Cliff and Ian say they needed work?" he asked.

"No, but they started paying with food stamps last week. It's a little earlier than usual."

"They should stop spending all their money betting on pool games and poker. And calling those 900 porn numbers."

"I don't know anything about that."

"Yes, you do. They ran up a thousand dollars on those calls last winter."

Alice had done her best to forget the incident, when the men ran a phone line through the window of one of the summer places and spent every night on the phone sex lines. The phone company forgave the bill after protest by the owners, who declined to press charges. She could not figure out how you had sex over the phone. The whole thing was so strange and sordid, she had pushed it out of her mind.

"I can come and help you in a while," Nick said. "I just want to get the debris cleared out at the Lundborns so I can get it carted off on the ferry."

"That's all right. I'll be done in another hour or so."

Nick said goodbye and left. The table was clear now, empty of the bits of trash and nails and screws, too. Alice listened to him driving off as she carried the bucket of dirty water outside and dumped it in the grass. She could make out a cloud of dust on the road, though she could not see the truck itself. After a few moments, the dust cleared when Nick took the bend by the cove, the sun glinting off the shiny hood of the vehicle. She watched the truck fade from view and thought of her other son, the one Nick did not know about. Back in the cottage, she filled the bucket and carried it into one of the bedrooms.

He came to her at odd times, when she was stepping out of the shower or switching off the light beside the bed, convinced that her mind was absorbed in something else entirely. Even now, after so many years, she saw her other son as an infant – the tiny red face, wrinkled and splotched, the miniature features squashed together as he let out a rending cry, the little hands balled together in fists she could not pry open. As she took the sponge to the wall in the bedroom, she played an old and familiar game, trying to imagine what he might look like today if he were still alive. A big if, one that hung over her, though she felt certain he was still out there, in the world somewhere. The sense of him had never left her. Whether he ever thought of her, wondered who she was and where she might be, she could not say. She might be a complete blank to him, someone who had never existed. It was his right to think of her this way.

She called him Peter when he was born, and she still called him this, though he had been given another name by another mother. Alice had imagined every stage of his life over the years—his first steps, his first day at school, and later, his graduation from high school, maybe his marriage and the birth of his own child. She had not imagined the parents who adopted him. That was too difficult, too cruel. In her mind, he grew up in a bubble, alone, a spirit barely touching his feet to the earth. They would have called him Peter if…another one of those *if*'s. Her life was littered with them. She remembered the lookout tower, where she and Lydia had perched, searching the sky for planes during the war. The lookout tower had become so rickety and unsafe that it had been torn down. When she thought back over her life, it was like being in the tower again. She stood far above the years, gazing down on them like the road circling the island, and at each turning point, there was another *what if*. What if her father had not fallen overboard on that cold March day when she was nine and drowned? What if Ethan Cunningham had not been so tall and slim, so mysterious and handsome? What if she had not been so young?

Ethan was a stupid, misguided mistake, but she had long since forgiven herself for that foolishness. It was harder to forgive herself for being so blind to Pete Giberson. What if she had said yes to Pete when she had the chance? And what if Pete had come home from the war? She would have led a different life. Nick and Ellen and Lizzie would not have been born. She would not have grown into the comfort of her marriage to Brock.

The dirt ran down the wall behind the bed. Alice knelt on the mattress, catching the rivulets before they fell behind the headboard. The bucket of water was already clouded and dark. It was better, she knew, not to go back over the past, but she could not stop retelling the story of her own life. To others she realized it must appear ridiculously simple, a straight line from beginning to end. She had lived for sixty-five years on the island, except for the brief time during the war when she went to the mainland ostensibly to make money, though it was really to have her child and give him up for adoption. As a girl, she had helped run the store and then taken over managing the place when she married. That added up to many seasons of hauling boxes of supplies up the porch steps, stocking the shelves, and sorting sacks of mail. She had been married to Brock for forty-five years; Ellen and Lizzie were now married themselves, and she was a grandmother to five grandchildren. All of this made up a life story that took only a minute to tell, but it was not, of course, the whole story.

Alice Daggett McGarrell appeared entirely settled to outward eyes. Alice, she's such a solid sort, everyone thought, dependable and responsible and sensible and, well, just plain Alice. Like a rock, she was always there, seated behind the store's counter, waiting for the ferry, answering the absurd questions the summer people asked, giving directions, handing out mail, taking orders. What you saw was what you got with Alice. She sometimes chafed at the idea of how others viewed her, but in the end she didn't want the summer people, or anyone else, prying beneath the surface.

Finished with the walls in one room, Alice emptied and refilled the bucket. In the second bedroom, the one Nick had entered, she found a blanket draped over the mattress and sheets underneath. She studied the pattern of roses on the sheets and realized they were an old set she had given to Nick. Why would he sleep out here? He had never mentioned it, though she was aware there was plenty he had never mentioned. She and Brock only learned about his radio show when they accidentally stumbled on the broadcast one night.

She stared at the bed, trying to make sense of it. Surely Nick would have known that she would find the sheets and wonder. Or perhaps, it occurred to her, he had come to the cottage hoping to retrieve the bedding before she arrived. There were so many things she did not know about her own son, so many times she felt that he was evading her, slipping away. Mystified, she folded the blanket and gathered up the sheets. They gave off the faint smell of soap and deodorant. She held the corner of a sheet to her face for a moment, drinking in the scent, before stuffing it into the pillowcase.

Chapter Eight

Ruth stood next to the bathtub in the darkened room, peering at the sheet of paper floating in the tray. Gradually the patches of light and dark took on substance, and the image sprang to life, coming up from the depths of the blank paper as though it had been hidden there all along: a close-up of a tide pool, the gray water surrounded by a circle of rocks. Even here, under the subdued red of the safelight, the print had a luminous quality. The silvery water seemed to contain the sky's light, though it gave back no reflection. The closely cropped view suggested what lay beyond—open water, and the play of wind, and winter closing in.

She used the tongs to pick up the print and move it from the developer tray to the stop bath. Stillness emanated from the photo, but the image was not static. It could shift from an abstraction to a simple view of a tide pool and back if you studied it long enough. More than one thing at once—wasn't that what her professor in art school had said years earlier? The best art revealed one world layered on top of another or contained within another. The best art suggested multiple ways of seeing, though it accomplished this without appearing to do so, without claiming to do so. She thought of Alfred Stieglitz and his "Equivalents," photographs of clouds rendered as pure abstraction without backdrop or context. She would do something similar with her compositions of water and rock and sand.

It took ten attempts to get the right balance in the blacks and grays. When she had perfected the tones, she set the print to wash in a tray beneath the faucet in the claw-foot bathtub and turned on the overhead light. The prints she had made that morning hung to dry from a clothesline. With the rush of excitement she had felt at sixteen, when she first worked in the darkroom, she studied the photographs bobbing beneath the running water and the ones clipped like socks to the rope. In the days she had spent wandering around the island, questioning her own sanity and judgment, she had broken through to the basic act of seeing again. Working exclusively in black and white, in thirty-five millimeter, something she had not done in years, she had captured the haunting quality she desired, but there was more to the photos than the island light. You cannot leave, the images seemed to be saying, at least until the ferry comes in the morning. You are held here where time has stopped.

She had printed the photos in a random order, starting with the ones that interested her most, but saw now that there was an image for each day during her time on the island so far. The lines traced in the sand. A wide angle shot of marsh and cloud-scudded sky. A crab's claw against gray rock. The gleaming circle of the tide pool. Together they formed a visual diary.

In the kitchen, Ruth heated up soup and some canned spinach. She added crackers and cheese to another plate and carried her meal to the long table that filled the space between the living room and kitchen. Everything on the island, including food, was gloriously stripped down to the essentials. She felt like a monk, or at least as she imagined a monk might feel, living a daily rhythm of such quiet and simplicity. Her room on the first floor of the inn was like a monk's cell with its single bed and dresser and chair, nothing more, and the long window, uncovered, looking out over the lighthouse and the water.

She finished eating and carried the dishes to the kitchen. Maybe she was going to keep the appointment she had made with herself years ago in art school, when she set out to shoot not commercial advertising shots but something the world might actually need, images of the hidden beauty of hidden places. When she had planned her stay on the island, it was a fantasy, one she barely trusted. Now it felt real. She slid the dirty dishes into the sink, went to the front door, and pulled on her jacket.

Outside, she took the bicycle from its place on the porch and set off for the dock.

Down below, the waves lapped at the shore with a quiet hiss. She strained to hear something else in the darkness, but the air was still, the distance empty of sound. She was the only person staying on this part of the island. Closer to the dock, scattered lights appeared in the houses on the hillside above the water. Snow Island could not be said to have a town, but it did have a center—the network of dirt roads above the dock, the collection of little houses, the old Union Church with its white clapboard front, the store and the parking lot.

The idea took shape as she pushed her feet against the pedals. A visual diary. It was simple but brilliant. She would have to produce a photo for each day, regardless of weather or light, her own interest or inspiration. She would set herself the task as if she were a monk following the daily order of prayer. It would be as much a spiritual discipline as an artistic one.

Ruth dismounted and walked her bike down the gravel-strewn hill. The single streetlight cast a circle of yellow light on the road above, but the store was shrouded in darkness. She propped her bike against the porch railing and fished in her pants' pocket for the phone card.

The telephone booth sat open to the elements, its door missing. She deposited a quarter and peered at the phone card in the half-light. The buttons on the phone felt greasy beneath her fingertip, and for a moment she wondered if they would simply stay down after she depressed them, stuck in their grooves of dirt and sand, but they gave way, and the call went through. She punched in another set of numbers when she was prompted by the recorded instructions and waited for the ring.

"Hello?" Liza said.

"Lize, hi, it's me."

"Ruthie. You're kind of fuzzy."

Ruth spoke more loudly. "I'm on the pay phone. I tried to call you last night."

"I was at the dance."

"How was it?"

"Okay. Sissy and Jude and Laurie were there. And that cute thing Kristin took up with. I swear that girl's sixteen. I didn't stay too long. I was kind of tired after staying up all night to finish that project. You know how it goes, everybody else holds up the job and then the designer has to haul ass. My boss thinks I can turn everything around on a dime. She doesn't care if I have to take it home and work all night."

"Was Melissa at the dance?"

"She came just as I was leaving. We went and had coffee."

"You better be careful. She's still got eyes for you."

"Ruth." Liza let out an indignant noise that came through the crackling on the line. "Melissa and I are close friends. End of story."

"Listen, I've figured out what I'm doing with the photographs. I'm going to make a visual diary."

"A visual diary?" Liza's echo of the words made the idea sound small and silly.

"A diary in photographs. I'll take one for each day I'm here. Well, I'll take more pictures than that, but I have to come up with one really good shot each day. No cheating. I'm thinking it could be a book. 'Living by Island Light: A Visual Diary.' How's that sound?"

"Nice, but are you going to have enough pictures for a book?"

"That's the thing. I've got to stay longer."

Liza took in this information. When she didn't respond, Ruth plunged on. "I've got enough in savings to pay my share of the rent. You don't have to worry about that."

"How long are you talking about?"

"A couple of months at least, maybe more. Maybe until spring."

"Until spring? You're kidding."

"It'll be a real challenge. An artistic endurance test. A marathon. It's not just the photographs. It's the process. It's like a zen exercise. It will make the book more saleable. There's an idea behind it. This place is so incredible. I mean, there are no restaurants, no stores except Alice's, nothing. There's hardly any place like this left in America. Well, maybe out west in Wyoming or something, but not on the east coast. The book would be a document that somewhere like this still exists. And it would be a book of art photographs. And it would be a sort of novelty, the idea of taking a photo a day."

"Were you planning on asking my opinion about this?"

Ruth was not sure how to respond. She did not think she needed Liza's permission. "It's not so terrible to be apart for a while."

"Don't be ridiculous."

"You know what I mean."

"No, I don't."

"I just mean that maybe it's not the worst thing. You can come up on weekends."

"Christ, you make it sound like we're in high school and going steady."

"Did you go steady with any women in high school?"

"No."

"Neither did I."

"You're missing my point."

Ruth propped the phone against her ear and wrapped her arms around her chest, determined not to sound defensive. "It's been a long time since I've done my own work."

"Done your own work? Jesus, you spend all day Saturday and Sunday in the darkroom. I never see you."

Is that, Ruth thought, how it felt to Liza? To Ruth it seemed that she never had time for her work, that she was always putting Liza first. She gazed beyond the dock at the dark surface of the water, overwhelmed by the sense that Liza was bent on seizing what was most essential, the bedrock core of her being, and strangling the life out of it. She tried to keep her voice steady, but it came out in a shaky squeak. "I'm totally distracted in the city. I need to focus, to do this and nothing else for a while."

"I'm sorry I'm such a distraction."

"I didn't say that."

"You implied it."

There was no answer Ruth could make to this accusation. Liza was a distraction.

"So when am I going to see you?" Liza said.

"If I'm really going to do this, I can't leave the island. I have to be here every day."

"We'll only see each other if I come to the island then."

Ruth had not thought of it in precisely these terms, but it was, she had to admit, what she was suggesting.

"You've really got chutzpah, sweetheart," Liza said. "I've got to hand it to you."

"Listen, I've worked my ass off for the last ten years. I've barely taken a vacation. I've forgotten what it's like to take photographs for myself. If I don't do this…" For a moment, Ruth did not think she could speak, but then she went on. "I'll just be a hired hack for the rest of my life."

"I thought we were in this together."

"We are. Who said I wasn't?"

There was a long silence on the other end. Finally Liza said, "I've got to go. I have to finish a job tonight."

"I'll call you tomorrow."

"I won't be home. I'm going to a forum on what's happening with Iraq. They're trying to organize a protest before that idiot Bush marches into Kuwait."

"I miss you."

After another pause, Liza said, "Yeah, all right, I'll talk to you later."

Ruth set the greasy receiver back into place and stepped from the phone booth. She walked the bike up the hill, thinking how wonderful her idea had seemed just moments earlier. Now it felt stupid and self-indulgent. In an instant, Liza had shredded the whole thing to bits.

Ruth rode off toward the lighthouse. She should have considered how Liza would feel about her staying on the island. She had given this part of her plan little thought, but she did not believe it was asking too much for Liza to understand what this might mean. Ruth felt the old frustration and anger rising in her throat. If she had been at home, she would have left without telling Liza where she was going, stomping out of the apartment and closing the door with a satisfying and dramatic slam. She would have stayed at the coffee shop until midnight and returned to slide silently into bed beside Liza. Here she could only slam doors in her mind, though the sound of her anger did seem audible, a hurt that hummed in the air as she rode along, louder than the waves breaking against the rocks.

She was almost to the inn when she saw the glow of eyes at the side of the road. A cat, she thought at first, but then the animal darted from the grass and ran in front of her. She put on the brakes and came to a stop. The animal was small and low to the ground, like a cat, but its shape was different. She held the gaze of the glowing eyes for a long moment and realized, as she studied the thick tail, that it was a fox. The fox did not appear to be scared, but curious, as curious as she was, before he turned and slipped into the dark.

Chapter Nine

She heard the car before she saw it coming around the bend. The headlights swung over the road, and she realized that it was a truck, not a car. She was still standing with the bicycle balanced between her legs, gazing at the spot where the fox had vanished. She waited for the piercing light of the headlights to go by, but the truck stopped beside her, and the driver rolled down the window.

"Nice night for a bike ride," the man said.

Ruth dipped her head, vaguely embarrassed, and then realized it was the man she had met at the twin houses. "It is, isn't it?"

He smiled. "You ride around like this every night?"

"I was just down at the dock using the pay phone."

"Your aunt never had a phone put in that place?"

"No. She was kind of stubborn about it."

"She was stubborn about a lot of things." He ran his fingers over the top of his head, fanning the short strands of his hair. "I see you all over the place with that camera."

Ruth registered this comment with a certain discomfort. She was not aware that he had been watching her, though she supposed that everyone on the island was watching her.

"You want a tour?" he asked. "Hop in. I'll give you the insider's island tour. We can throw your bike in the back."

On another night, Ruth later reflected, she would have found a polite way to refuse the offer, but after the conversation with Liza, she felt defiant, freed of ordinary constraints. She agreed and watched as he got out of the truck, leaving the engine running, and lifted the bike with what appeared to be almost no effort into the flatbed. She climbed into the passenger seat.

"So your mother is Lydia Giberson?" he said as he got in beside her.

"Yes."

"Your mother and my mother were friends. When they were teenagers."

"You're Alice's son?"

"Yeah."

He gazed at her across the seat as though taking satisfaction in revealing this key piece of information withheld at their first meeting. He shifted into gear and moved off down the road, toward the dock. When he reached the store, he turned down the hill and circled the parking lot, then went back along the road in the other direction. "We'll start at the south end," he said. "At the old Navy base. You been down there?"

"Once. I haven't been through the whole place."

"That's our little piece of island history. World War II and all that."

"My mother used to talk about the sailors."

He did not respond, but drove on, his gaze set straight ahead. He drove into a wooded area and pulled up to a metal gate across the road. They sat in silence for a moment with the engine running.

"There," he said, pointing. A deer darted through the path of the headlights on the other side of the gate and bounded off into the woods. "You always see deer down here."

The animal leapt out of view with a deft grace, back arched and legs taut. Nick turned the truck around and retraced their path. He told her that the Navy base was a state park now, but this past summer the campgrounds had been closed because of Lyme disease. There were so many deer ticks, it wasn't safe.

The truck rattled over the dirt road. He pointed out the old ferry dock and turned up the hill onto Broadway. There was an Indian burial ground in this stretch of woods. He said he used to find a lot of arrowheads there when he was a kid. At the bottom of the hill, he took the bend and followed the road along the water. "That's my house," he said, gesturing toward a patch of lawn.

Set back from the road, she could make out a small two-story house with a light shining in a downstairs window. She thought he was going to pull in and invite her to see the place, but he kept going without glancing to the right or left. She didn't know what she was doing, riding around with this guy, even if he was Alice's son, though it was better, she told herself, than wandering around the inn alone, obsessively reviewing the conversation with Liza.

"Have you always lived on Snow?" she asked in an attempt to break the silence.

He balanced his fingertips on the wheel, steering with a light touch, and took the turn out toward Gooseneck Cove. "No. I was gone for a long time. I just moved back three years ago." He turned into a clearing and brought the truck to a stop. Reaching into the well behind the seat, he produced a six-pack of beer. "Come on, I'll show you the beach."

He opened the door and jumped out. Ruth followed. She struggled to keep her footing on the sandy path and kept her eyes fixed on the broad outline of his back.

The beach was long and narrow, a light strip between the dense blackness of the brush and the dark surface of the water. Nick gestured toward the distant point where the sand gave way to a rocky shoreline below a tangle of thick growth. "I flipped a car there once," he said. "I got it going at top speed and drove it off the road, jumping out at the last minute. Thing rolled right over like a top. It's still there."

He plunked the six-pack onto the sand and sat beside it. When she was seated next to him, he handed her a bottle. "You like this stuff? This Canadian beer?"

"It's okay."

"Hell, I spent seven bucks for it. It better be okay."

Ruth grasped the bottle cap, keeping her hand covered by her coat sleeve to protect it from the sharp edges. The beer let out a soft hiss as she opened it.

"There was nobody at the quonset hut tonight," he said. "Good thing

I ran into you so this beer didn't go to waste."

"What's the quonset hut?"

"The local hangout. Guy named Gary runs the place. He's got a pool table and a woodstove and a bunch of scruffy characters who are regulars. They must all be over at Cliff's. He just got a satellite dish. Three thousand channels and not a damn thing on any of them."

Ruth took a sip of the bitter beer. She tried to make hoisting a beer with a man, a man she didn't really know, feel normal, but she could not remember the last time she had been in such a situation.

"How old are you?" he asked. "I mean if it's not too forward a question." He brought the bottle to his lips and took a long swig.

"Thirty-one."

He tapped himself on the chest. "I'm forty-two. Does that sound old?"

"Not too old."

"Sometimes it seems way too old to me. I used to think I would have a little repair shop, repairing radios and televisions, things like that. And I would spend every weekend in the woods, tracking animals. I thought that would be the perfect life when I was seventeen."

"What happened?"

"I went to Vietnam." He drank the rest of the beer in a long gulp and took another from the six-pack.

"Forty-two isn't old," she said.

"It's middle-aged, or close to it."

"You're only middle-aged if you think you are."

He gave her a sidelong glance. "That's easy for you to say."

He smoothed his hand over the sand in front of him, creating a swirled circle. She watched him with the sense of reaching back, into a past so far that she could barely locate it, but he was not the boy of her fourteen-year-old summer fling, and she was not the confused and hesitant girl she had been then.

"How long were you in Vietnam?" she asked.

"A year. Sixty-six to '67."

"You went early."

"Yeah."

He didn't speak for a moment, and she thought that was all he would say. "I was lucky," he continued. "I spent most of my time on base. I got some jungle duty, but not a lot. You know all the shit you see in the movies. It wasn't like that most of the time. We were bored out of our gourds and so hot we wanted to die. I was in charge of the gook detail. That's what we called it. The villagers came and worked on the base doing k.p. and other stuff. I don't mean it the way it sounds. Gook was more like a term of affection. I had to go pick them up every day and drive them back, and make sure they were doing something while they were there. The Army is the pits. I hated it, every minute of it."

He spoke slowly and evenly, as though reciting memorized lines.

"Most of the villagers spoke a little English. We joked around a lot. It was a good deal for them. They got paid a dollar a day, which was good money, plus we'd give them the garbage for their pigs. That was as important as the pay, getting that garbage. There was this one guy who was on gook detail with me. He was at the end of his tour, and he'd been there too long. You could spot the guys who'd been there too long right away. They got just plain nasty, didn't give a shit about anything anymore. We took the villagers home at the end of the day, and instead of letting them come around and pick up the pails of garbage the way we usually did, this guy dumped all the garbage on the ground over the side of the truck. The whole place went crazy. Everyone in the village came running, and they're all on the ground fighting over the garbage and screaming at each other. I was so disgusted. What was the point of doing that? It made me sick. There were a lot of times like that, small stuff, but it made you sick.

"We used to run out of water on the base. The supply people wouldn't get through. One time we came back from jungle duty, and there was no water. It's over a hundred degrees, we're all just sitting there baking. I thought, well I'll just go get one of the coconuts from the trees in the village right by the camp. What you wanted was one of the green ones—they weren't as good to eat, but the juice was better. I went over, by the edge of the camp, and cut down a coconut, and this woman came out and said I had to pay for it. I shook my head. I wasn't about to pay for that thing. She didn't own those trees. She kept yelling and throwing her hands in the air and saying I had to pay for it. I thought, I'll shoot her. I'll just take my gun and shoot her if she won't let me have this coconut. One of the guys from my battalion came running over and threw some coins at her and grabbed me. He knew what was in my head. I could have done it. I could have killed her. When you're that hot and thirsty and disgusted, you could do anything. That's what you find out. You can do anything."

Ruth studied his face in the darkness. He continued to stare out over the water, his expression shorn of emotion. He told the stories as if on autopilot. She was drawn into his trance, feeling the heat and thirst, seeing the woman screaming about the coconut. Except that she couldn't see her, not really, or know what it must have been like.

With a quick motion, as though dispensing with his own words, Nick brushed his hands together, freeing them of the sand. "I don't know why I talk about this shit. So you make money as a photographer back there in the city?"

"I'm a food photographer. I shoot ads and magazine spreads, but I've sworn off pictures of food for a while."

He took a swig of beer. "A while?"

"Well, as long as I can stay here."

"Most of the artists who come here don't stay more than a month." He said the word *artists* with a healthy dose of disdain.

"What happens?"

"They go stir-crazy. They can't stand the quiet. They think it's paradise, and then they get here and realize it's not."

"But you don't go stir-crazy?"

"No. Everyone has this fantasy about living on an island. They want to get back to a simple life and all that crap. I didn't come back with any fantasies. I knew what it was like. I used to be a civil engineer. I traveled all over the place doing bridge construction, highway projects, that kind of thing. I was a consultant." He grimaced as he said the word *consultant*, as though it was overly pretentious. "I decided I didn't want to do it anymore. Living out of motels and everything. Gets to be old. I do construction here now. I built an addition for this crazy lawyer over on the other side of the island this summer. Now I'm doing a kitchen renovation."

"I'm not sure I've ever met a civil engineer."

"I'm not sure I've ever met a food photographer."

"We're a rare breed."

"So are civil engineers."

Ruth had not traded witty observations with a man in a long time. Her circle of friends in the city did not include many men, except for those she met on photo shoots. She felt off-kilter, as though she were impersonating someone she was not.

"You must be freezing," he said. "This sand's like ice."

She braced herself for what would come next, an arm around her shoulder to keep her warm, and tried to think what she would say, but he reached for the six-pack, got to his feet, and headed for the path. She followed, feeling the sand seep into her shoes. He was so tall and his shoulders were so broad, she could see nothing on either side of him once they entered the wooded area.

When she was settled beside him in the truck, he turned the key in the ignition and reached for the volume on the tape deck. Music filled the cab of the truck, a song with a lot of horns and a heavy beat, and a female singer with a belting voice.

"Who's this?" Ruth asked.

"Etta James."

She did not want to admit that she wasn't familiar with Etta James. The woman sounded like someone she should know.

They made the turn onto the main road and passed the dump. They were almost to the dock when they met another truck coming toward them. Nick raised his hand in a wave. The driver of the other vehicle, a man, returned the gesture.

"That's Eddie Brovelli," Nick said, "keeping us safe."

"Safe from what?"

"The bogey man. He's the police chief and the entire island force. Spends all day driving around spying on people. There's not a lot of illegal activity on Snow, but if there is, he's got a knack for sniffing it out."

Nick pulled over by the inn and shut off the engine. If he made a move now, she would be ready to rebuff him, but he looked at her for a moment before asking, "Would you do me a favor? Would you walk on my back?"

"Walk on your back?"

"Yeah, it's killing me. I strained it hauling lumber. If you walk on it, it'll get the kinks out."

This struck Ruth as a fairly strange come-on ploy, if it was, in fact, one at all. She stepped out of the truck. He came around and lifted the bike from the flatbed.

"You want this on the porch?" he said.

"Yeah, that's fine."

Ruth opened the door. The knob was still loose. She thought for a moment of asking him to fix it. He went back to the truck and got the beer. Inside, he deposited the six-pack on the table by the couch.

"This place always had so much atmosphere," he said.

"It was like a palace to us when I was a kid."

"How's the roof?"

"You were right. It leaks. I've got buckets set up. I think my aunt just let the water run all over. The floorboards are a mess."

"It's kind of a white elephant, huh?"

"Kind of. I want to hang on to it, but…I don't know."

They were standing in the living room. Without saying more, he lay face down on the worn rug. Ruth slipped off her shoes and cautiously stepped onto his back, first one foot, then the other. She wobbled unsteadily, feeling his body shift beneath her, then settled into place. His back was oddly like a table. She could not imagine having such a substantial, muscled body. Men took up so much room, commanded so much space. They made her feel small and insignificant.

Inching her feet forward, she moved up toward his neck and then back to his waist, careful not to bring her full weight down at once. She could hear his back cracking, not just once but over and over. He let out a low groan.

"Enough?" she asked.

"No, don't stop."

She continued to move slowly up and down his back until, at last, he mumbled, "Okay."

He rolled over and sat up. "That was great."

She smiled in spite of herself. "Glad you enjoyed it."

"You've got a real touch. Or your feet do."

"It's a skill I didn't know I had."

Nick stood up, went to the hall, and pulled on his jacket. "Thanks a lot. Really." He ran his hand over the back of his head to smooth his hair into place and headed for the door. "I'll see you around."

He was about to pull the door closed when he turned back. "Don't tell my mother I stopped by, all right? She can be a little too nosey."

"All right." Ruth gave the response automatically, though it struck her as a strange request.

He said goodnight and closed the door behind him.

It was a moment before she noticed the beer still sitting on the table, three bottles left in the cardboard container. She was about to go after him, but then she heard the truck's hum as he drove away.

Chapter Ten

Nora had always hated boats. There was the slick surface of the deck, waiting to trip her up, and the endless rolling that even on the calmest days left her legs feeling like they were made of water hours after she was back on land. The sudden snapping of the sails, signaling that something was about to happen, unnerved her. Gerald had claimed that she was so hopeless, there was no point in taking her out at all. She agreed, avoiding the sailing trips whenever she could. She didn't care for having her hair blown in ten directions at once, or her face turning a ruddy shade of red, or her stomach roiling and heaving like the waves. She had only joined Gerald on that trip to Narragansett Bay because he insisted. The Whittet couple were coming, and he didn't care what she had to say, he needed her to act as the hostess for once. She would be his wife.

Words were like fish, Nora reflected as she stood on the deck of the ferry waiting for it to pull away for the run to the island. Slipping and slithering through your hands, their meaning could shift at the slightest turn. She had resisted the word *wife* for years, refusing to get married and become nothing more than some man's property, or if that was too severe a way of viewing it, a simpering helpmate. Once married, she had resisted being a wife in other ways, having her own friends and taking her own vacations. Now the word meant nothing. For most of her life she had been a widow, a term she hated almost as much as she had once hated wife, but she would never be a wife again, Gerald's or anyone else's. There was a certain satisfaction and relief in this fact. The word no longer haunted her.

The ferry's horn sounded, and it chugged away from the dock. Riding a ferry was different, naturally, from going out on Gerald's sailboat. The movement was gradual, almost imperceptible, until the ferry reached the channel and rolled gently. Nora thought of that day when she first saw Isabelle on the deck of the boat. She knew immediately that she would like this petite woman whose gestures were at once so free and so precise. Isabelle did not conform to the standards of beauty of that time, which favored pouty lips and ample breasts. The lines of her face were arresting, and the delicate shape of her frame suggested a reserved strength. "Nora," she said, extending her hand as she stepped on board. Already in that moment they seemed to be alone, just the two of them. The men went off to the bow, fiddling with the lines, and it seemed to Nora that Isabelle understood. The men were superfluous, easily overlooked and ignored.

When the ferry gathered speed and the wind picked up, Nora went inside the passenger cabin, where she perched on a narrow metal bench crusted with spilled soda and who knew what else. Among the other passengers that afternoon were two men who remained in their cars parked on the deck and a young woman wearing a thick down jacket with a camera slung round her neck. Through the smeared window, Nora studied the water beyond the bow, flat and gray, stretching off to the obscured horizon. Gerald would have said she was slumming it, had the expression existed back then, and he would have been right. She was indeed slumming it, taking the ferry and sitting in the close, overheated cabin. There was a sense of the forbidden about this trip back to the island, which Isabelle's absence only exaggerated. Isabelle had gone home to Henry, as Nora knew she would, though Henry was not there waiting for her anymore. He lived in the nursing home now, where bit by bit his mind had slipped away until he no longer recognized her, although she visited daily.

When she and Isabelle were together, waking side by side at Nora's house, luxuriating in the feel of a warm bed and a morning containing only what they wanted, it was simple, but once they stepped from the enclosed world of the bedroom, fear raised its head. They began the complicated dance that went with daylight, careful to hold up the wobbly façade. There were disguises they wore for the neighbors and even the mailman. Now, on the island, Nora could give up sidestepping through the days to the dizzy tune of a lie. It was not her fault. Isabelle was the one who could not let go of the elaborate subterfuge. She refused to move in with Nora because God knows what everyone would think. Everyone consisted of almost no one now that their parents and their siblings were dead. Only Isabelle's children were left, and they would be nothing but relieved if Isabelle went to live with "Aunt Nora."

Nora went out onto the deck, unable to bear the stifling smell and heat any longer. The island came into sight at last. The woman with the camera had retrieved a bicycle from a rack beside the passenger cabin and was waiting at the railing, a large backpack at her feet. Nora went to stand beside her. Neither of them spoke as they gazed together at the approaching shore.

The woman broke the silence. "The island looks so small from a distance."

"It is small," Nora said.

"Six miles long and a mile wide. Not that small, actually. But from here, it looks like nothing. Are you on the island year-round?"

"No, but I'm staying for a while."

"So am I. I saw you getting off the boat last week."

Nora nodded. She thought the woman had looked familiar, though bundled up in her jacket, it was hard to see much beyond the circle of her face, a fringe of short hair, and a pair of brown eyes. "You've been shopping?"

"Groceries. You can't get everything you need at Alice's."

"How do you manage groceries without a car?"

The woman appeared momentarily embarrassed by this question. "I use the crate." She gestured toward a plastic crate strapped to the back of the bike, in which a paper bag sat. "And the knapsack."

"Well, if you need to go shopping again, let me know. I can drive you."

The woman thanked her for the offer as the ferry chugged to a stop, and the men came down from the wheelhouse.

"I'm down at Gooseneck Cove. The little cottage behind the big house," Nora said.

"You mean the mansion?"

Nora flinched at the word. "Yes, I guess that's what they call it."

"I'm at the inn." The woman pointed in the direction of the lighthouse.

"We'll see each other then," Nora said, certain that they would. In this young woman, she suspected she had found someone who might be compatible, someone who did not appear to be, though she was sorry to think in such terms, an islander.

Nora got in her car and followed the directions of the man at the head of the ramp, who signaled to the cars one at a time. In her rear-view mirror, she saw the woman push the bicycle down the ramp with the unwieldy knapsack hanging from her shoulders. It was too late to offer the woman a ride right now, though she should have. Nora was already at the top of the hill, about to turn down Bay Avenue, and there was a man in a truck behind her waiting impatiently.

The wind churned up the waves. The tide was high, the rocks along the shore barely visible. Nora rolled down the window, so the cold air hit her face. How alive it made her feel. She glanced into the back seat at the box of books she had brought and the stack of drawing pads and her bag full of brushes and tubes of paint. These would be her companions.

She reached the cottage and slipped the key in the lock. Nick's mother had performed miracles. The interior of the cabin was transformed, the walls no longer a dingy black. With the new furniture, it was positively cozy and entirely respectable. Who's slumming it? she asked Gerald, for she felt him watching over her shoulder in triumphant satisfaction. I knew you would return, he seemed to be saying.

She worked quickly, though it took all afternoon to unpack the boxes of pots and pans and dishes, to make the bed and arrange the new towels, and to get a fire going in the little woodstove. She felt capable and resourceful. She felt strong. Only late in the day, as the sky began to darken, did her energy fade, and she slumped on the new couch, wondering for the first time how she would fill the evening. On the nights when she and Isabelle were together, they cooked dinner and then watched television, the news and maybe a movie or a nature program. They went to bed early and sat side by side reading. There was a predictable rhythm to it all, from what they would fix for dinner and the time they would sit down at the table to who would use the bathroom first before bed. They went through the routine like an old married couple, except that of course they were not a married couple.

Nora pulled on her jacket and headed outside. No getting maudlin, she told herself. No lying around wondering what to do next. She had nothing but time, it was true, but she did not have time for getting stupid and cheerless and tired. She owed it to herself, to the ghost of Gerald and even the shadowed presence of Isabelle, to seize the solitude and empty beauty of the island and use it, make it hers.

The wood was stacked neatly outside the cottage, the packed rows speaking of comfort and readiness. She would give Nick and his mother a little extra for all the work they had done. The islanders were wonderfully industrious and accommodating and reliable. How lucky she was to have these people who were happy to have the work and the money. It was the same in Gerald's day. Islanders were the best damn workers he had ever seen, she remembered him saying, though she would try not to mimic his swaggering delight, his interest in buying the whole island.

She skirted the big house, crossed the field, and took the path out to the cove. The wind, stronger now, made the tops of the pines sway. She watched a chickadee dart from branch to branch, so quick and light and seemingly happy. She walked faster to keep the bird in sight. At the top of the hill, the view of the bay opened before her. A tanker inched toward Providence, the long gray body of the boat appearing balanced atop the water, barely touching the surface. The chickadee let out a series of cheeping calls from a branch above her head and took off over the marsh.

She thought of the wind that night they had spent riding out the storm in the boat. They had just made it into Gooseneck Cove, safely anchored, before the storm unleashed, and the swells deepened. The wind sounded like people furiously yelling instructions back and forth out on the deck. They huddled in the cabin to eat the last of the sand-wiches and cookies and divide what was left of a bottle of scotch. Nora could remember the moment when she handed a glass to Isabelle and their eyes met for longer than necessary, and in some distant region of her mind and body, she recognized a flicker of interest and desire, and knew that it was returned. Months would pass before they acted on the under-standing that had moved so surely between them that night, when they sat balanced on the edges of the bunks, and Gerald and Henry rattled on about golf.

She had never asked Isabelle about that look or many things because, she supposed, she feared the answers. The undercurrent of doubt remained near, an animal waiting to spring. She had lived too long inwardly preparing herself for Isabelle's turning away, steeling herself against the small acts of denial that stung so routinely and the final denial she felt sure would come one day, though over time it seemed less likely.

The look they exchanged that night at Gooseneck Cove was con-summated on afternoons when they met in an attic room beneath the eaves and took pleasure in a quick, nervous lovemaking, ready to pull on clothes and flee down the stairs at any moment. They made love without words, in a hushed and watchful silence. Their breathing kept beat with the swift passing of minutes and the knowledge that for them the only kind of time was stolen time. They were so very young then, so lithe and daring; the memory of their slim bodies twined together was dazzling. For a brief span of months, anything seemed possible. They talked about leaving their husbands, and Isabelle made Nora believe, foolishly, that she would have the courage to do it. Such wild ideas died when Isabelle announced she was pregnant.

With the birth of Burt and then Heather, Nora took on the role of Aunt Nora, a role cemented by Gerald's death. She joined Isabelle and Henry and the kids for Thanksgiving and Christmas and trips to Europe. The afternoon and late-night trysts ended. Nora told herself she was con-tent with simple friendship and companionship, and being attached to a family. She found consolation with women she met in a dark hole of a bar in Boston and a few scattered relationships, none of which lasted long. She spent less time with Isabelle and Henry as the children got older, though she still joined them for a week in Maine each summer. When the intensity of what she and Isabelle had shared threatened to come to life again, even for a moment, they snuffed it out. Only later, after the children were off in college, did Isabelle return, tentative and anxious, and timid as a prepubescent girl at first.

Henry and Isabelle were forever throwing dinner parties after the children were gone. She would shoot Nora looks of anxious pleading across the crowded dinner table, begging Nora to be cautious. Nora hated her then, something she was not ashamed to admit. Isabelle had driven her to hate and driven her back again to love, again and again. Maybe all lovers experienced something equally complex, but she could not assess how much they were like others. The odd parameters and twisted rules of their relationship dictated everything, down to the clothes they wore. For years, Isabelle feared that a "mannish" jacket or button-down shirt would give them away and insisted they wear unfailingly feminine skirts and tailored pants.

When Henry went into the nursing home, feeble and confused, Nora assumed that Isabelle would move in with her. There was nothing stopping her now, but Isabelle surprised her yet again. She was still married to Henry. She wouldn't risk it.

Nora pulled her jacket close against the wind and turned back down the hill. How foolish people were with their constant worry about what others thought of them. Isabelle was particularly afflicted with this idiocy, though Nora supposed she was no worse than most. To have happiness within your grasp and to let it slip away was criminal. She wanted her happiness out in the open, a glass of wine ready to be drunk to the last dregs.

PART TWO
November

Chapter Eleven

When the children left for the day, the schoolhouse fell into an abrupt silence, though the empty room still seemed to echo with shouts of glee and the scraping of chairs on linoleum and the pounding of footsteps headed for escape. Rachel stood in the center of the sudden stillness, surrounded by papers that had spilled over the sides of desks and pencils scattered like pick-up sticks across the floor. She bent over to retrieve a stray piece of construction paper and told herself she really was getting too old for this. How, she often wondered, had the Hershels and the Mannings persuaded her to go back to work? She must have lost her mind when she agreed to it. Running a one-room schoolhouse took the sort of stamina and naïve optimism only a young teacher fresh out of school could muster. She was long past the time in her life when the daily grind of lesson preparation and test grading could seem new.

The pencils were sticky. She gathered them up gingerly. Rachel was strict about food in the classroom. Snacks were only allowed in the kitchen; candy and gum were off-limits entirely. Somehow the children managed to get a sugary mess on everything anyway. The stuff clung to them, she supposed, a residue they brought with them from home—or they were sneaking in pieces of candy buried in their pockets.

While setting the pencils in an old coffee can on her desk, she heard the throaty hum of a vehicle approaching. When the engine went still, she moved to the front window in time to see Nick swing down from the truck. The canvas jacket he wore fit him tightly, and a fine dusting of sawdust was visible on the sleeves. He moved with a taut ease that made her long to be somewhere else, the moon maybe, far enough away that the simple sight of him would not fill her with a debilitating mix of desire and fear.

He disappeared around the side of the schoolhouse. This was a business call, or at least the appearance of one. She went to meet him on the back porch, where she found him beside the woodpile.

"You've been going through this wood," he said.

"It's been cold in the mornings."

"I can get the delivery over here before you run out. Four cords. You think that will do it?"

"Is that what we got last year?"

"I think so."

"That should be enough then. Has the price gone up?"

"Probably."

"I don't want the School Department hassling us about it."

"I'll call that woman in the front office. She doesn't seem to have it in for us like the School Board." Nick took a notepad from his jacket pocket and wrote a few words on a blank page. "Who helps you start the fire these days?"

"The Hershel boys do sometimes. They're not as reliable as you used to be."

"I was a real brownnoser, wasn't I?"

"No. You were just...helpful."

Nick slid the notebook back in his pocket. "A little too helpful."

She smiled. "Maybe."

Rachel turned and went back inside, and he followed her into the schoolhouse kitchen.

There were no curtains on the windows, and she was aware that someone could drive by and see the two of them there. Someone, of course, meant Eddie, though their secret wouldn't be safe with any of the islanders. She took the accounts book from the cupboard and spread it open on the kitchen table. Nick came up behind her, cupped his hands around her hips, and kissed the back of her neck. She slipped out of his embrace.

"Don't get me started," she said.

He hooked a finger through the belt loop on her jeans as if to pull her back to him.

"Nick."

"Nobody could see us if we lay on the floor."

"You're crazy." She flipped through the accounts book and felt the heat rise into her face. He had the power to undo her in an instant. She finally found the figure she was looking for. "Here it is. November of 1989. We spent five hundred on wood."

"Could be a little more this year."

She looked up from the column of figures. "You're a bit of a mess." She reached over and pulled some slivers of wood from the ends of his hair.

"I'm always a bit of a mess."

He submitted to her grooming, head lowered, a smile on his lips. She loved that sardonic expression of his.

"Mrs. Venable has moved into the cottage," he said. "It's kind of nuts, but she seems determined to live there."

"For how long?"

"She's not saying."

"So now what do we do?"

"You can come over to my place."

"No," she said, instantly and sharply.

"I'll come and get you and drive you back."

"It's too dangerous."

"There's always the twin houses."

"Nick."

"We can go to the Lundborns, where I'm working. They've got a queen-sized bed."

Rachel closed the accounts book and held his gaze. He raised his hand to her face and touched her cheek. They remained motionless, both, it seemed, holding their breath, until she moved to the far side of the table, putting it between them.

"I took the radio equipment over to my house, but I don't like broadcasting there," he said. "I'm afraid the Hershels are going to tune in some time and bust me."

"I don't think they allow radio in their house. Radio or television. Or music."

"The work of the devil, huh?"

"It's amazing what those kids don't know. It's like they've spent their whole lives in an incubator. They are truly unspotted from the world."

"What's that mean, 'unspotted from the world'?"

"It's an old prayer. 'Lord, keep us unspotted from the world.' You know the church. It's all about being soiled or stained or dirty."

"At least those kids don't give you much trouble."

"No, but sometimes they scare me. Jenny tried to save me the other day. She said, 'Have you accepted Jesus Christ as your Lord and savior?' A six-year-old. I nearly fell out of my chair."

"What did you say?"

"I told her I accepted Jesus Christ as my Lord and savior a long time ago, and I'm Catholic."

"It must be hard for them, not really having anyone they can convert here on the island," Nick said, glancing at his watch. "I better be getting over to the dock."

"Is the poker game on for Friday?"

"No. Cliff's going off island for the weekend. They're playing next Wednesday, before Thanksgiving. I'll wait at the Lundborns."

"All right. As long as Eddie goes."

"He never misses a poker game."

He glanced toward the window and pulled her toward him again, over against the wall, where they could not be seen. He kissed her long and slow, making her legs turn to jelly. He smelled vaguely of gasoline and sweat.

She broke away. "You better go," she whispered.

He kissed her once more, short and quick, on the lips. "See you around."

He left through the back door and crossed the lawn. She watched him with the sick sense that she had to put an end to this, though she knew she could not. She wanted him too badly.

Rachel returned to the schoolroom and sat at her desk. She opened a folder full of spelling tests and stared blankly at them. The childish scrawl of words down the page moved before her eyes without registering. There were times when she was able to convince herself that her nights with Nick were entirely justified, payback for the years of being a mother and running the house and answering to Eddie. Today was not one of those times. She felt hollow, riddled with doubt.

She reached for her red pen and went through the spelling tests mechanically. Her students were diligent. They did their homework and got uniformly good grades under the watchful guidance of their parents. They made it seem almost too easy.

She had finished with the spelling tests and moved on to arithmetic papers when she heard another car outside. This one was a new vehicle, in good shape like Nick's, with a high-pitched purring engine and an intact muffler. She knew, before it came into sight, that it must be Eddie's truck. He raised his hand in an absent-minded wave as he went past. She did not bother to return the gesture. He was already gone.

Rachel glanced at the clock and saw that it was time for the ferry's arrival. She didn't feel the need to join the other islanders at the dock. She finished the grading and rose to go.

She took the road toward Snow Park, in the direction away from the dock. When she crested the hill, the water came into view. It was a sight she had come to love over the years. The presence of the water on all sides was quieting, even comforting, though in the dead of winter, it took on a bleaker, more lonely aspect. No two days were the same, even then. Each day sky and water and sun came into play in a different combination. This was hard to explain to someone who had never lived on an island. She would be the first to admit that there was monotony to island life, but the landscape itself was dynamic, always changing.

When she reached her house, she carried the canvas bag with her lesson book inside and went directly to the kitchen. She turned the dial on the oven to three hundred-fifty. Through the window above the sink, she searched the trees that bordered the yard. Most of the birds were gone now. Just a lone crow sat in one of the top branches.

She had not sought Nick out, not at first. When he returned to the island, they had kept their distance. Both of them were wary; the memory of his senior year at the schoolhouse, when his eyes tracked her from one side of the room to the other, hovered just beneath the surface. She had not given in back then, despite being tempted. Though just eighteen, he seemed like a man with his lanky height and deep voice. Day after day that year, she steeled herself against the question in his gaze. The one time he crossed the boundary and reached out to touch her, she made it clear that nothing was going to happen between them.

By the time Nick returned to the island, she and Eddie had raised two children and sent them off to college. Eddie had become the police chief when his brother, who had held the job for years, moved to Florida. She dismissed the idea of Nick and told herself that she barely remembered the strange time when he was her student. Neither of them, she supposed, had imagined meeting over her desk at the schoolhouse again. It had been closed in the mid-seventies and only reopened when the Hershels and Mannings arrived with their large families and lobbied her to return as the teacher. After staying at home with her children and not working for so long, she did not expect to be in the classroom again, but there she was, back at her desk and looking for a handyman at the schoolhouse. It seemed natural enough for Nick to take the job. Other things came to seem natural over time, like lingering to talk in the kitchen and finding the hint of something (desire?) in his gaze.

The chicken she had left to thaw that morning sat on the top shelf in the refrigerator. Rachel took the pieces from the package, rinsed them at the sink, and set them in the baking pan. Deception, she had found, was far easier than she would have thought. In fact, she barely saw it as deception now. Small lies were just the accommodations she needed to make for this new life to work.

She opened the oven and slid the pan onto the rack. Outside, she heard Eddie pull up in his truck.

Chapter Twelve

Rachel hurried up the stairs before Eddie came through the door. By the time the door slammed, she was pulling on the lycra leggings she wore for running. She traded her blouse and sweater for a tee shirt and sweatshirt, tugged on her sneakers, and went tumbling back down the stairs. Eddie stood at the kitchen table sorting through the pile of mail he had brought in.

"Nothing but these damn catalogs and credit card offers," he said without glancing up. "I should just recycle the whole pile without bringing it home."

Rachel surveyed the catalogs to see if there was anything that interested her.

"How do all these people get our address?" he said.

"Mailing lists."

"There should be a law against it."

"I'm going running."

Eddie glanced up and gave her a quick kiss on the cheek. "You gonna be warm enough?"

"Yeah. I'll wear some gloves."

"The wind's kicking up."

"I'll stay on this side of the island."

Rachel fished a pair of gloves from the pocket of a coat hanging in the closet. "There's chicken in the oven. I'll be back before it's done."

Eddie nodded and continued flipping through the catalogs.

Outside, the cold air hit her face. Rachel started at a slow jog down the driveway and picked up the pace as she turned onto the road. She kept her eyes on the uneven surface and rolling pebbles, running carefully, until she reached the smooth asphalt past the bend and lengthened her stride. She felt fluid then, her arms and legs loose, her body moving in one seamless motion. She became a machine when she ran, lean and efficient, her breathing hard but steady. It was the one time she knew herself fully and completely, without doubt or guilt or confusion.

She ran the length of the east side of the island. No one was left down at the dock, except for Brock and Alice still hauling boxes into the store. Brock raised his hand in a wave as she went past. Rachel peered into the windows at the inn, thinking she might get a glimpse of the photographer, but she could make out only the vague shapes of furniture in the darkened front room. She had spoken to the woman once down at the store. The photographer's city look, with her short hair and cargo pants, made Rachel feel old and frumpy.

When she reached the old Navy base, Rachel turned around and ran back the way she had come. She needed the idea of Nick, the possibility of him, even if he stayed on the margins. The times when they were able to meet made her feel so alive it was as if her skin had been turned inside out. For days afterward, she was like an instrument still vibrating to a music no one else heard. Sometimes she wondered if what went on between them had anything remotely to do with love, but to say it was made only of lust was too simple. He gave her a second life; it was this she could not give up, no matter how many times she swore that she would.

The last bits of light were draining from the sky by the time she came to the turn for her house and made the transition onto the dirt road. She passed Mary Lou Danks' house and the pull-off for the sandy beach. The sky was a purple shade of black now, with the first stars glinting overhead. It was, she thought, the color of cold.

Inside, Eddie had the television tuned to the news. Slumped back in the La-Z-Boy, his feet covered in a pair of bulky wool socks, he looked like a hibernating animal. Rachel pulled off her gloves and went upstairs for a shower. In the bathroom mirror, she saw how bright her face had become from the chill air. The flush of exercise obscured the wrinkles around her eyes and the blotchy spots on her skin. If only she could run all the time.

Showered and dressed, she made her way downstairs in a pair of slippers and took the chicken from the oven. Eddie pressed the button on the remote and changed the station. "God, those public television people drone on," he said.

"I don't know why you watch that. All you do is complain."

"They tell you something about what's going on other places in the world, which is more than the networks do, but then they tell you way too much."

"What's going on elsewhere in the world?"

"War, mostly. Or the threat of it."

Rachel opened the dishwasher and began stacking the clean plates on the counter. Eddie got out of the chair, went to the refrigerator, and took out a beer.

"Bush is really dragging his feet about Iraq," he said.

"I'm sure a show of force will improve things."

"We can't let Hussein get away with invading anybody he feels like."

She finished removing the plates and started on the silverware, not anxious to get into a discussion of the situation in the Gulf. Eddie, a Korean War veteran, believed that fighting for American interests was always justified.

"Donna called," he said. "She said to call her back. Probably some trouble with that boyfriend of hers."

Rachel raised her eyes to meet Eddie's look. "He's not that bad."

"Did I say anything?"

"I know what you're thinking."

"He can't sponge off Donna forever."

"He's looking for work. She says he's sent out something like a hundred resumes."

"I didn't kill myself to send her to college so she could be a waitress and live in some dump with that jerk."

"They're young. They're just getting started. The economy's terrible. Nobody can find a job."

Eddie shrugged. "He's too picky. There's jobs if you want them."

Rachel turned to the refrigerator and took out the ingredients for a salad. Eddie went back to his easy chair in front of the television. She knew that he was only an overly protective father, but these conversations took on a circular nature, with Rachel always the one to defend their daughter and her quirky choices. Rachel did not like Matt, the boyfriend, any better than Eddie did, but she knew that her approval or disapproval was of no consequence to Donna.

When Rachel had finished preparing the food and set it on the table, Eddie switched off the TV. On his way to join her, he turned on the radio and fiddled with the knob. He found a piece with a lot of high-pitched harmonica, coming through with a clear signal, and left it there. Rachel suspected, as she knew Eddie did, that this was Nick broadcasting, but neither of them said anything as they began eating. They were halfway through the meal when Nick's voice sounded in the room, announcing that they had just been listening to "It's My Life, Baby" by Junior Wells.

"I knew that was him," Eddie said. "No other stations come through that clear."

Rachel continued eating.

"He plays some pretty interesting music," he said.

"Yeah, he's got quite a collection."

"I guess that's all he does when he goes off island, goes to all the record stores. So how much longer will he be working on that kitchen renovation?"

"I don't know."

"You think he's got time this winter to do ours?"

"He might have other jobs lined up."

"He does decent work. I went inside that place over by Snow Park he did this summer. It was very clean, very professional work. All we need is a design. We could probably do that ourselves. Just make up a plan for him to follow."

Rachel took a sip of water and tried to think of a good reason why

Nick shouldn't work for them.

"I'm not sure winter is the best time," she said. "I mean, how are we going to live without a kitchen?"

"You move the appliances into the living room, set up a microwave and hotplate. We won't starve."

"I know. It would just be easier in the summer, when I'm not working."

"He might not have the time then. I'll ask him when I see him down at the dock tomorrow."

She ran through objections in her mind, trying to come up with something that sounded plausible. Anything she could say struck her as a signpost pointing at her and Nick, saying *look more closely*. She felt her face getting hot and quickly collected the dirty dishes and carried them to the counter.

"I'll do the dishes," Eddie said. He came up behind her and put a hand on her shoulder. "Are those kids at the schoolhouse wearing you out?"

She turned to face him. "A little. I'll go upstairs to call Donna."

"Don't want me to hear, huh?"

"No. I thought you were going to watch the hockey game."

Eddie smiled. "I'm just kidding. Go on. I'll take care of this mess."

As she climbed the stairs, she heard the radio go off and the television start up. She had thought, as she sometimes did for brief moments, that he must know, that the conversation about Nick working on the kitchen was just the prelude to an angry parade of accusations. Eddie would leave her, she felt certain, if he discovered the affair. He would not be one to forgive. She wouldn't blame him. She could not imagine staying if the roles were reversed.

Rachel dialed the mobile phone and waited for Donna to answer. After several rings, she picked up. She began crying almost as soon as she heard Rachel's voice.

"Sweetie, what is it?" Rachel said.

Donna went on crying, sucking in breath like a child.

"What's happened?"

It took Donna a few moments to get control of her voice. Rachel wandered around the bedroom picking up Eddie's socks and underwear and dirty blue jeans from the floor.

"We had a fight," Donna said finally.

"You had a fight? What about?"

"Matt wanted to go to a movie and I said we couldn't afford it and he just left. I mean, like he left three hours ago, and I don't know where he is."

Rachel lifted the lid of the clothes hamper in the closet with the phone cradled against her ear. She dropped the pieces of clothing one by one into the hamper. "I'm sorry."

"I don't know if he's coming back. I really don't."

"Was it that bad?"

"He said I was a controlling bitch."

"Oh." Rachel knew she would not be repeating this to Eddie, who would take the next ferry off the island, find Matt, and beat him senseless. She had to admit she would wring the guy's neck herself if she had the chance.

Donna made a snorting noise. Rachel wanted to hand her a tissue through the phone. "Where do you think he's gone?" she asked.

"I don't know. He's never done this. Downtown maybe."

"He took the car?"

"Yeah."

"Are you sure you want him to come back?"

"Mom."

"It's just something you might want to think about."

"Yes, I want him to come back."

"Okay, so when he comes back, you need to talk. If he's not bringing in any money, he needs to respect how you feel about spending it. That's not unreasonable."

"So you don't think I'm a controlling bitch?"

"Donna, don't even talk like that."

Rachel crossed the hall to the bathroom. She sat on the closed toilet lid and reached for a nail file in the cabinet.

"He gets so mad," Donna said.

"He doesn't hurt you, does he?"

"Mom, I'm not a battered woman."

"You have to watch out with men who have tempers."

"Dad has a temper."

"He does. Most men do. But your father's never hit me." Rachel studied her nails a moment before beginning with her index finger and smoothing the nail into a rounded moon.

"You and Dad fight."

"It's normal to fight. You just need to make sure you talk about what's making you fight, that you work through things."

"Okay, I gotta go."

"You have to go?"

"He's back," Donna whispered. "He just came in the door. I'll call you later."

Before Rachel could say goodbye, the line went dead. She set the phone on the toilet tank and continued filing her nails. How earth-shattering it all seemed at Donna's age. She supposed this was part of the appeal of her time with Nick. For an hour or two, Rachel felt the old sense of urgency and excitement again, but in the end, small doses of that heightened state were enough.

Donna was right. She and Eddie did fight, but they fought far less these days than in the past. She chalked it up to age and being comfortable enough, in their own skins and with each other, to let go of the conflicts that had once felt so monumental. She recognized the irony; since she had been with Nick, she and Eddie were getting along better than any time she could remember in the twenty-four years of their marriage, and not because she expected less of Eddie now. If anything, she expected more. The time she spent with Nick made Eddie's strengths sharper and sweeter, more precious. Rachel told herself she should be sickened by such thoughts, but she wasn't. They remained a riddle, one she could not defend, a riddle that, for the moment, was as close as she could come to the truth.

She replaced the nail file in the cabinet and went to the top of the stairs, where she stood for a moment before going down. The racket of the hockey game filled the space below. She did not like hockey. It was a brutish sport, worse than football, but tonight the slap of the sticks against the puck and the raucous cheering of the crowd sounded festive, even reassuring.

Chapter Thirteen

Ruth plunged her hands in the soapy water and swabbed at a pot with the sponge. She followed the track of the lighthouse beam beyond the kitchen window as she scrubbed the crusted remains of macaroni and cheese from the rim of the pot. Sometimes she found the presence of the lighthouse comforting, but tonight its cold eye, and the dogged repetition of its rounds, made her feel more alone. The telephone that had been installed the day before hung on the wall beside the refrigerator. As soon as the thing was hooked up, she had called and left a message for Liza, the third she had left since their last, disastrous conversation. If Liza didn't call tonight, she would call at midnight and let it ring fifty times if that was what it took to wake her up. Liza's silence was worse than her anger. Ruth felt it following her around all day.

She rinsed the pot, set it in the dish drainer, and dried her hands on a towel, then crossed the living room to the tape player and turned up the volume. This was the third time that day she had listened to Dvořák's "New World Symphony." The music mirrored her roiling mood, until the final movement with its elegiac tone. She found, at that point, there was nothing to do but start the tape over again.

A battered copy of *War and Peace* lay on the coffee table by the couch. She stared at the book as though it were an adversary in a contest she had unwillingly joined. She had brought a cardboard box full of books to the island with the plan of working her way chronologically through all the classics she could not remember reading or had missed entirely, starting with Homer's *Odyssey*. This lasted less than a day. Homer was simply too dense and slow going. She would come back to *The Odyssey*, she told herself, but there was nothing wrong with jumping ahead, to the nineteenth century, which was how she had landed on Tolstoy.

Ruth flopped on the couch, pulled an old afghan her aunt had crocheted in garish shades of orange and green over her, and reached for the local newspaper, *The Barton Crier*. She had taken to reading it cover to cover, even the police log. It was amazing how fascinating the car accidents of people she didn't know could be. She was making her way through an article about a field trip by elementary school kids to clean up the beaches when the ringing phone caused her to jump up, spilling the newspaper onto the floor. The ring was shrill and high-pitched and far too loud. She wondered if she could control the volume. She tossed aside the afghan and went to turn down the music.

She answered the phone with a tentative hello, ready to hear Liza's chastened voice.

"Ruth? Is that you?" Joan said. "God, you sound like you're under water. The connection's terrible."

Ruth muttered a surprised apology for the bad connection, wondering how her sister had gotten her number so quickly. Apparently their mother had made fast work of letting the world know there was now a phone at the inn.

"You must be freezing to death," Joan said. "Is there any heat in that place?"

"There's electric heat downstairs. I keep the upstairs closed off."

"Electric? That's going to cost a fortune."

"I'm paying for it, Joan." Ruth did not add that she was keeping the thermostat set at sixty.

"Is the place a wreck?"

"No, not really. I had to do some cleaning. There was a lot of stuff to go through—Aunt Betty's clothes and piles of papers, but I've gotten through most of it. The inn is pretty much the way you would remember it."

"And that's a good thing?"

Ruth ignored this question.

"Mom says the roof leaks," Joan said.

"There are a few leaks upstairs, if there's heavy rain. I've got buckets set up."

"I've been doing some research. Property values on Snow aren't what they are other places, like Block Island, but I still think we could get at least $200,000, maybe more with the right buyer. You think we can get the inn looking good enough to put on the market in the spring?"

"I don't want to put it on the market. I don't want to sell."

There was a long silence on the other end of the phone. "Ruth, there's no way we can support that place. It doesn't make any sense. I know you've got a sentimental attachment to the inn, but it's just crazy to think we can do the maintenance and come up with the money for the taxes and…I'm not putting a dime into it. It's not worth it."

"Then I'll have to buy you out."

Another long pause. Ruth thought she could hear Joan breathing angrily into the phone, though maybe it was just the fuzziness of the poor connection.

"Where are you going to come up with the money?"

"I don't know. But I've got a year, right? Aunt Betty paid the taxes. I'll figure something out."

"You've done a lot of crazy things, and I've kept my mouth shut, but this is insane. How are you going to support that place? It's like a black hole. It's going to eat money."

"If I buy you out, that's my problem, not yours."

"You're right about that. Listen, I've got to go. The boys are tearing the living room apart. I'll call you later."

Ruth set the receiver back in the cradle. A *sentimental attachment* to the inn. She felt powerless to respond to such a gross caricature of the truth. The island was the one constant of her childhood, the place where she had always been most herself.

At the end of that last summer, when Ruth was sixteen, she boarded the ferry certain she would be back the next year. In January, the news came that Grammy Giberson had died and left the inn to Aunt Betty.

One inheritor, Grammy Giberson believed, was simpler than three, though she expected Betty would share the place with the rest of the family. Ruth's mother and her aunt began arguing in the lawyer's office, when the will was read, and did not stop until they were no longer speaking. Betty took possession of the inn and made it clear that her sister and her family were not welcome to visit. Ruth's mother claimed she didn't care about going to the island anyway.

Ruth used to dream that she was wandering through the upstairs rooms of the inn. When she recounted her dreams at the breakfast table, Joan laughed at her. Why did she want to spend a whole boring month of the summer on Snow? After that, the island became nothing more than a collection of brittle memories, fingered so often they were yellowed and frayed around the edges. Ruth did not expect to return, not for a long time at least. Aunt Betty's sudden death of a stroke was the first surprise, followed by the news that she had left the inn not to her sister Lydia but to her nieces.

Ruth could not give a rational defense for keeping the inn. She simply felt that losing it would be like cutting off a limb. She and Joan remained locked in their roles: Joan, the disapproving older sister, determined to make Ruth see reason and grow up; Ruth, the free-spirited and reckless baby of the family, given to flights of whimsy and not planning for the future. Added to this (always added to anything) was the fact of Ruth's being gay. In her politically correct way, Joan had never been anything but accepting and supportive, but beneath this veneer, Ruth sensed the unspoken but ever-present implication that Joan, with her husband, children, career, and two-story house, lived a real adult life, while Ruth, with her female partner and Soho loft, dabbled with the alternatives like a confused teenager trying on so many roles.

Ruth returned to the couch, took up the newspaper, and slid beneath the afghan. Her eyes moved over the page, but the words didn't register. She couldn't shake the image of Joan storming through the front door, pointing out everything that was wrong with the inn and sneering at her for being so ridiculous as to think she could raise the money to keep the place. She fell asleep with the afghan wrapped around her shoulders. Her first thought when she woke in the morning—still on the couch, the rough wool scratching her neck—was that Liza had not called.

She dressed quickly in the chill air of the bedroom, made herself a cup of tea, and ate a bowl of cereal. The sun was bathing the glass of the front windows when she headed out to the porch with her camera bag slung over her shoulder. The air was so clear and still, it seemed to shimmer. She gazed up at the lighthouse, remembering the time she had climbed the circular stairs to the top, when the Coast Guard men came to check on the light and let them inside. The sweep of the view was so great, she grabbed the railing, afraid she might fall through the glass into all that space and light, all that blue. The long, skinny finger of the island spread below and the winking surface of the bay seemed to belong to her alone. She came down from the light and declared that when she grew up, she would be a lighthouse keeper, but her mother explained, with a touch of exasperation, that the keepers didn't exist anymore. The automated lighthouses ran themselves.

Ruth heard the hum of a motor in the distance and scanned the water. A small boat was putting along past the lighthouse. She recognized the low-riding boat with its little box of a wheelhouse as a quahog skiff. She caught a glimpse of the quahogger in his yellow slicker, his profile visible through the window of the wheelhouse. As a girl, she had watched the quahoggers return to Snow on summer afternoons, back from selling their haul over in Barton. Everything about those men was tough and weathered, as though they had taken on the character of the sea itself. Nothing daunted them—hurricanes, nor'easters, the falling price of clams. They went out seven days a week, in any weather. She imagined it as a magical life and thought that if she couldn't be a lighthouse keeper, maybe she could be a quahogger.

The rattling hulk of an island car came down the road and went past the inn. Ruth raised her hand in a wave. The man behind the wheel, a scruffy-looking character with gray hair hanging in a ponytail down his back, raised his fingers so that the tips showed above the steering wheel. Moments later, another vehicle without a muffler rumbled past, and Ruth knew either the ferry was arriving or the dump was open. These were the only occasions when more than one car drove by in a row.

She zipped her jacket up to her neck and set off down the road. This morning, the strong sunlight and the quahogger out on the water made her feel certain that she would find a way to keep the inn. When she reached Our Lady of Snow, the Catholic church, she turned up the hill toward the small chapel. With its white clapboard sides, the building looked more like a camp lodge than a church, if you ignored the cross above the door. In the morning light, the place had an abandoned feel. She took her camera from the bag and zoomed in on the sharp lines of the cross against the sky. She circled the building a couple of times, snapping close-ups of the little squares of window and the domed metal top of the propane tank against the back wall.

The ferry had come and gone by the time Ruth finished taking her pictures. She could see the white dot of the boat across the water, headed back to the mainland. She went on down the road toward the store and found Alice inside, rummaging through boxes, with the old man who sat on the porch on warmer days slumped in a chair by the woodstove.

"You're out early," Alice said.

Ruth gestured toward the camera bag. "I need to take advantage of the morning light." She leaned forward, lowered her voice, and pointed at the old man. "Is he asleep?"

"Yes. Silas gets more sleep here than he does at home. I have to wake him up when I close for lunch."

Ruth set her camera bag on the counter and went up and down the store's narrow aisles examining the dusty tops of soup cans and cracker boxes. The plain planks of the floor were unfinished, the rough wood dulled to a dirty black. At the end of one aisle, she found a large orange and white cat curled in a ball. She selected cans of green beans and peaches, thinking how strange it was to be eating like this. She couldn't remember eating canned peaches since the grade-school cafeteria, but until she could get to the mainland on Friday, when two ferries ran in the afternoon, she didn't have a choice. It was Alice's canned food or nothing.

Silas let out a prolonged snort as she passed him on her way back to the counter. A bristled stubble of white hairs covered his chin, and he wore a bulky plaid wool jacket whose sleeves were stiff with a layer of dirt. If Ruth had encountered him on the streets of New York, she would have assumed he was homeless, but here he merely looked like an older and more disheveled version of the other islanders.

"You still have a cat," Ruth said as she set her purchases on the counter. "We loved that tabby you had when I was a kid. We used to smash the muscle shells and feed the raw muscles to him."

"I think that must have been Arthur. He was the best mouser we ever had. Chester here falls down on the job sometimes."

Alice reached for the cans of food and squinted at the price stickers. Ruth watched her ringing up each item on the old cash register, a big thing that looked like it might date from the early 1900s, and wished that her mother had remained friendly with Alice. She knew that Alice still sent a Christmas card every year. She didn't think her mother ever sent one to Alice.

"It was pretty cold last night," Alice said as she unfurled a paper bag and placed the cans in it. "At least we've got the sun this morning."

Ruth fished in her pocket for a ten dollar bill. "I've got blankets hanging over the doorway to the second floor to keep the heat in downstairs. That staircase is like a wind tunnel."

"I used to go visit your aunt. I remember it got a little chilly in there in the winter."

Alice gave Ruth the change as Silas let out another loud snort. He shook his head from side to side like a horse, but did not open his eyes.

Ruth thanked Alice and scooped up the groceries with her camera bag. She was almost to the door when Alice said, "Stop by sometime. I have a picture of your uncle to show you."

"Uncle Hank?"

"No. Your other uncle. Pete"

Her mother rarely mentioned Pete, who had been killed at the age of eighteen in the war. Ruth couldn't remember the last time anyone in the family had so much as said his name. "I'd like to see that."

"Come for lunch some day."

Ruth said she would do that and went on out to the porch. Nick stood beside his truck in the parking lot, talking to another man. He glanced in her direction for a moment, but did not give any sign that he recognized her. She had not seen him, other than driving past, since that night when he gave her the tour. Ruth clutched the paper bag to her chest and climbed the hill to the road.

Chapter Fourteen

Through a haze of sleep, she became aware of sounds: a car door slamming, a knock on the door. Nora raised herself from the pillow and squinted at the clock. Eight forty-five. For a moment, she couldn't think if it was morning or night, unable to believe she had slept so late. It must have been the darkness. The small bedroom was completely enclosed, shrouded in dark, and beyond the curtain, the sky remained overcast. Isabelle lay on her back with one arm flung toward Nora. She opened her eyes when Nora stepped from the bed.

"What is it?" Isabelle said.

"Someone's at the door."

"What time is it?"

"Nearly nine."

Isabelle ran her hands over her head as if checking the condition of her hair. "You're not going to the door like that, are you?"

"Why not?" Nora stood there naked, watching alarm take possession of Isabelle's face before pulling on her robe and shoving her feet into a pair of loafers.

She went out to the porch and unlatched the door. Nick stood on the top step.

"Mrs. Venable," he said. "I'm sorry. I didn't mean to—"

She raised her hand, cutting him off. "I don't usually sleep so late. It must be the sea air."

"That's what they say. It makes you sleepy."

"It doesn't make you sleepy?"

"No. I'm used to it. I came to check on your propane, see if you need more." He gestured toward the side of the house. "I'm going to order a cylinder. This one's almost out."

"Do you need money?"

"You can just pay the bill when it comes."

Nora thanked him and asked if there was anything else.

"Not really, but I just thought I should tell you there was a fire out here a few weeks ago. I found the remains of one in the grass by the mansion. This morning it looks like there was another one. You haven't heard anyone or seen anyone, have you?"

"No. You mean like a campfire? Who would be out here doing that?"

"I think it's some kids. I'll do some asking around. If you see anyone out here, let me know."

Nora said she would and thanked him again. When she shut the door, Isabelle emerged from the bedroom tying the belt at the waist of her bathrobe.

"What did he say?" Isabelle asked. "Something about a fire?"

"Some kids have been having campfires out here. Harmless, I guess. He said to keep an eye out. He's going to try to figure out who it is. I can't imagine there are too many kids on the island who could be wandering around at night setting fires."

"The big house must be an attraction."

"More like an eyesore." Nora went to the sink and filled the coffee pot with water. "The coffee's in the fridge."

"Nora, how long are you going to keep this up?"

"Keep what up?" Nora turned to find Isabelle facing her, hands sunk in the pockets of her robe.

"Staying in this godforsaken place."

"I like it here." Nora went to the refrigerator and rummaged around until she found the coffee. "I think I've made this place quite comfortable."

"Comfortable for how long?"

"I don't know. I don't have a plan. As long as I feel like it. You're welcome to stay."

Isabelle gave her another annoyed glance, went out to the porch, and slammed the bathroom door behind her. After a moment, Nora heard water running in the bathtub. She spooned the coffee into the filter, emptied the contents of the coffee pot into the coffee maker, and sat at the table, watching the thin black liquid drip down. She didn't know why Isabelle had bothered to come if she was only going to start up again with old arguments.

After Isabelle's arrival on the afternoon ferry the day before, they had cooked a dinner of roasted chicken and mashed potatoes and consumed a bottle of wine. Warm and drowsy by the woodstove, they made love on the couch, for the first time in what felt like months. Isabelle exclaimed over Nora's paintings. The one of the cove was lovely, she said. In all of it there was approval and understanding, a tacit agreement that they were done with a past littered with recriminations. Now Nora felt like she had been duped. She should have told Isabelle not to come.

The thick aroma of coffee filled the small room. She had made it strong, the way she liked it. When Isabelle emerged from the bathroom, a towel around her head, Nora was leaning back in the chair, her feet propped on the edge of the table, drinking the coffee.

"You're going to kill yourself sitting like that," Isabelle said.

"That's what you want, isn't it? You want me to keel over dead, so you don't have to deal with me anymore."

Isabelle touched the towel wrapped around her head, as though checking to see that it was still in place, and bit her lip, a nervous habit Nora sometimes found endearing but at the moment found exasperating.

"I've left everything to you," Nora said. "You'll be well off when I'm gone."

"Don't do this, Nora."

"Shouldn't I be saying that to you? You're the one who won't move in with me but doesn't want me to stay here on the island. You want me to go back to that house by myself, so I'm there when you deign to visit, like I'm some sort of animal at the zoo."

Isabelle gave her a pained look, and Nora felt that momentary surge of satisfaction, thinking, *good, I hurt her.*

"I asked you how long you were staying, that's all," Isabelle said. "You can do anything you like. That's quite obvious. You already do anything you like. I'm not trying to stop you."

Nora took another sip of coffee and watched Isabelle march into the bedroom. She made the maximum amount of noise possible, it seemed, going through her suitcase and straightening the sheets, as though the business of dressing and putting the room in order could say the things she would not.

Isabelle returned in an old pair of jeans Nora had not seen her wear in some time and a bulky sweater. She poured herself some coffee, took a drink, and went to the sink, where she dumped the contents of the cup down the drain.

"What's wrong?" Nora said.

"I can't drink that. It's strong as mud."

"Should I make another pot?"

"No."

Isabelle went to the refrigerator and poured orange juice into a glass. She drank it standing next to the counter. Nora could not face an entire day of this. "I'm going to go see about the fire," she said.

She went to the bedroom and got dressed, and stopped in the bathroom, where she splashed water on her face and ran a comb through her hair. Isabelle was waiting for her on the porch, outside the bathroom door.

Nora pulled on her jacket and stepped outside. Isabelle followed. They were going to check on the fire together, it appeared. The grass was still wet with dew, and the smell of the pines filled the air. Nora felt better instantly. She strode across the lawn toward the big house, grateful for the bracing cold.

The charred patch of grass was visible from a distance, a black, flattened circle. Other flattened spots surrounded it, where people had clearly been sitting. Nora stood over the remains of the fire, studying the exposed mound of dirt as though it might give up some clue, although to what she was not sure.

"Maybe we should tell the policeman," Isabelle said. "There is a policeman on the island, isn't there?"

"Yes. He shows up every time the ferry comes in."

"I worry about you, Nora."

Isabelle's voice took on a squeaky tone. Nora recognized the words, and the tone, as an overture, even an apology. "I can take care of myself."

"I know that. But you can't control other people."

Nora laughed. "I'm not afraid of some prepubescent island boys."

Quahog boats often appeared in the cove in the morning, but today the circle of water was empty. Pebbles rolled beneath the soles of Nora's shoes. She walked quickly to the bend and kept going, staying in the tire tracks made by the few cars that came out to the cove. She felt Isabelle behind her, taking long strides to keep up.

They walked for a good half mile without speaking, before Isabelle asked in her small voice, "Where are we going?"

"To the beach. I walk there every morning."

Nora said these words without looking back, but she could hear Isabelle behind her, dislodging stones as she made her way. When she reached the pull-off for the beach, Nora took the path through the brush. Narrow and enclosed, the path was dark, until suddenly it opened onto the wide space of sand. They were not alone. A woman stood down by the water, a camera held to her face. Nora recognized her bulky down jacket.

Isabelle scanned the beach. "I feel like I've been here before. Did we swim here, when we came, that first time?"

"I don't think so."

The woman down by the water turned and saw them, and raised her hand in a wave.

Nora called hello as the woman approached.

"Good morning," the woman said. "We've got some sun at last."

"Yes," Nora said. "At last."

They stood awkwardly, the woman glancing back toward the water. Nora broke the silence. "I'm Nora. This is my friend, Isabelle."

"I'm Ruth."

"You're always taking pictures," Nora said.

"That's why I came here, to do a photographic study of the island."

"Really? I'm doing some painting while I'm here. It's such a wonderful place. The light is terrific."

Ruth smiled, as if to say she knew just what Nora meant.

"I'd love to see your photographs," Nora added.

"Stop by sometime."

"I'll do that."

They stood for another moment, glancing at each other and then toward the waves breaking on the shore.

"Well, I guess I'll be off. Good to see you again," Ruth said. "And nice to meet you." She nodded toward Isabelle.

"Nice to meet you," Isabelle replied, her voice barely audible.

Ruth made her way across the sand. As soon as she disappeared, out of earshot, Nora said, "You could have been friendly."

Isabelle returned her look, eyebrows arched. "I wasn't unfriendly."

"You weren't friendly either."

"Maybe it was the way you were flirting with her."

"God, Isabelle, that is truly ridiculous. I was not flirting with that girl."

"I'd love to see your photographs." Isabelle repeated the phrase, deepening her voice so it sounded like Nora's.

"Well, I would like to see her photographs. That's not flirting."

"She's a member of the church."

"What church?"

"You know, *the* church."

Nora rolled her eyes at Isabelle's use of this code phrase. "You mean she's a lesbian?"

"Yes."

"How do you know?"

"The hair, the clothes. The way she slings that camera around. Take a look at her. It's obvious."

"So she's a lesbian. That doesn't mean if I'm friendly to her, I'm flirting."

"You flirt with everyone."

"I don't think you understand the difference between common friendliness and flirting. Just because a person is outgoing, has a little bit of personality, does not mean she's going around flirting with everyone she meets. I saw her on the ferry last week. She's staying at the inn over by the lighthouse. She's not an islander."

Nora gave Isabelle a long look, but Isabelle did not raise her eyes.

"What is wrong with you?" Nora said. "Why am I getting this interrogation this morning?"

Isabelle smoothed the sand with the tip of her shoe. "I think Henry's dying. I want you there."

Nora paused to take this in. "Have they said he's dying?"

"No. I can just feel it. It's like he's slipping away a bit more every day."

"If he's dying, of course, I mean...I'll come."

When Isabelle looked up, Nora wasn't sure what she saw in her face, manipulation or true need, but it was clear that Henry was still there between them, as he always had been, an unyielding presence. She was afraid death would not break the hold. He would continue to watch over them, nudging them into self-conscious guilt at every turn.

"You want me there at the nursing home with you?" Nora asked.

Isabelle had never allowed her to come to the nursing home, too preoccupied with what the nurses and aides might think, what everyone might think.

"Yes."

"All right, then, I'll come. We can go today. We can take the afternoon ferry."

Nora turned away from the water and made her way back across the sand, her feet sinking into the soft surface. Isabelle caught up to her and reached for her hand, giving it a quick squeeze before letting go.

"I wouldn't ask you to come, Nora, if I didn't think—"

"I know."

When they came to the road, Nora slowed her pace, and they walked side by side in a silence that, if not companionable, was at least devoid of anger or accusation. How many kinds of silence there could be between two people, Nora thought, and how hard this was to understand. She resisted the urge to reduce the silence to one simple emotion that could be recognized and categorized. Fury or disdain. Contempt or indifference. The silence between them contained too many strands, each negating the other.

"I'm glad you're coming," Isabelle said when the cove came into view.

Nora nodded. She was not glad, but she would do this because it was what needed to be done.

Chapter Fifteen

The red brick building came into view only when the street was left behind. Elaborate cast-iron gates framed a curved drive lined by apple trees. Nora was reminded of a college campus. They parked in the area marked for visitors and made their way down a walkway brightened by the purples and oranges of potted mums. Isabelle's heels clicked against the pavement.

A wave of heat met them as they stepped through the door. Isabelle stopped at the receptionist's desk and exchanged a few muted words with the woman seated there. The lounge area was furnished with overstuffed couches and chairs covered in bright florals, and framed Matisse prints hung on the walls. The air of forced cheer was oppressive.

Nora followed Isabelle down a hallway. They turned a corner, past rooms where patients sat in wheelchairs staring blankly at nothing or lay on beds, immobile. Nora tried to contain the panic that overtook her when she looked into those rooms. She told herself to keep her eyes on Isabelle's back, but she could not stop turning her head.

The curtains were open, giving a view of the lawn and flowerbeds beyond the window, and Henry sat in an easy chair in sweatpants and a baggy cardigan sweater and slippers. The room smelled faintly of disinfectant, a repellant but acceptable odor, but beneath this scent there were others—institutional food served in the dining room down the hall, and a vaguely human smell that brought to mind skin that does not come clean, no matter how many scrubbings. The chair in which Henry sat was covered in a stiff vinyl that made a crackling noise when he turned to watch Isabelle cross the room to the window. Henry gazed at her with unfocused eyes. He reminded Nora of a bird, his head moving so slowly and deliberately.

"Henry, it's me," Isabelle said.

"Who?" His voice, weak and wobbly, was nothing more than a faint imitation of the voice Nora remembered.

"Isabelle."

"Isabelle. She's my wife."

"That's right. I'm Isabelle, your wife."

He stared at her, his mouth hanging open, and shook his head. "You're not my wife."

"Yes, I am. It's me, Henry. Isabelle." She took his hand, but he pulled it away and returned to staring out the window.

Isabelle attempted to get his attention again. "Henry, I've brought someone to see you. Nora. You remember Nora."

He shook his head back and forth until Isabelle grabbed his hand again, and he went still.

She looked over at Nora. "He does this," she whispered. "Shakes his head so much you think he's going to hurt himself."

"He doesn't want to see me," Nora said, her voice low.

"No, he does this with anyone."

Nora remained by the door. She had not seen Henry for two years, since he'd entered the nursing home. He was hardly recognizable, a shell not just of himself but of a human being. No one should be allowed to go on living like this, Nora thought, overwhelmed by repulsion and the terrifying thought that she could end up in such a state.

Isabelle motioned for her to come over. Nora crossed the shiny linoleum, the soles of her shoes squeaking. "Hello, Henry," she said.

He gazed up at her, and for a moment, she thought she saw comprehension in his eyes. He said nothing but began shaking his head again. Isabelle wrapped her hand around his. "It's okay," she said softly. "It's okay, Henry."

Henry rocked back and forth, making a guttural sound in his throat.

After a moment, he stopped rocking and took up shaking his head again. Isabelle ran her fingers over the translucent skin covering his hand. Nora thought of the Indian pipes they used to find hidden in the woods in Maine, the tubers coming up from the moss, bleached an unearthly white.

"I should go," Nora whispered to Isabelle.

"Just stand over there." Isabelle motioned vaguely toward the door.

Nora moved away and found a bare spot of wall to lean against. She tried not to move or make the slightest sound while Isabelle stroked Henry's hand. Finally he stopped shaking his head.

"Look at those nails," Isabelle said, speaking to Henry in a voice you would use with a child. "We need to do something about that."

She took a pair of nail clippers from a drawer in the table by the bed and pulled a chair up beside his. "Put your hand out, Henry. Like this."

He looked down at Isabelle's hand uncertainly. She guided his arm away from his body and took his fingers one at a time, holding them in place while she clipped the nails. He flinched at the sound the nail clippers made, trying to pull back, but Isabelle held on.

"We don't want your nails to get too long, Henry. You can hurt yourself. We want to make you look nice. Like the barber. You remember the barber who comes and gives you a shave. He makes you look nice, doesn't he?"

She finished with one hand and started on the other. Nora wished that she could vanish, suddenly transported from the place. She was not up to walking back down those hallways, but she was not up to staying, either, watching Isabelle go through this pathetic routine. It was clear what Isabelle was trying to do. She wanted Nora to feel as guilty as she did, to live for a few minutes in her skin. All right, Nora wanted to scream, I get it.

Isabelle set the nail clipper back in the drawer. "Okay, time for a walk. Henry, we're going for a walk. Down the hall. We're going to look at the leaves."

Henry gazed up at her, his mouth hanging open.

"Come and help me," Isabelle said to Nora.

Henry began shaking his head as soon as Nora stepped forward. She shrank back against the wall.

"Ignore him," Isabelle said. "It doesn't mean anything." She moved a wheelchair next to Henry. "Just take him under the elbow. If we both hold him, he can get into the wheelchair."

Nora would have done almost anything at that moment to avoid touching Henry, but she went to his side and placed her hand beneath his elbow. His arm was thin and brittle as a chicken's wing.

"Okay, Henry, now stand up," Isabelle said. "We're going for a walk."

Henry tottered unsteadily and fell into the wheelchair. Isabelle placed one foot and then the other against the rests and took a blanket from the bottom of the bed, which she draped over his legs. "Let's go look at the leaves."

Isabelle pushed the wheelchair from the room with resigned but cheerful efficiency. As they went down the hallway, past more rooms with open doors, Isabelle called out hello to the nurses and aides they passed. One of them, a woman wearing hospital scrubs in a garish pink, patted Henry on the head as they went by and said, "Taking a little walk, Henry?"

At the end of the hallway, they came to a lounge with double glass doors leading to an outdoor patio. Isabelle pushed Henry up to the doors and pointed. "See the leaves, Henry?"

There were a few bright yellow leaves still clinging to a poplar in the center of the courtyard. "Leaves," Henry said.

Nora stood behind Isabelle, thinking of all the years when Henry sat in his favorite chair reading the paper and watching sports on TV. It was easy to deceive him then, when he controlled everything about Isabelle's life except the hours she stole with Nora. It was easy to have contempt for him then.

"He always loved the fall," Isabelle said. "He still does. If I don't bring him down here, he'll say 'leaves' over and over."

As if on cue, Henry said again, "Leaves."

"Yellow leaves. Just like at home," Isabelle responded.

She stood with her hands on his shoulders and gazed out at the courtyard with him. They made a touching tableau, Nora thought, as long as you didn't know the long struggle that had been the truth of their marriage.

"How about another walk?" Isabelle said as she swiveled the wheelchair and set off down another hallway.

Nora wondered where they were going now, until she realized that the place was laid out in a square. They made the circuit back to Henry's room, and an aide came in to help get him out of the wheelchair. She was a large woman from the islands, with an accent Nora assumed was Jamaican.

"Now there, ain't we happy?" the woman said as she settled Henry in the armchair and set the blanket over his legs. "Henry's the happiest. All the time, he's happy." The woman laughed and rubbed Henry's cheek. "You ladies have a nice day now."

She went clomping out of the room in her white clogs. Nora checked her watch. Hadn't they been here long enough?

Isabelle straightened the bedspread and went through the closet, collecting clothes to take home and wash. She took her time with each task, stopping to talk with Henry and pat his knee, as though intentionally prolonging Nora's discomfort. Nora was about to announce that she would go out and wait in the car when Isabelle leaned down to plant a kiss on Henry's forehead and told him she would be back soon. Nora followed her out of the room without saying goodbye to Henry, afraid he would only become agitated again. This time she did not look into the open doors as she went past. She kept her gaze straight ahead, on a large potted plant at the end of the corridor and the nurse coming down the hall with a cart covered with little paper cups full of pills.

The air outside, so cool and fresh, seemed to carry off the disgusting smells that clung to her skin. The women made their way to the car in silence. Nora climbed into the passenger seat. For a change, Isabelle was driving. As they moved down the long drive, Nora tried to think of something to say, but there were no words. She simply wanted to be gone, free of the place.

"They're really very caring," Isabelle said as she turned onto the avenue. "Everyone who works there. They treat Henry like family."

"I don't think I should go again. He doesn't like seeing me."

Isabelle gave her a quick glance and looked back at the road. "He gets like that sometimes. You can't tell what it is. Usually he won't let me cut his nails, but today he was calm about that."

"But there was something about me. He didn't want me there. It was as if he knew."

"How could he not know?"

"You were always convinced that he didn't know."

"That we were sleeping together? Yes, I was convinced he didn't know that. Henry didn't have enough imagination to figure that out. But he knew there was something between us, something out of the ordinary. He wasn't a completely blind idiot. He was jealous."

"Of what?"

"Everything. The time I spent with you, the time you spent with us, all of it."

"He acted like he didn't care."

"He didn't care, and he did. That's the way he was about most things. Now, well, you saw for yourself. He's like a child."

They came to a red light, and Nora saw tears sliding soundlessly down Isabelle's face.

"Pull over," Nora said. "I'll drive."

Isabelle did as instructed and turned into the parking lot of a convenience store. She shut off the engine and handed Nora the keys. By the time they had switched seats, Isabelle was crying convulsively, her nose red, her shoulders shaking. Nora sat for a moment before starting up the engine.

"Did he seem worse today?" she asked.

Isabelle fished for a tissue in her purse and blew her nose. "No, not really."

"Do you really think he's dying?"

"I don't know. Nobody knows. He could go on like this forever."

"You shouldn't visit so often. It's too upsetting to you."

This set Isabelle off on another crying fit. Head bowed, she made a sort of mewing sound that Nora hated, and blew her nose again. Nora sped out of the parking lot and drove on to Isabelle's house.

Chapter Sixteen

Some days the photographs mocked her. If she stared at the images too long, they went dead. The black-and-white prints seemed small and insignificant—mussel shells scattered in a pile, the plain front of the Union Church. The images did not surprise her. Predictable, even sentimental, they took on a flat quality.

Ruth stood back from the bathtub and studied the prints pinned to the clothesline. She wanted to have a collection ready to show Liza, but now it seemed she had nothing, that her weeks of roaming the island added up to a few prints an amateur could have shot. How had she ever imagined she could take a photograph a day and produce anything worthwhile? The idea was foolish and self-indulgent, fated to failure. She unpinned the prints one at a time and set them under the press. Something was missing: an intensity of vision, the full force of the light. None of it came through in the photos as she had hoped.

Ruth made her way down the hall to the kitchen, where she opened the oven and checked on the lasagna. The cheese on top had melted, but the sauce wasn't bubbling yet around the edges. She ran water in the sink and set about washing the pot she had used for the tomato sauce. The traditional black-and-white images she was making were passé. The art world wanted "edgy" and experimental work that tested the boundaries of technique and taste—huge color polaroids, prints so manipulated they no longer looked like photographs, fragmented triptychs. She found much of this work slick and gimmicky. She longed for the purity of such masters as Edward Weston and Imogen Cunningham, who were not afraid to make photographs that were beautiful. In the current age of irony, beauty had become something to be mocked, unless it was the "beauty" of emaciated super models. Ruth remained convinced that making black-and-white images which relied on pure shooting and printing technique was more difficult than creating the sensational stuff. She would readily admit that she was a traditionalist, when it came to photography at least, yet how hard it was to create photographs in this vein with true force.

The quick excitement of clicking the shutter had always been what she loved. In that fluid instant between raising the camera to her eye and capturing the image, she was alive to the slightest nuance in her conversation with trees and sky, sand and water, sun and shadow. She released the shutter with a surge of certainty, thinking *that's it, I got it*, but once she entered the darkroom, she confronted the truth. She would mix the developing chemicals with a heady sense of anticipation only to find that what she had captured on film did not match what she had seen through the camera's lens. Sometimes, of course, the experience went the other way, when images she shot randomly, not thinking they would amount to much, ended up as the most interesting ones on the roll, but today was not one of those days.

Finished with the dishes, Ruth took the lasagna from the oven. The rich smell of tomato sauce and cheese filled the room. At least she could make a decent pan of lasagna. She tossed the potholders on the counter. Ten minutes to boat time.

She heard a car outside and glanced at the window in time to see a shiny Nissan truck go past. She caught a glimpse of Nick behind the wheel, his large shoulders and the profile of his face. He did not turn his head. He drove past ten times a day, but he had not stopped by again, which surprised her. She had expected he would be back.

Ruth waited until he was on down the road, then headed out the door. After an overcast day, the sun had broken through, shooting tendrils of orange light along the edges of the clouds on the horizon. The ferry emerged from the vivid color, a bit of white against the glowering sky. Ruth kept her eye on the back of the Nissan as it rounded a curve and disappeared from view. She felt lighter already. Out in the chill air her grand plans of publishing a book of photographs didn't seem that important. She thought of the days ahead, of how wonderful it would be to have Liza with her, to talk, to laugh, to shed the oppressive silence of being alone.

Liza had finally returned her phone calls and, after a series of tentative conversations, agreed to come up for Thanksgiving. The last time they talked, Liza seemed ready to accept Ruth staying on the island, ready even to embrace the idea of saving the inn. A couple of cars passed, headed in the direction of the dock, people Ruth had seen down at the store but didn't know. She waved to each one, and the drivers waved back. The island had taken on a flurry of life, with the holiday the next day. People had been arriving on the ferry or leaving to visit family on the mainland.

Ruth covered the last stretch at a slow run. She came down the hill as the ferry was tying up and spotted Liza on the deck. She stood a ways back from the others gathered in the parking lot. Nick's truck was parked off to the side. He sat in the cab with the window open, his gaze fixed straight ahead on the ferry.

Liza drove down the ramp and pulled up beside her. As Ruth opened the door and slid into the seat, Liza reached over and grasped her hand. "Sweetheart."

"Honeypie," Ruth answered.

They laughed at the familiar exchange, which had started as a joke, an imitation of straight couples, but then took on a life of its own as real terms of endearment they used with each other.

When they reached the top of the hill and made the turn onto the road, Liza brought Ruth's hand to her lips and planted a wet kiss. "I could eat you with a spoon."

"Me, too. But first there's lasagna for dinner."

They exchanged a glance that suggested maybe dinner could wait.

"I got one of those free-range turkeys." Liza gestured toward the cooler in the back seat.

"Is it frozen?"

"Yeah. I just tossed it in the cooler. It probably hasn't thawed yet. Ten pounds. We're going to have a feast."

The light drained from the sky as they drove the distance to the inn. It was almost dark by the time they had carried Liza's bags and the cooler inside. Once the door was closed behind them, Ruth wrapped her arms around Liza and gave her a long kiss. She felt Liza's hands sliding beneath the layers of clothing until they found her bra strap and unhooked it. Liza's fingers traced a path down Ruth's back, over the knobs of her spine, the light touch making her shiver.

"You're like the Michelin man in all these clothes," Liza said. "I can't get to you."

Ruth unbuttoned her jacket, dropped it to the floor, and pulled Liza back into a kiss. She reached beneath her blouse to cradle the soft skin of Liza's belly and inched toward her breasts, drawing out the slow touching.

"Maybe we should go to the bedroom," Ruth whispered.

Liza responded by shrugging off her jacket and stepping from her pants and shoes. A tightly fitting tee shirt brushed the band of her underpants, and her feet were swaddled in thick wool socks. She went sliding down the hall, pulling Ruth by the hand, and Ruth could not help but think how foolish people looked half-dressed, though in the tee shirt and underpants Liza left her breathless. When they reached the bedroom, Liza removed the tee shirt in a deft motion and climbed into bed. Ruth peeled off her sweater and shirt and pants, and let the bra fall from her shoulders. In the gray light, the smooth mounds of Liza's breasts waited.

They began slowly, as they always did. Ruth straddled Liza and leaned down to give her small kisses. She eased the underpants down past her hips, and Liza wriggled free of them, kicking them to the floor. She felt Liza's tongue moving over her neck like a wet snake. A wave of gratitude swept over her at the thought that someone could give her such pleasure and such peace.

They made the tantalizing build-up last as long as possible, an exploration that seemed to go on for hours, balanced between a teeth-gritting intensity and pure delight. When they could not hold back another moment, they gave in. The sensation was exquisite and exhausting. Ruth had forgotten how much she needed this, how much she missed it.

Sinking back against the pillows, they lay side by side with the sheets tangled at their feet. The window had gone dark, the black pool beyond the glass broken only by the beam from the lighthouse swinging out over the water and back.

Liza reached over and took Ruth's hand. "I guess we haven't lost the touch."

Ruth squeezed her hand. "I guess not."

"Did you say there was lasagna? I'm starving."

Ruth raised herself on one elbow, leaning over to give Liza a kiss flat on the mouth, and climbed from the bed. She reached for the sweatpants hanging from a hook on the back of the door and pulled on her shirt and sweater. In the front hallway, she switched on the light and found Liza's overnight bag by the door. She knew, without opening it, that the bag contained Liza's battered hairbrush missing half the bristles and the little pillow she brought with her when she traveled.

Ruth carried the overnight bag to the bedroom, where she sat on the edge of the bed and watched as Liza dressed in a pair of pajama bottoms and a sweatshirt. She took a schoolgirl's delight in everything Liza did, from tying the drawstring at her waist to smoothing her hair into place. She could not, at that moment, remember why she had ever felt impatience or annoyance with Liza, or reconstruct what it was they had fought over. The idea of fighting about anything was inconceivable, a bad dream from a hazy past.

"I brought four bottles of wine," Liza said. "Will that last us?"

"Maybe. I baked two pies. Pumpkin and apple."

They exchanged another kiss, and Ruth made her way to the kitchen. She had gone to the mainland on Sunday, spending the hours between ferries sitting at the coffee shop, reading and drinking one cup of tea after another, before setting off for the grocery store. This time she had walked the mile to the store and taken a cab back to the ferry with her bags of groceries.

She held her hand over the lasagna. Still warm. If she set the oven on two-fifty, she could heat the lasagna through without drying it out. She turned on the oven and took the lettuce from the refrigerator. She was ripping the lettuce over the salad bowl when Liza emerged from the bedroom and went to the refrigerator. "Beer?" Liza said as she opened the door. "What are you doing drinking beer?"

"Oh, that. Somebody brought it over one night."

"Somebody?"

"Alice's son. Nick."

"I didn't know she had any kids on the island."

"Neither did I. He came back a few years ago. He's a carpenter. Well, an engineer, but now he does carpentry work. He was in Vietnam."

Liza took a bottle of cranberry juice from the refrigerator and poured herself a glass. "How old is he?"

"Forty-two."

"You know his exact age?"

"He told me."

"What's his status?"

"Single. He lives by himself over on the other side of the island."

"Did you tell him you're not on the hetero team?"

"It didn't exactly come up."

"He's probably got designs on you."

"I don't think so. I ran into him a couple of times, and I haven't really seen him since."

"I think we should move to the island."

Ruth looked up from the salad bowl.

"I mean it," Liza said. "We could live right here in the inn. We could run the inn in the summer and live here in the winter. We could have a bunch of kids and send them to the schoolhouse."

They had never discussed having children, and though there was an implicit assumption between them that they were both in this for the long haul, what Liza described sounded much more final, much more settled than anything Ruth had imagined. Ruth shredded the last leaf of lettuce and reached for the cutting board. She sliced a cucumber in thin slices that fell in an even row.

"I don't know," Ruth said. "It's a lot quieter here than I thought."

"You want to go back to New York?"

"Yes and no."

"I don't. The minute I stepped off the ferry, I thought, this is it. I want to stay here forever."

"I just don't know that I would want to stay year round. It's very…" Ruth tried to think of a word for the leaden emptiness of the island, but she couldn't. After a pause, she added, "Still."

"Still is fine with me. The city makes me dizzy these days. Are you having second thoughts?"

"No." Ruth answered quickly, automatically. She could not admit to having doubts, not to anyone else, at least. The whole idea of her visual diary would disappear in a puff of smoke.

Liza sat at the table, her feet propped on a chair, and drank the cranberry juice. It felt like home to have Liza there while she prepared the salad, but Ruth wasn't sure that the sprawling inn with its rows of rooms and beaten-up furniture and rattling windows could become a permanent home. She could not imagine a baby, here or anywhere else. She definitely could not imagine packing a lunch and sending a child off to the schoolhouse for the day.

Liza went to the sideboard and turned on the radio. "Can you get anything on this thing?"

"There's the college station on the mainland. It's not bad. They've got a good folk show on some nights."

After a moment of fiddling with the dial, Liza found a station, and the sound of guitar music filled the room, followed by the crooning voice of a female singer. Ruth finished assembling the salad and put the lasagna in the oven while Liza opened one of the bottles of wine. There were no wine glasses, so they drank out of thick-rimmed juice glasses. The plates were chipped, too, but none of this bothered Ruth. She was going to eat a meal the way it was meant to be eaten, with another person to savor the food, with the rich taste of red wine to wash it down.

She took the lasagna from the oven and served the plates as the music came to an end.

"That was Rory Block doing Willie's Brown's 'Future Blues' off her *Best Blues and Originals* album," the DJ said. "What a voice that woman has. Well, I hope it's a good night for everyone out there. You're listening to Jolly Roger, the voice of the bay, on WBAY radio. That's right, folks, I'm a music pirate, not a pirate of gold doubloons, and I'm here to keep the records spinning for you. Okay, up next, I've got Muddy Waters doing 'I Just Want to Make Love to You.'"

Ruth stopped with a plate in each hand.

"What's wrong?" Liza said.

"That voice. On the radio."

"What about it?"

"It's Nick. Alice's son."

"Did he tell you he had a radio station?"

"No."

"You're sure it's him?"

"Pretty sure."

"Well, he said he was a music pirate."

"He must be broadcasting here, on the island."

Ruth set the plates down and took the seat across from Liza. The sound of Nick's voice, suddenly in the room, was unnerving.

"God, I'm really starving," Liza said. "All I had for lunch was a bag of potato chips." She raised her juice glass. "To the Snow Island Inn."

Ruth touched her glass against Liza's. It made a distinctly clunky sound.

"So did I tell you about the rally last week in Washington Square?" Liza said.

Ruth shook her head.

"Martie called me about it. That group at Cooper Union organized it. Peace Action or something like that."

Only a couple of hundred people showed up, Liza explained, but they were planning another one for December. Bush was going to just roll into Iraq without anyone saying a word if they didn't try to stop him. Here he was talking about democracy and freedom and human rights when Kuwait, the country they were supposedly defending, didn't let women vote.

Ruth tried to follow what Liza was saying as she brought a forkful of lasagna to her mouth, but here on the island, the possibility of war seemed utterly remote, and she was distracted by the radio, waiting for the sound of Nick's voice again.

Chapter Seventeen

The headlights shone on the road, two needle-like beams of light. Everything else fell away into darkness. He could see the surface of the pavement, but not much more beneath the clouded sky as he passed the dock and went on toward the lighthouse. The downstairs windows of the inn were awash in yellow. Nick caught a glimpse of two people, both women, seated on the sofa.

He had seen Ruth a couple of times down at the dock. They had exchanged brief looks, but that was all. She seemed to understand that he did not want to talk to her there, in public, where everyone would take note. This was the curse of living on an island. If he so much as smiled at her, it would be the talk of the quonset hut for the next week. Islanders lived on rumor and the scantest bits of evidence that something, anything, of interest might be going on. They dreamed up scandals and created elaborate intrigues where none existed because there wasn't anything else to do. He tried, as much as possible, to stay under the radar.

When he reached Broadway, he turned and downshifted as the truck labored up the steep grade. He was not about to stop at the inn when Ruth had a guest, no matter how curious this made him, though he had intended to go by again some night. He liked her aloof independence.

Nick went over the high point past the schoolhouse and took the side road to the twin houses. He parked at the edge of the grass, feeling the wind, steady and cold, the moment he stepped from the truck. He swung the beam of his flashlight over the windows and doors of both houses as he circled the places. Imprisoned in time, perfectly preserved, the twin houses sat there like posts keeping guard over the past. They were an extension of George Tibbits, a physical manifestation of his fixation on the denial of change in any form. People might say he was entitled to this, being ninety. Once you reached such an advanced age, change was hard to take, but George had never liked change. He had been wedded to keeping everything just the same for as long as anyone could remember.

Back in the cab of the truck, Nick took out the notepad and wrote, "Moonless night." He tucked the notepad in the glove compartment and drove off, toward the cove. He saw a figure ahead of him on the road when he was almost to the sandy beach, a silhouetted form in the headlights, and as he drew closer, her silver hair was visible against a dark jacket. He pulled alongside her.

Neither of them spoke as she climbed into the truck and ducked down to crouch on the floor, out of sight. Nick kept his eyes on the road, gave the truck gas, and went on.

"'I Just Want to Make Love to You'—nice touch," she said.

"I thought I'd give the poker players something to listen to for a bit. Mrs. Venable's gone. We can go out to the cottage."

"Is that okay?"

"I'm still the caretaker."

"But she's coming back, right?"

"I guess." He could just make out her eyes in the dark beneath the seat.

"Eddie said he had a headache tonight and he wasn't going to play poker, but then he changed his mind."

"Will he stay for the whole game?"

"Yeah, after a couple beers he'll forget the headache."

Their conversations about Eddie were confined to this sort of exchange, the trading of necessary information. Nick didn't want to know more.

"Why did Mrs. Venable leave?" she asked.

"She said there was something she had to attend to back home."

"Kind of mysterious. She just shows up here after all these years."

"She's rich."

"So?"

"She thinks she can do anything she wants. And she can. Tear the mansion down, build a new house, whatever."

Nick parked beneath the pine trees and shut off the engine. The mansion loomed over the field, a blank square. He reached for Rachel's hand and pulled her up beside him. They kissed for a long moment. He thought of stripping off her clothes there in the truck, but he knew she would not like that. He was so trigger-happy when he saw her, he had to force himself to slow down, to savor what was to come.

He took a blanket from the well behind the seat, and they crossed the field without touching, until they came to the cottage. The little house felt familiar and welcoming, even in the dark, a piece of the landscape. It did not cry out for notice the way the mansion did.

He unlocked the porch door and then the interior door. When he flipped the light switch, they saw the new furniture, a couch and chairs covered in upholstery splashed with pink and red flowers. There were new lamps and end tables as well, and a framed Georgia O'Keefe print on the wall, and a fancy coffee maker on the counter.

"Cute," Rachel said. "She really fixed this place up."

"Spare no expense."

"Do you automatically hate anyone with money?"

"No, just intensely dislike them."

Rachel went to the little hallway and glanced in the bedrooms. "She got new beds, too?"

"New everything."

"I liked that old lumpy mattress."

"Me, too."

Nick went to her and kissed her again. The smell of her skin, sweet and yeasty, overwhelmed him. He tugged at the buttons on her blouse.

She pulled away. "I don't want to use the bed."

"I brought the blanket. We'll put it on the couch."

He managed to free the last button on her blouse and to unhook her bra. He felt an almost crazed need to see her naked. He was rewarded by the view of her breasts as the bra straps fell down her arms.

He pulled her to the couch, draped the blanket over it, and stumbled out of his own clothes. She lay there naked save for a pair of lacy underpants he knew she had worn for him.

"Turn out the light," she whispered.

"I want to see you."

"It's shining in my eyes."

It seemed to take an eternity to cross the floor and switch off the overhead light, but then he was back, stretched beside her on the couch. He ran his fingers lightly over her skin. The window let in no more than a murky light, but he could make out her body clearly—the white of her belly, the muscled shape of her legs. He felt a terrific happiness at having her there beside him, even if it was wrong, though he couldn't in the end convince himself of this. What they did together felt too good, too right.

He kissed her arms and the soft place between her breasts. She returned his kiss, letting out that low, satisfied sound he loved. He knelt beside her and removed her underpants slowly and deliberately, so he could watch the journey down her legs. She had taught him how to love her. She had shown him, more than any other woman he had been with, how her body worked.

The air in the room was cold. He felt the goose bumps on her skin and rolled on top of her, covering her with his warmth. He made the teasing of fingertips and tongue last as long as possible before slipping inside her. She arched her back and breathed hard. He tried to extend the intensity, but they both came quickly, shuddering together in one long breath. He covered her in kisses and lay beside her, spent. Within moments, he drifted off into an easy sleep, aware of the weight of her head against his chest. They could stay like this forever, it seemed, animals curled together in tired happiness.

He was roused by her hand on his shoulder.

"Nick. I hear voices outside."

He lurched up. "How close?"

"Not close. Over by the mansion maybe."

He retrieved his boxers and jeans from the floor, pulled them on, and went to the bedroom. When he pushed the curtain back, he had a view of the field beyond the mansion. The boys were there, seated in a circle on the ground, their bikes beside them. He could make out the lit ends of cigarettes in their mouths.

"It's the Hershel and Manning boys," he said when Rachel joined him. "They were out here a couple weeks ago."

"What are they doing?"

"Smoking."

"Rascals. Will they see the truck?"

"Probably not. You can't see under the trees from there."

"Where did they get cigarettes? Your mother wouldn't sell them cigarettes."

"No. But somebody bought them. Or stole them, more likely."

"If their parents had any idea they were out here, they'd kill them. How'd they get away?"

"Told their parents they were going over to each other's house or something."

"Those Christian children wouldn't lie."

"Of course they wouldn't."

The murmur of the boys' voices rose and fell, followed by laughter. Nick felt a rush of envy for them. He remembered when something as simple as smoking a forbidden cigarette could seem so potent and daring.

"You want to go out there and bust them?" Nick said.

"Sure."

"Wouldn't they be surprised to see Mrs. Brovelli appear out of nowhere?"

"Yes, they would. We're not going anywhere until they leave."

Nick wrapped his arms around her and kissed her ear. She had pulled on her pants and bra, but not her shirt. He stroked her shoulder. She took his face in her hands and brought him to her. Her tongue darted between his lips, and he thought they were headed back to the couch, but then a shout came from beyond the window.

"Get the bikes," one of the boys yelled. "Come on."

Nick saw the glow as soon as he turned back to the window. The dry grass had caught fire, and the wind had taken the flame and spread it in an instant. A huge swath of lawn was ablaze. Rachel grabbed his arm. They stood side by side, transfixed, before turning at the same moment and rushing back to the living room. Quickly they pulled on their remaining clothes. Nick grabbed the blanket.

Rachel gave him a look of confused fright and followed him out the door. He took the time to make sure both doors were locked and ran for the truck. He could just see the boys weaving down the road on the bikes. They had cleared the circle of the cove and would be past the marsh in a moment. He felt the heat rising from the ground already. With the wind blowing out of the southwest, straight for the mansion, it would take five minutes for the fire to reach the place.

They jumped into the truck. Nick was about to start the engine when she grasped his hand.

"They're on bicycles," Rachel said. "They'll see us."

"You can hide under the seat."

"Right, but they'll want to know where you were, why they didn't see you. Everybody will want to know that. If you were there, why didn't you stop them?"

"We can't just sit here and watch the whole place go up."

"She's planning to tear it down anyway."

Nick set the key in the ignition and turned it, but she grabbed his hand again. "Rachel, I'm not going to just sit here."

"There will be too many questions."

Nick shut off the engine, slumped back against the seat, and closed his eyes. The light of the fire raged in his head. He saw grass burning, a whole swath of jungle ablaze, and helicopters hovering, bodies strewn over the ground. No, not bodies. One body. The lieutenant, his legs blown off, nothing left but the stumps.

She wrapped her hand around his. "It'll be okay."

"No, it won't."

He withdrew his hand and rubbed his eyes. He felt the smart of smoke in his eyes already, though whether it was real or imaginary smoke, he couldn't say.

"You're shaking," she said.

"Yeah." Nick opened his eyes and stared through the windshield, at a spot off in the trees, away from the fire.

She ran her fingers over the back of his hand. "You can go get the men in a minute, once the boys have a head start. You can drop me at my house." She moved across the seat, closer to him, and wrapped her other hand around his. "Those stupid kids. If it weren't for the wind…"

"There's always wind out here."

He pulled his hand away and inserted the key in the ignition. This time she didn't try to stop him. He drove as fast as he could on the bumpy road. As they approached Rachel's house, she took his hand again. "I'm sorry."

"You didn't start the fire."

He stopped at the end of her driveway, and she jumped out. He took off the moment she cleared the truck. He gunned the engine and hugged the curves as he barreled on down the road. With wind from the west, there was no saving the place, even if the fire truck were to arrive right now. He and the rest of the volunteer firemen practiced the drill once a year: unrolling the hoses from the truck and setting up a human chain, running the hoses down to the water, pumping the water from the bay into the lines. They had the whole operation down to eight minutes, but that would not be fast enough. He thought ruefully of how he had remarked that they needed a good fire to test their technique.

He made the turn onto Bay Avenue and went past the dump. The boys on their bikes had vanished into the side roads. He met no one all the way to the firehouse.

Chapter Eighteen

The fluorescent light over the kitchen sink gave the table a green hue. She shuffled the cards and dealt them, resisting the impulse to turn on more lights. She was not really playing solitaire at three in the morning. She was not really awake. The dim light seemed to confirm her sense of being present but not present.

She reached for her mug of tea and took a sip. The tea was cold now, the taste of peppermint pungent on the tongue. She went through the deck and turned up every third card. The game was stupid, but it passed the time. She had been playing for nearly an hour now without winning once. Was this a sign?

Nora found herself mentally lighting a cigarette. She longed for the calming smoke in her lungs and the feel of the cigarette between her fingers. She had not smoked in years, nearly thirty of them, but at times like these, the urge returned. If there had been a cigarette in the house, she would have smoked it. Henry, of course, did not allow cigarettes in the house. She and Isabelle used to sneak off like schoolgirls after dinner and hide behind the bushes in the backyard. The one time Henry nearly caught them in bed, Isabelle jumped from beneath the covers, pulled on a robe, and lit a cigarette. By the time he opened the door, she was seated in the easy chair with her legs crossed, puffing away. He was so angry to discover her smoking that he gave no thought apparently to finding the two of them in the bedroom, undressed in the middle of the afternoon.

It was summer, and they were at the house in Maine. Henry had returned from a fishing trip early. They heard his footsteps on the stairs and then he was there in the doorway. He took in the sight of the two of them for a long moment before speaking. "I'm disappointed in you, Isabelle," he said, his voice gruff and officious. He sounded like a father rather than a husband, so reprimanding and righteous. Nora had to stifle a laugh.

Isabelle's lower lip had quivered, and Nora feared, as she often did, that once Isabelle started crying, she would confess everything to Henry.

"I gave her the cigarette," Nora said. "She was just keeping me company."

Nora was seated on the edge of the bed in Isabelle's bathing suit, which she had grabbed from the floor and tugged on. "Swimming always makes me feel like having a cigarette."

Henry stared at them. His bermuda shorts bagged around his knees, and the fishing vest hung from his shoulders, loaded down with gear. He looked more foolish than usual, an impression reinforced by his furrowed brow.

"Well, if you must smoke, do it somewhere else."

He directed this warning at Nora. It was clear from the look he gave Isabelle that he would deal with her later. He stood there a moment longer, a moment in which they all seemed to be waiting for the next move to be revealed, and then he lifted his shoulders, so the vest rattled. "I've caught a good-sized striper for dinner," he said. He turned and went back down the stairs.

Isabelle ground out the cigarette in a clam shell on the dresser and left the room. Down the hall, the bathroom door clicked shut behind her. Nora wondered if Henry had noticed that she was wearing Isabelle's bathing suit, which did not quite fit her.

Nora used to think of the three of them as characters in a Marx brothers movie. She was always running out one door as Henry came through another, and there was Isabelle, the straight woman, watching Nora duck out of sight while she composed her face. The straight woman was a pun, even back then, and Nora had taken a sort of perverse enjoyment in using the phrase to describe Isabelle, though only to herself.

Isabelle would not have found it funny, but she was the straight woman in the act, in more ways than one.

Nora gathered up the cards and shuffled them. The snapping sound the cards made hung in the air. It was past three-thirty now, and Isabelle had not called. This could mean anything. Henry was dead, and there were too many details to attend to, too many decisions to be made, no time to get to a phone. Or Henry was alive, and there was nothing to report. Nora had considered going with Isabelle, but it had taken her such a long time to pull herself from sleep after the phone rang, and she did not think it was her place to be there, not now. By the time she had lifted her head from the pillow, blinking at the light from the hallway, Isabelle was standing beside the bed, dressed. "They say he's taken a turn for the worse," she said.

A turn for the worse. That could mean anything, too, or nothing, though the nursing home would not call in the middle of the night if it was not serious.

"I can drive you there," Nora had offered.

"No. I better go by myself."

"You're sure?"

"Yes."

Nora leaned on her elbow and watched as Isabelle ran the comb through her hair and pulled on a sweater. "You'll call me, right?" Nora said when Isabelle moved toward the door.

"I'll call if there's anything to tell you."

Nora puzzled over these words now as she dealt out another hand of solitaire. *If there's anything to tell you.* The ambiguity was typical of Isabelle. Who was to say what would constitute something that Nora should know? Only Isabelle held the keys to this mystery.

Nora had assumed she would fall back to sleep, but after lying there for close to half an hour, she got up and went down to the kitchen. If Henry was dead, wouldn't she sense it somehow? She peered at the cards laid across the table as though looking into a crystal ball. They told her nothing. She felt simply jittery and sleepless, anxious for what would come next. No clues came back to her when she gazed across the room at the black surface of the windows overlooking the garden.

When Gerald died, she was taken completely by surprise. The call came from his mother, not in the middle of the night but the middle of the morning, when Nora was still in bed. She had returned the night before from her tour of the big house on the island, and she was luxuriating in the feel of a warm bed, the silence of the bedroom with no one else present, the knowledge that she had another week to spend as she liked before Gerald came home. Then she heard the ringing of the phone, followed by his mother's raspy voice, as worn as if she had been coughing for hours. Even then, after his mother told her, Nora did not believe Gerald was dead. She remained convinced, for a long time, that any minute he would walk through the door and slap everyone on the back, full of the old bravado. Being released so suddenly and completely did not seem possible. She dreamed once that his death was a trick he had played on them all. *You bastard*, she said in the dream, playfully punching him on the arm. She was glad to see him and relieved the whole thing amounted to nothing more than a practical joke of the sort he had always loved, but when she woke, a sick dread took hold of her. A train crash was too neat, too stupid and improbable. He might still waltz into the house with that adolescent grin on his face and fill the room with his overly robust laughter. For the better part of a year, she went on expecting just such a sleight of hand, until at last, she began to believe it. He wasn't coming home.

When her father died, the experience had been entirely different. She knew, though an ocean lay between them. She was seated in a café in Aix-en-Provence with Anne, a friend from college. The trip was her father's graduation gift, but he insisted she travel with a group. She and Anne bumming around Europe on their own would not do. That day, they slipped away from the group, missing a tour of some Medieval church to wander through the shops and the open-air market. She remembered the dates they bought at the market, plump and delicious, unlike any others she had eaten before. They took a table at an outdoor café and sipped the thick coffee that made them feel so adult and ate the dates from a paper bag. As she watched the pigeons pecking at the crumbs beneath the café tables, her father suddenly seemed to be there, beside them, and she was filled with the urgent need to speak with him. The only public phones were in the post office, which was closed in the early afternoon and would not open again until four o'clock. By then, she and Anne were back at the hotel, surrounded by the other girls, who bab-bled on about the sites they'd seen. She forgot her father entirely until the next day when the telegram came, and she knew it must have been at that moment, when she sat watching the pigeons, that he died.

Over the years, Gerald came back to her in dreams, but the dreams were sporadic and not especially vivid. He became a minor character, someone who showed up occasionally on the edge of a crowd, or stepped forward on a sidewalk and said hello. She woke thinking of Gerald as an old classmate she might have encountered at a reunion. "Oh, it's you," she was tempted to say. "I remember you." The dreams of her father took hold of her in an entirely different way. For fifty years, her father had appeared at least once a month, a healthy man in mid-life, handsome in his neat shirts and slacks. She woke convinced that she had seen him and heard him speak. The sense of him was so palpable, so eerily real, that she came to think of the dreams as visitations. The two of them met in that in-between place, a third realm, where they continued conversations begun when she was a child. He placed his hand on her shoulder and gave her that chiding look, as if to say, "Is that really what you think, Nora?" He led her over the rocky path to the beach. He poured a glass of wine and raised it in a toast. Who was to say that these things had not actually happened? They were as real as if they had occurred, more so, in fact, than much of what passed for daily life.

Nora did not believe in magic or ghosts or supernatural occurrences. She was not interested in shamans or medicine men or gurus, as everyone else seemed to be these days. For many years, she had attended the Episcopal church, and she could not say she had ever experienced a mys-tical moment, in church or out of it—but the dreams of her father had their own life, a life she did not ordain or control. She wouldn't call them mystical, though there was mystery in them.

She did not expect Henry would haunt her the way her father did, and she doubted she would feel the moment of his death when it happened, though of all the men in her life, Henry had been the most constantly present and taken up the most space. He was the oversized piece of furniture in the center of the room, around which she was forced to maneuver, again and again.

Nora considered calling the nursing home. They would not tell her anything, of course, but perhaps they could bring the phone to Isabelle or relay a message. She gazed at the tan-colored wall phone beside the sink, testing out the words she might say in her mind, and gathered up the cards, but instead of going to the phone, she crossed the darkened room to the den and slumped onto the couch. She took a throw from the back of the couch, draped it over her, and fell into a shallow sleep. She was still there on the couch when the phone rang just after eight.

Nora went to the kitchen and reached the phone just before the answering machine picked up.

"Hello." The voice belonged not to Isabelle, but to a man, a man she did not know. "I'm trying to reach Mrs. Venable," he said.

"This is she."

"Mrs. Venable, it's Nick. Nick McGarrell, from the island."

For a moment she entertained the confusing idea that Nick was calling to tell her Henry had died.

"Nick. How are you?"

"Fine. But I have some news. Not such good news. There's been a fire. Out at the mansion."

"Another one?"

"Another one, but this one spread. Quickly. The winds were high, and there wasn't much we could do. The fire truck got there as fast as possible, but it really caught. There's not much left."

"Not much left of what?"

"The mansion."

"And the caretaker's cottage?"

"It's okay. We kept the fire from spreading to the cottage. We were out there all night. The inspector's coming over this morning from the fire department in Barton. I think it was the kids again, but we'll see what the inspector says. It looks like the fire started in the field, not in the house."

"No one's stepped forward?"

"No."

"What right did they have to go trespassing like that to begin with?" Nora was as angry at the kids as she was at herself for not addressing the situation sooner. "I'm assuming someone will be talking with the boys' parents."

"I guess so."

"Well, I would like to talk with them."

There was silence on the other end. After a long moment, Nick said, "Sure."

"I don't know when I will be able to get over to the island. Can I call you later?"

"Call my mother. You've got her number at home, right? She's there cooking the turkey."

"This isn't much of a Thanksgiving for you. I'm sorry."

"We were lucky there were a bunch of us on the island. Most of the guys aren't going anywhere."

Nora thanked him and, as she hung up the phone, considered what she would say to the parents of the wayward boys who liked playing with matches down by the haunted mansion. She owed those thoughtless boys nothing but gratitude, really, for saving her the trouble of tearing the place down, but she would not let them, or their parents, know that their irresponsible stupidity fit her plans.

Chapter Nineteen

Liza lay on her side, on the edge of the bed, with the covers mounded around her shoulders. Her face appeared smaller when she slept, the features scrunched together, and she balled her hands in tight fists like a child. Ruth resisted the urge to cross the room and run her fingers over the tangled strands of hair matted against her cheek. Instead, she went quietly down the hall and slipped out of the inn.

A steady wind blew off the water. Ruth tugged the hood of her jacket into place and wheeled the bicycle up to the road. She pedaled slowly and scanned the shoreline for changes – an unusual piece of driftwood, new deposits of seaweed and shells. She had learned to study the beach carefully. She had seen how much it changed from one day to the next. This morning the tide was high, so the rocks were covered by water. Nothing in particular caught her eye, though she rode with the camera bag slung crosswise over her chest, ready if needed.

The cold air made her eyes water. She blinked back the tears and reached into her pocket for a tissue to blow her nose as she approached the dock and the store. The ferry was just a speck across the water, a good ten minutes away, but the parking lot was full of people standing in clusters. She spotted Nick, and beside him, the policeman. The two remained hunched together in conversation and did not glance up as she parked her bike by the porch and went into the store. Inside, she found Alice alone, in her chair behind the counter, knitting.

Ruth crossed the worn floor boards, which were covered in a thin layer of sand. "That's pretty," she said. "What are you making?"

Alice held up the square of tightly knitted rows in yellow wool. "A baby blanket. My daughter Ellen's expecting."

"Ellen was about eight the last time I saw her. She was always here behind the counter."

"She used to say she wanted to run the store when she grew up. We thought she would be the one who stayed on the island, but she didn't. She met a man off island. Nick was the one who was supposed to go away, and now he's back." Alice shrugged, as if to say there was no predicting children, your own or anyone else's.

"You didn't expect him to come back?"

"No." Alice resumed knitting. Her fingers moved quickly, gathering the yarn, and the needles made a faint clicking noise that could be heard over the sound of voices outside.

Ruth glanced out the window with its view of the parking lot. "What's with the crowd this morning?"

"There was a fire last night, out at the Venable mansion. By the time the men got there with the fire truck, the place was pretty much gone. Just the stone walls are left."

Ruth had heard the siren, but had not been sure what it signaled. "You mean the place that belongs to that woman? Nora, I think it is."

"Nora Venable. It's her place, or it was."

"I hope she wasn't there."

"No. She went back to Massachusetts last week. It's terrible for Nick. He's the caretaker. He drove out there last night and discovered it. It's hard to imagine anyone would deliberately set a fire, but how else did the thing get started?"

Ruth considered the possibilities. One of the younger men who did construction work could be fascinated by fire. She couldn't think of any other likely candidates. The year-round population was so small, it limited the number of suspects. Whoever had done this must have realized how hard it would be to hide on Snow Island. That, or the person was crazy.

"It's awful to think someone set it intentionally," Ruth said as she took a basket from the stack by the newspaper stand.

"Maybe it was a stupid accident, but I don't think the place spontaneously combusted."

Ruth went through the aisles and placed a box of corn flakes in the basket along with a carton of milk, a jar of peanut butter, and, on impulse, some chocolate chip cookies that didn't look like they had been sitting on the shelf too long. She would take the groceries back to the inn, but she didn't care about having breakfast now. She wanted to get down to the fire as fast as possible.

"I was up all night," Alice said when Ruth set her purchases on the counter. "Everyone was. It's going to tear this place apart, unless someone steps forward."

"You don't have any ideas?"

Alice glanced toward the door, leaned across the counter, and lowered her voice. "Nick thinks it was some of the kids, but we've got to wait for the investigator to get here on the ferry before he says anything. The old dance hall burned down one summer. Everyone thought it was some of the summer kids. They never caught them. That was bad enough, but this is island kids. That's worse."

Alice rang up the groceries. The paper bag made a loud rattling as she shook it open, the sound intensifying the silence of the store and the sense Ruth had that there was not much she could say in response. She was a summer kid, or had been one at least. She could only begin to imagine what something like this would mean to the islanders.

Ruth took the bag of groceries, thanked Alice, and made her way out of the store. A woman with two young girls, each holding one of their mother's hands, waited at the foot of the porch steps. Ruth said good morning to them. The woman grunted a hello and went on up the stairs.

As she set the bag of groceries in the plastic milk crate tied to the back of the bike, Ruth studied the small groups of people scattered over the parking lot. Their faces were pulled tight, emptied of ordinary gesture and expression. She felt guilty for not sharing their dread and confusion. Already in her mind she was composing close-ups of charred ground and fallen beams.

She rode quickly back to the inn. She heard the shower running in the guest bathroom when she stepped inside. She deposited the milk in the refrigerator and went down the hall. The big bathroom she used for her darkroom was at the end of the corridor. This smaller one, with its shower stall, was nestled between the narrow rooms that once housed the paying guests.

The confined space was warm and steamy, and smelled of Liza's shampoo. Liza peered around the edge of the shower curtain, her hair white with soap bubbles. "Did you go get milk?" she said.

"Yes. You won't believe what happened. The mansion burned down. Last night, down at Gooseneck Cove."

Liza ducked back behind the shower curtain. "That's terrible."

"It's the place that belongs to that older woman I met, the one I told you about, the dyke."

"God, do you think somebody set it? Maybe it was a statement."

Ruth had not thought of this. "It doesn't sound like it."

Liza said something in a garbled voice.

"I can't understand you when the water's running down your face," Ruth said.

"I said there could be people on the island who don't want gays here."

"Alice thinks it was some kids playing with matches. I bet no one else would spot that woman as a lesbian. She's pretty in the closet."

"But you spotted her with your gaydar, huh?" Liza turned off the water and pulled back the curtain. "Hand me that towel, will you?"

Ruth reached for the towel draped over a hook on the back of the door. Liza stood there a moment with beads of water sliding down her breasts and her hair shiny and sleek. Ruth knew Liza was trying to entice her, but she was not about to fall for the sight of Liza's wet, naked body, not now.

"I've got to go out there," Ruth said.

"Go out where?"

"To the mansion. I want to get some photos before they do any cleaning up."

Liza wrapped the towel around her shoulders and stepped from the tub. "I thought we were going to make the stuffing and put the turkey in."

"We were. I mean we are. After I get back. Okay?" Ruth added the final word as an afterthought, and she knew that was just how it sounded, but she wasn't going to miss this.

Liza pulled the towel tight around her body and gave Ruth a leveling look.

"This won't take long," Ruth said. "I'll just ride there and back."

"And spend an hour or two taking pictures."

"I'll be right back, Lize."

Liza took a hand towel from the rack by the sink, leaned over, and let her hair fall forward. She rubbed the towel over her head in a vigorous motion that conveyed her displeasure as clearly as the set line of her mouth.

"I have to photograph this. It's like…like a gift from God."

"Jesus, that's beautiful, Ruth." Liza righted herself and draped the towel around her head, turban-style. "A horrible thing that's probably ruining someone's life is a gift from God to you."

"That's not how I meant it. I'm sorry about the fire, but I'm not going to pass up the chance to shoot it. I can stand here having this inane argument with you, or I can go take the pictures before it's too late."

Ruth held Liza's gaze a moment longer and then reached for the door knob. The sweet smell of the shampoo wafted into the hallway as she closed the door. On her way down the hall, she grabbed her camera bag. Outside she jumped on the bicycle and pushed off. The ferry was just pulling away from the dock. If Nick and the investigator and the policeman stood around talking for a few minutes, she could beat them down to the mansion, or what was left of it.

She gulped in the clean, cold air as she pedaled hard down the road. The ache in her lungs felt good. It purged the plaintive tone in Liza's voice and the hurt look in her eyes. Ruth went past the dock. Nick was still there with the other men, in a circle in the center of the parking lot. She picked him out, taller than the others, with his dark hair and tight blue jeans.

Beyond the dump, she took the dirt road. She bounced along, over the rough surface, listening for cars coming behind her, but the road was silent all the way to the cove.

Ruth was not prepared for the sight that met her as she rounded the bend. The stone walls, black with soot, enclosed empty space. The smoldering hulk gave off an acrid smell that coated her nostrils and throat as if she had swallowed handfuls of ash. What had been lawn was now singed dirt covered in chunks of white and black debris, none of it recognizable as what it once had been. A few beams lay on the ground, just as she had imagined, like the skeleton of a ship's hull, but much of the interior of the house appeared to have evaporated, literally to have gone up in smoke. Two men stood off to the side, water buckets beside them. She recognized them from down at the store and nodded a hello. She got off her bike awed by the power of such quick and sure destruction; then she reached inside the bag for her camera.

After a few long shots that took in the whole scene, she shifted her focus to the ground and zoomed in on a pile of rubble. The debris was, as she had expected, strangely beautiful, full of texture in shades of gray and white. A pile of burnt wood might be mistaken for layers of black rock, though the mess quickly revealed itself to be something less natural and more sinister. She felt that exultation of finding exactly what she wanted, an image that gave way to other images, horrible and gorgeous at the same time, arresting but repellent. These were the images she was seeking now, ones that turned back on themselves and left something for the viewer to imagine beyond the frame.

She circled the blackened field shooting the ruins from every angle. The grass around the stone walls was still smoldering. She wanted to cross the flattened ground and come right up to the stone walls that were left reaching toward the sky like open arms, but she knew the men would stop her. The whole area was potentially a crime scene. She confined herself to shooting the edge of the fire-ravaged grass as she moved back and forth to capture the close-ups where one texture met another. It was all rather sculptural. She snapped the shutter without pausing to think as she searched for what could be revealed by a new slant of light, a different cropping.

"You gonna sell those to the newspaper?" one of the men called.

Ruth lowered the camera. "No. I'm just taking these for myself."

"They'd pay you. The paper won't get anybody here till tomorrow, if they send someone. You should call them up."

She was not used to thinking of herself as a news photographer, though she could see the man's point. She was the photographer on the island now, documenting this bit of news.

Ruth skirted the burned grass and came to stand beside the men.

"You're Ruth, right?" the man said. "I'm Ian." He extended his hand and then withdrew it with a laugh. "I guess I'm a little dirty. This is Cliff." He jerked his head toward the man beside him.

Both of them, Ruth saw now that she was closer, were covered in soot, their canvas jackets stiff and smeared with black.

"Have you been here all night?" she asked.

"Pretty much," Ian said.

"It went up fast, huh?"

"Yeah, the wind was bad. We saved the caretaker's cottage, but that was about it."

The sound of approaching vehicles carried down the road, and an assortment of trucks arrived.

"See you around," Ian said as he and Cliff went to join the others, including a fire inspector in an official uniform, clipboard clenched in one hand.

Ruth did not say anything as they moved off. The niceties of ordinary speech did not seem necessary beside the smoking remains of the house. It occurred to her, with an odd thrill, that she was the only woman present.

She stayed off to the side and snapped an occasional shot. After a few minutes, Brock lumbered over in his green work pants.

"I guess you got something to take pictures of now," he said.

"I guess."

"What a waste. It's a damn shame this place burned down, but it was an accident waiting to happen, if you ask me. That Venable family just left it sitting here for all these years. Nobody cared about the place besides Nick, and you can't blame him. He kept an eye on it."

"Alice said Nick thinks it was some kids on the island."

Brock looked startled for a moment, then assumed a blank expression. "We don't know what happened. We have to see what the inspector says." He gave her a short look, as though warning her not to say more, shrugged his jacket into place on his shoulders, and walked away.

The investigator removed a roll of yellow tape and a bundle of stakes from a duffel bag. He and the policeman went around the perimeter of the burned area setting the stakes in place. When they were done, the investigator looped the bright strands of tape from one stake to the next. Everyone else watched in silence. This act, marking the area as off limits, suggested that there was an answer and that it would be found. Ruth surreptitiously took a last shot of the tape against the black ground. She was going to retrieve her bike when she noticed Nick standing a ways apart from the other men. She went over to him. Head bent, he seemed to be searching the charred grass for clues.

"I'm sorry about the fire," she said.

He looked up, clearly surprised to see her, and nodded. The clenched line of his jaw did not give away much.

"I hope they can figure out what happened," she added.

"I think we'll get to the bottom of it," he said.

He moved off without saying more, and she felt, as she had with his father, that she had crossed a line. This was the islanders' business.

The back of Nick's jacket was dotted with soot, and his hair stuck to his head as though it had not been washed in a week. She felt a surge of regret that she had not come up with something more helpful to say.

When she reached the bike, she could not get the kickstand to lift up. She struggled to move it with her foot, and finally resorted to crouching beside the bike and forcing it with her hand. The kickstand gave at last. She caught the bike against her shoulder before it fell over. Ruth got to her feet quickly and glanced around, certain that all the men were watching her, but they were turned toward the ruins of the mansion, fanned out in a semi-circle around the police tape, eyes on the investigator as he picked his way over the site. She climbed onto the bike and rode off with her fingers, cold inside her gloves, clenched around the handlebars.

Chapter Twenty

Nick woke with a start, hands pressed to his forehead, the air squeezed in his lungs. *Get off me*, he wanted to shout, but the breath would not come. He forced his eyes open, struggling to grab hold of something real. He listened to the refrigerator humming in the kitchen downstairs and told himself the sound was reassuring, though it wasn't. He got out of bed, took a pair of jeans from the floor, and pulled them on over his boxer shorts, then crossed the room to the window.

A metallic ache ran down his throat – the rot of the jungle, the charred taste of burning. The thwack, thwack of the chopper blades circled overhead, and the medic was yelling, except he could not hear him, only see his lips furiously moving. He was reaching for the lieutenant, ready to hand him up, and then he saw the stumps of the man's legs hanging there like pulverized chicken meat. He hesitated, and the chopper was gone, leaving him in a tunnel of wind, his ears filled with a rhythmic throbbing.

Nick stared at the gray and white shapes of the geese huddled in a mass at the edge of the lawn, heads tucked beneath their wings, their bodies pressed together for warmth, and wondered if they would ever go. They showed no signs of preparing to migrate. He touched his fingertips to the cold glass and turned away.

He thought he had shaken the dream. Since returning to the island, he had managed to push the dreams away, most of the time. He made his way downstairs with the old argument running through his mind. *We got him in the helicopter. He was alive.* Or was he alive? Chances were the lieutenant was already dead, and they didn't know it, but this wasn't the point, if there was a point. The helicopter came within minutes. In the dreams he could never get the body inside, but back then, when it happened, he grabbed the lieutenant around the middle and helped hoist him to the medics without hesitating, without thinking.

Nick filled a mug with water and set it in the microwave. Lieutenant Jankins. That was all he could remember, the man's name. He could not recall a face or the color of his hair. Nick had known the lieutenant for two weeks, if that. Two weeks in which it became numbingly clear that the lieutenant would get them all killed if they gave him the chance. Two weeks, long enough for the lieutenant to learn, except he didn't, and this was not, as he kept pointing out to the phantom jury that followed him around, Nick's fault.

When the microwave shut off, he spooned instant coffee into the cup. Through the window, he watched trails of fog lift from the ground. The doe emerged from the fog like another dream. She stood at the edge of the lawn, just beyond the trees, head cocked as though watching him through the glass. He sipped the coffee and thought of how he and his father used to go hunting on the island. Even then, he had hated it. Now the idea was unthinkable.

He ate a couple of pieces of toast standing at the sink, letting the crumbs fall into it. His stomach wasn't up to more that morning. He grabbed his coat and went out to the truck. The geese barely moved.

Nick drove straight to the Lundborns' without stopping at the store and, for the first time since the fire, did not continue on to the cove. There was nothing, he reminded himself, to check on at the mansion. The lieutenant was young, a few days past twenty-one at most, but they were all young, far younger than they knew at the time. This was not an excuse, just the truth. The lieutenant thought he would show them who was in charge, and they let him. They stood by and watched. It was a sin of omission rather than commission, if it was, in fact, a sin. Nick didn't believe in sin. Everything consisted of sin back then in Vietnam, or nothing did. There was no sense in singling out one act or another, but this act—or lack of action—had singled him out. This one wouldn't leave him alone.

The guts of the Lundborns' kitchen lay strewn over the lawn—the old cabinets with their chipped green paint, the 1950s refrigerator. The stove and the sink sat off to one side, oddly forlorn out of context. He thought of the wrecked hulk of the mansion. Even though no one had wanted the place, the sight of the burned ruins called up an involuntary wave of regret. People might have lived here, the blackened walls seemed to say. The phantom shell of the house loomed over the rubble as though it had a message for the men who stood at the edges of the site. Ruin was coming to all of them one way or another.

Inside the Lundborns', he surveyed the kitchen. Only the floor remained. He wondered what had possessed the designers who created the linoleum in a pattern of fake bricks. The linoleum was faded and, in various spots, flaking into a residue of orange crud. Even new, it could never have been convincing as a "brick" floor. The orange and brown squares looked like an arrangement of Lincoln logs.

Nick used a scraper to pry the linoleum free. Once it was loose, he could peel it back in large chunks, though repeatedly, the pieces broke off in his gloved hands and splintered into dried-up shavings. As he worked, his mind went to another place, free of the lieutenant, free of the smell of smoke. When he had pulled up all the linoleum, he carried the pieces out to the yard and returned to inspect the sub-flooring. He had planned to save the sub-floor, but black areas of mold dotted the wood. Around the edges, it was nearly rotted through. He was surprised they had been able to walk on the mess without it giving way. Now he would have to get this up, too, a job that was tougher than dealing with the linoleum. He lost himself in the pure physical nature of the work as he took the crowbar to the wood and forced it away from the beams underneath. The morning was gone by the time he had gotten the floor up and dragged all the old wood outside.

Nick started up the truck and let it run while he carried the last pieces of wood out. The cab was warm when he climbed in. He took off his gloves and held his hands in front of the heater vents. The electric radiator he used while he was working in the house didn't throw out much heat. On the other side of the windshield, the sky pressed close, its steely tone suggesting snow. Days like these, there was no difference between morning and afternoon. A state of twilight lasted from dawn to dusk.

He turned out of the Lundborns' driveway, passed the sandy beach, and drove on toward the store. His father's truck was the only vehicle parked out front. A blast of warmth met Nick as he stepped inside.

"You've got that thing cranking," he said to his mother, with a nod of his head toward the woodstove.

She looked up from her knitting. "I can't stand the cold air coming through the cracks."

Nick went behind the counter and poured himself a cup of coffee. "Where's Dad?"

"He went up to the house for lunch. Are you hungry?"

Nick shrugged. "Hungry. Tired."

"You weren't out at the mansion last night, were you?"

"I went out to check on things around midnight."

"You need to sleep, Nick."

He fell into the easy chair by the stove and sipped the coffee. "Somebody has to check on the place."

"The other men can take turns."

"I don't trust those guys—Cliff, Ian. They drink too much."

"Fred Hershel should have been the one to stay out there, if you ask me."

"We don't need him in the fire department."

"Don't need him or don't want him?"

"Both."

Footsteps sounded out on the porch, and Brock came through the door. "Got that kitchen done yet?" he said to Nick.

"I've got the floor torn up. I'll get the new sub-floor down this afternoon."

"You're making progress."

"Ripping everything out is the fast part. This is where it starts going slow."

Brock took the other seat beside the stove. "You been down to the mansion this morning?"

"No. I think it's safe to say that fire is out."

"Now that the wind's finally died down. I hope Mrs. Venable appreciates what you did."

"She said she'd pay for the extra time I spent down there, but I told her forget it, just make a donation to the fire department."

"That's big of you. You had lunch?"

"No. I'm living on coffee."

"There's some beef stew in the crock pot up at the house," Alice said.

His mother glanced up from her knitting and gave him a quick smile. She looked young, almost girlish, when she smiled like that, despite the lines around her eyes. He knew, from the flush of pleasure on her face, that she had made the beef stew, his favorite, for him. It was a peace offering after the last few days, when she wouldn't stop asking him if he'd gotten any sleep, and he kept snapping at her.

"Beef stew," Nick said. "I guess I could eat some of that."

"There's some pumpkin bread in the bread box."

Nick downed what was left of the coffee and dropped the cup in the trash can behind the counter. Alice reached for him as he brushed past her. He felt her hand on his arm for a moment, and then he was free, heading for the door.

He climbed the hill to the road. He was about to cross over and walk up to his parents' house when Fred Hershel pulled beside him in the van, his window rolled down. For a moment he simply stared at Nick, and Nick had the fleeting thought that maybe Fred was going to get out of the van and hit him.

When Fred spoke, his words came out short and clipped. "That fire inspector came by. He said you sent him."

"Yeah, I did."

"I don't appreciate you telling people my boys started that fire."

"I saw them out at the mansion." Nick tried to keep his voice even.

"The night of the fire? Or some other night?"

"It was another night, but they were out there, and they made a fire."

"So you jumped to the conclusion that it was them?"

"I didn't jump to any conclusions, I told the fire inspector to check it out, that's all."

"You don't know my kids."

Nick decided this did not require a response.

"You don't know what they would do and what they wouldn't do. I do. And I know they couldn't have set that fire."

"Nobody said they set the fire. I just said they were out there before, and they were playing with matches. Maybe it was an accident. Did you ask them?"

"I don't need to ask them. I know my kids. Next time use your head before you start spreading rumors."

Fred rolled up the window and sped off. Nick watched the van go down the road in stupefied wonder. If it wasn't the kids, who did Fred think started the fire? Of course Fred believed his children could not have played a part. They did as they were told. They read the Bible and knelt beside the bed to pray every night. Fred and his wife had brought their children to the island to protect them from just this sort of thing. On the island, they could not be corrupted by the evils of modern day life, by the lure of the mall and teenage parties and drinking and drugs. They could not get in trouble on the island because there was no trouble to get into. What would you expect the boys to do under the circumstances? They created their own trouble.

Nick sat at the kitchen table in his parents' house. He watched the chickadees darting to the feeder his mother filled outside the kitchen window as he spooned the thick chunks of meat and carrots into his mouth. Maybe the fire inspector would drop the investigation, that is if Nora Venable didn't want to pursue it. She didn't strike him, though, as the sort of woman to let something like this go.

He left the empty bowl in the sink and cut a hunk of pumpkin bread, which he ate as he walked back down the hill. He climbed into his truck and took off down the deserted road. After the days of excitement, cars and trucks driving back and forth to the cove in a constant parade, the island appeared abandoned. Not that he wanted the excitement back. That sort of excitement he didn't need.

When he reached the Lundborns', he took a bag of pot from a hidden compartment at the bottom of his toolbox and went inside. With the sub-floor gone, the house was open to the air. He stood on bare ground, though he was inside what was left of the kitchen. Like most of the houses on the island, the cottage had no basement, and the foundation consisted of nothing more than joists and cinder blocks, and an open space of air between the flooring and the ground. He would need to work fast to get the new sub-floor laid by dark.

Nick crossed the threshold into the rest of the house and sat on the floor. He balanced the opened bag on his thigh, scooped the pot into a rolling paper, and twirled the paper. When he had licked the edge, securing the paper, he lit the joint and inhaled. The sheets of plywood were stacked in the back of the truck. He could get them in one at a time without too much difficulty. First he would fix a large piece of plastic over the ground, beneath what would become the floor, to keep the moisture out. Nick smoked the joint to the end, pinched the stub to make sure it was out, and dropped the roach in the plastic bag. He slipped the bag in his breast pocket before heading outside to get the roll of plastic sheeting.

He listened to the college radio station from the mainland as he worked, the only station he could stand. Everything else was pure bubble gum. The college DJs were erratic and unpredictable in their musical taste, but they could be counted on for interesting stuff most of the time, and white kids going to school in Rhode Island had not discovered rap music, thank God. This afternoon some student was playing 1950s and '60s oldies recorded well before he was born. Chuck Berry and Little Richard suited Nick's mood somehow.

He was almost finished setting the squares of plywood in place and nailing them down when he heard a car outside. He dropped the hammer and went to the door. Through the glass he saw Rachel getting out of her car. He had not spoken to her, other than brief exchanges at the store, since the night of the fire. At first he felt the familiar wave of pleasure at seeing her, but then he remembered that stopping by his work site was not something she normally did.

Nick opened the door as she approached and stepped outside. "What's going on? Eddie's going to see your car here."

"He's over at Silas Wardell's going over some new hunting regulations. I just wanted to tell you the boys are acting strange, but they haven't cracked."

"I figured that. Fred stopped me and chewed me out. He said to stop spreading rumors."

"I asked Daniel if he knew anything about the fire, and he gave me this guilty look and said no. The rest of them ducked their heads and avoided looking at me. But maybe I can keep working on them."

Rachel moved closer to him. He could see her breath hanging in the air in white puffs.

"Fred Hershel will calm down eventually. The boys will confess. It'll all blow over," he said.

"I wish they would confess."

"I'd give them a few more days at most. They'll crack. All that praying and guilt will get to them. Thinking they're going to hell, Jesus doesn't love them anymore. It's got to be torture for them."

"You sound like you're enjoying it."

"Not for their sake but their parents'. It's hard not to when they're so full of themselves."

She gave him a wistful look. "I worry about how we're all going to live together after this. I have to see the Hershels and Mannings and their kids every day."

"That's their problem, not yours. Their kids started the fire. You're just doing your job."

She nodded, though she did not look entirely convinced. "I'm sorry you couldn't go get the men sooner. It was so stupid to be stuck out there like that."

"The place would have burned down anyway. It didn't make any difference."

She fixed her gaze on him, as though she had just noticed something odd about his face. He thought maybe he had a smear of beef stew left around his mouth, but when she spoke, he realized she was searching for a different sort of clue.

"You're high, aren't you?"

Nick shrugged. "Why do you say that?"

"Your eyes are bloodshot. And I can see the bag sticking out of your pocket. You told me you weren't doing that anymore."

"It's just once in a while."

"This makes me crazy. You know it makes me crazy."

"Why?"

"Because it's not safe. You're doing construction work. Alone."

"The pot doesn't make any difference."

"That's ridiculous."

She gave him her stern look, and he imagined her at the school-house, in front of the blackboard, jabbing a finger at the unfurled map of the world. What he did on his own time was none of her business.

"I can't stop you from endangering yourself and God knows who else," she said, "but I don't want to be a part of it."

"You're not a part of it."

Now she looked hurt. Without saying more, she turned and walked toward the car.

"Rachel," he called after her.

"I'll talk to you when you're not high."

She got in the car, slammed the door, and before he could think what to do, she was gone.

Chapter Twenty-one

He finished up at the Lundborns' with darkness falling and drove out to the cove. As he approached the Brovellis', he gunned the engine. Only one car sat in the driveway and a single light shone in the kitchen window. She was there by herself and would hear him driving past.

When he reached the cove, Nick pulled the truck under the pines and got out. An owl hooted off in the trees, but he could not spot the bird. He circled the ruins of the mansion and went to check on the cottage. The door was securely locked. He found no signs that anyone had been there. He didn't imagine the boys would be coming out this way again anytime soon. Back in the truck, he turned up the volume on the tape deck and listened to the latest Van Morrison. The beat filled the small space, along with the singer's bluesy voice. He passed the Brovellis' again. Eddie's truck was parked beside Rachel's car now. He caught a glimpse of Eddie's silhouette through the window and thought that the big old lug was what Rachel deserved.

Nick felt looser, more fluid, after smoking a joint. He could manage a hammer and crowbar better. It was actually probably safer for him to work with a slight buzz, though there was no convincing Rachel of this. She saw marijuana and alcohol as twin evils, two sides of the same coin. Her father's drinking binges had sealed her self-righteous zeal on the subject. Nick could do just about anything high. The drug made him easier with himself and others, but did not impair his judgment the way alcohol did. Maybe he moved a little more slowly when he was high, but that was about the worst of its effects. He didn't start shouting or hitting anyone, or get sloppy and fall down. He didn't become scary, the way Rachel's father had when he was still alive.

If Rachel planned to stay married to Eddie, as it appeared she did, she had no right to tell Nick how to spend his time when he wasn't with her. A couple of hours in the sack did not give her a say. She should be grateful for the sex, something she clearly didn't get much, if any, of from Eddie. She should keep her mouth shut.

When he came to the fork, he did not take the wooded stretch of road to his house. He went the other way, past the Improvement Center, and turned into a dirt drive that wound through a field. At the crest of the hill, he came to the domed shape of the quonset hut. A few cars were parked outside. He pulled alongside them and sat for a moment. The low beat of music came from inside. Probably one of those grunge bands Gary loved. He played almost nothing else. This was one reason Nick didn't frequent the hut as much as the other men. There were other reasons, too. Most of them were younger than he was. Some nights he couldn't find anything to say to them.

Nick grabbed a six-pack from the well behind the seat—warm beer, but it was all he had to offer. He brushed the sawdust from the front of his jeans and went inside. The doorway was so low, he had to stoop to keep from hitting his head. The men gathered around the pool table glanced up.

"Hey," Gary called.

"Hey," Nick said. He went to the refrigerator, set the six-pack inside, and helped himself to one of the cold bottles on the top shelf.

Cliff leaned over the pool table, his eyes narrowed in a squint. He took his shot and missed. "Shit. Now Ian's going to run out the game, aren't you?"

"Yes, I am. Stand back, boys."

Ian buffed the tip of his cue with chalk and circled the table, making an elaborate show of sizing up the position of each ball.

Nick went to stand beside Gary, who raised his beer bottle and clinked it against Nick's.

"That girl from the inn was out at the mansion taking pictures," Gary said.

"Yeah, I saw her."

"Kind of spooky the way she shows up everywhere with that camera. I feel like I'm watching my back."

"I don't think she's spying on you."

"Nah, she just seems to be everywhere at once. It must get kind of cold over there at the inn all alone."

"She came here to work I guess."

"So she doesn't get cold?"

Nick shrugged and took a long drink from the beer.

Ian sank one ball and then another. He worked his way quickly around the table, picking shots off with a sharp, resounding click of the cue. Nick watched with the others. He rarely participated in these games. They took it too seriously and bet too much money.

"Ian and Cliff actually got that girl to talk to them," Brad said. "I can't get her to say 'boo' when I see her down at the store. And she's always wearing that hooded sweatshirt. What would you say, she's thirty or so?"

"Something like that," Nick said.

"They should outlaw those sweatshirts on chicks," Cliff said. "You can't see a thing."

Ian finished sinking all the balls and held out his hand. "Pony up, guys."

The men each slapped a five dollar bill into his palm.

"Who's in?" Ian asked.

They all picked up their cues and moved around the table while Ian gathered the balls in the rack. No one suggested Nick join the game. The music was loud, the beat grinding. He didn't even try to keep these bands straight. They all sounded the same, like they were desperate simply to make noise, to fill the air with static. He drained his beer and went to get another. The curved walls of the hut were covered in posters of rock bands and Gary's collection of neon beer signs. Shelves filled with cassette tapes lined the back wall, along with a few compact discs. Gary knew some music, Nick would grant him that. The 1960s through the '80s (like that was the whole story of music), but Gary didn't know music the way Nick did.

Ian broke the pack of balls and circled the table, rapidly sinking three shots before missing. He stepped back to let Cliff take a turn. "Fred Hershel's not speaking to any of us," he said to Nick.

"Yeah, he chewed me out when I ran into him today, told me to stop spreading rumors about his kids."

"Hell, I didn't start that fire, and you didn't start it, so who did?"

"Fred's convinced it wasn't his little angels."

"Angels, my ass. That Venable woman could sue."

"It's probably not worth it to her. I don't think she exactly needs the money."

"You still babysitting those geese?" Ian said.

"Yeah, you want to take them for a while?"

"No, thanks."

"I was thinking of having a little auction. Raffle them off one at a time. I'll pay the winners to take them."

"Why don't you get Mary Lou Danks to take them over to her house? She loves the things."

"I know. She's been coming over to feed them. I'm thinking I'll poison her and the geese both if I get the chance."

"The animal rights people will come after you for the geese, but I don't think even they'll complain if you poison Mary Lou."

Gary missed a shot, and Ian returned to make quick work of the rest of the game. Nick watched as they fished in their pockets for more money. He wondered how they made this whole thing work. In the dead of winter, they would be buying their groceries with food stamps.

"Hey, I haven't heard you on the radio in a while," Brad called to Nick across the table.

"I've had some technical difficulties."

"Oh, yeah? Well, let us know when you're back on, so we're not tuning in to static every night."

Nick acknowledged the request by raising his beer. None of the guys at the hut would turn him in, but he didn't like to talk about his radio show, if for no other reason than it might bring bad luck.

The balls went rolling over the table with a hollow sound. Nick followed the game without following it. The beer, smooth going down his throat, would do for dinner.

Gary came over to stand beside him again. "So it looks like we're gonna have to bomb the shit out of Iraq, huh?"

Nick took a drink. "Saddam's asking for it."

"I don't see that we got a whole lot of choice. We can't let him invade Kuwait and get away with it. It'll be a piece of cake. Drop a few big ones, and he'll fold right up."

Nick suspected it might not be that simple, but he didn't say anything.

"I saw this article in the paper," Gary said. "They've got these new laser-guided missiles. They can hit a pinhead. Incredible. They can set the targets so they only hit what they want. No more blanketed bombing."

Gary didn't say it, but Nick knew that "blanketed bombing" was a reference to Vietnam. Everyone brought up war with him because Nick was the expert, the one who had been there.

"Hey, Gary, you're up," Cliff called.

Gary returned to the game. Nick downed the rest of the beer and told the men he would see them later. They glanced away from the pool table for a moment to register his departure. Outside he felt the cold air on his face and saw the stars overhead, crisp against the black sky. That was one thing to be said for the island. You could see the stars.

He took the dark road to the fork and followed the bend toward his house. He pulled into the driveway and sat for a minute staring at the space of lawn beyond the windshield. The geese were bedded down by the perennial bed. They let out a few sleepy squawks when he stepped from the truck. He felt a momentary affection for them, gathered together for the night like a heap of feathered kittens, before reminding himself that they were a nuisance, that they had destroyed the lawn and flower beds.

Inside, he hung his jacket from the coat rack and went to the refrigerator for a beer. He carried the bottle upstairs to the spare room where shelves of record albums lined the walls. Darkness fell earlier and earlier now, plunging the view beyond the window into a night so dense it seemed like not a phase of the day but another state entirely. He sank into the chair at the table and reached over to pull the shade.

The turntable and receiver sat in front of him, but he didn't feel like broadcasting now. He had hooked the antenna up to the tallest pine on the rise behind the house. It seemed to work. Rachel had found him on the dial anyway. He still felt uneasy about broadcasting from his house.

He took a Robert Johnson album from the nearest shelf and slid the record from the sleeve. He switched on the turntable, set the record in place, and lowered the needle. Johnson's raw crooning filled the room. The album was one of the first in Nick's collection. The day he brought it home from a shop in Boston he played it straight through three times in a row. He had been back from Vietnam only a few months. He worked nights as a dishwasher in a diner and spent the days roaming the record shops. Even the rare finds were cheap, or relatively so. The used bins were full of treasures, old blues '78s, records he could never replace now. The country was ready to explode, but he remembered it as an oddly peaceful time. He lived inside the music.

Nick collected the pile of roaches saved in a tin on the shelf and unrolled them one by one onto a sheet of paper. The shreds of rolling paper, brown around the edges, peeled into thin strips. The blackened bits of pot gave off the pungent odor of seasoned weed. He saved the second-generation joints, assembled from the rich leftovers of the roaches, for special occasions. Not that tonight was a special occasion, but he would allow himself the pleasure anyway, a salute to all those sorry men shipping out to a potential war in the Gulf.

He rolled a thin joint and lit it. The beer and pot made him fuzzy and a little relaxed, but he knew if he got up and started walking around the house, if he broke the spell, he would become a circuit of wakeful nerves.

The story he always told was that he had not seen any action in Vietnam, and it was, for the most part, true. There were just those weeks, after the lieutenant arrived, when he was loaned to another unit and sent out on jungle duty. They were supposed to sweep the village that day, maybe rough up the people a little, force them to reveal where the Viet Cong were hiding. Not necessarily a dangerous mission—that is, if no one did anything stupid. The lieutenant didn't know the difference between smart and stupid, though. He had already led the men on a couple of crazy trips, taking them so far off course in his zeal they were lucky to find their way back to camp, let alone get there alive. He was fresh out of West Point and ready to be a martyr for the cause. They didn't share his fervor.

The huts in the village stood in a ring around a circle of dirt, and in the center of the circle was a Coke can lying there like a discarded piece of trash. Nick knew, like every other man in the unit, that there was no trash in Vietnam. Everything got used somehow. And a Coke can was so obvious, it was the equivalent of a bad joke. The lieutenant strode toward the villagers in his officious way, waving his hands and yelling at them, "V.C. Where V.C.?" The villagers' eyes expanded until they seemed to fill their faces, and Nick felt a ripple of understanding pass between the villagers and the soldiers. They stood there as though set in cement, knowing as surely as the villagers what was about to happen. No one moved or breathed or spoke. The soldiers in their muddy fatigues, and the villagers in their pointed hats, showed no awareness of the lieutenant, who kept going, leaving the rest of the men behind. When he reached the Coke can, he hauled back with one leg and gave it a swift kick. The leg went back. There was time enough to shout, but no one did.

When the mine blew, it took off both legs. The lieutenant went sailing into the air and landed in his own blood. The shrieking villagers, certain the soldiers were about to mow them down, fled into the jungle. They could not know that the men would only look at each other, eyebrows raised, and radio for the medics, and once the chopper had come and gone, return to base with an unspoken agreement forged between them. They would not tell anyone the real story.

The record came to the end. Nick raised the needle, switched off the turntable, and made his way downstairs. He took a beer from the refrigerator, company for whatever the television had to offer. A basketball game popped up on the screen when he pushed the button on the remote. He took a seat on the couch, the cold bottle gripped in his hand. The players ran up and down the court. He watched for a few minutes, then turned it off. The basketball pounding on the parquet made him so jumpy, he'd never get to sleep now.

PART THREE

December

Chapter Twenty-two

"You are not going to stay on that island for Christmas."

In typical fashion, her mother made the observation as something close to a command.

Ruth propped the phone against her ear and traced the ridged lines in the dining room table with her finger. "I told you I can't leave. If I'm going to do this project, I have to stay here. I have to take a photo every day."

"So you miss a day or two, what's the difference? You can take the bus on Monday and go back on Wednesday if you want."

"The point is to be here every single day."

"The point for who?"

Ruth paused before answering. "For me."

"Oh, Ruthie."

She could see her mother on the other end of the phone, shaking her head, her mouth pulled into a tight line. It was the expression of her mother's she knew best.

"You can come here," Ruth said. "We can have Christmas at the inn. There's plenty of room."

"That is not anyone's idea of Christmas, freezing in that place. Does the oven even work?"

"Yes, the oven works. How do you think I've been eating?"

"I figured with all those vegetables you eat, you don't really cook. Is your roommate going to be there?"

"No. Liza's going to her parents'."

"So you're going to have Christmas by yourself." Her mother's tone conveyed both irritation and disbelief.

"I'm going to Alice's. She's invited me."

There was silence while Lydia took in this information. "How is Alice?"

"Fine."

"Is she still spending twelve hours a day behind the counter at the store?"

"She doesn't stay open such long hours this time of year."

"And Brock's still running the dump?"

"Yes."

"I guess some things really don't change."

Ruth was tempted to inform her mother that not only was she going to Alice's for Christmas, she was having lunch with her in just a few hours, but instead she said, "Her son lives on the island now. Nick."

"What does he do?"

"Construction work."

"He's not a quahogger?"

"No. Not everyone on the island is a quahogger, Mom."

"I didn't say they were."

"You implied it."

"Construction work, quahogging, what's the difference? Don't they all go on unemployment for the winter anyway?"

"I don't know." Ruth held the phone to her ear with a profound sense of fatigue. Talking to her mother was exhausting.

"Well, it's nice of Alice to have you for Christmas. Joan's kids will be crushed, you know. They love seeing you."

"I love seeing them, too."

"I guess we'll have to send your presents. Alice is still the post-mistress, I suppose."

"Yes, she is."

"That's my image of Alice, sitting there behind the counter sorting the mail. She's been doing that for her whole life practically."

"It's not a bad life."

Lydia let out a harrumph of disagreement.

"I should go," Ruth said. "I've got to get back to the darkroom."

"Call us some time. Your father's off at the dentist. He'd like to talk to you."

It was only ten in the morning, but Ruth could not escape the feeling that the conversation had blown her concentration for the day. Her mother loved to call early, after she had finished a leisurely breakfast and done her nails and make-up, precisely the time Ruth did not want to talk with her. She imagined one of those lists her mother was constantly making and the red check mark she would now place beside "call Ruth."

The print she had been working on was ruined, left too long in the developer. She shouldn't have answered the phone, but when she did not answer, her mother kept calling over and over, and she had to listen to the endless ringing. It was easier to get it over with.

She gazed at the photograph floating in the tray. It was an act of ego to think that her photographs made a difference. Or just plain narcissism. Her mother was right. Liza was right. She was self-centered and distracted and thoughtless. She didn't care about people. The ethereal business of creating something out of nothing meant more to her than gathering around a Christmas tree with her family.

For many years, she had been the dutiful daughter. She'd shown up for all the major holidays without Liza, who went home to her own family. When the celebrations were moved to Joan's house because she had young children, Ruth went along without complaint. Never once had she missed a major holiday, and never once had she hosted one. This year she thought she was entitled to do something different.

She fished the wet print from the developer, tossed it in the trash, and started over. Adjusting the focus on the lens, she slid a fresh sheet of paper into the easel and flipped on the timer. The negative image projected by the enlarger had an other-worldly strangeness—one of the quonset huts, down at the old Navy base, shot with a wide angle, marooned in the center of bare ground. There was a haunted emptiness to the image. Maybe she did love this more than any person in the world. Was that a crime?

The pictures she had shot down at the old Navy base the day before were the best she had made yet. That's how they struck her here, under the murky red light, at least. The domed frames of the quonset huts, and the abandoned workshops and garages, spoke of a place that once bustled with importance during the glory days of World War II. Snapping the shots of the oddly eloquent structures, she had felt she was doing exactly what she should be doing; if there was such a thing as a calling in a person's life, she had found hers.

The print did not disappoint her. When it was ready to be carried out into the natural light, she saw that the tones were just what she wanted. The corroded sides of the quonset hut shone ever so slightly against the backdrop of an overcast sky and the dark ground. The footsteps of those World War II sailors seemed to echo through the scene. She returned to the bathroom anxious to try other shots from the roll and pored over the contact sheet feeling defiant and hopeful. These photographs would take her somewhere. They would not languish in a dusty portfolio. She would have her show, maybe even her book.

The longer she spent on the island, the clearer it became that her commercial work had been both an excuse and a trap. Doing photography was acceptable when it was simply a job and a source of income. When she tried to make a claim for the work as art, it took on another character entirely. In recent years, her attempts at making "art" had remained nothing more than the Saturday afternoons Liza resented. The commercial work was the real work. Now she had cast that fiction aside. Ruth did not care about her mother's disapproval and disappointment. She had learned to live with that long ago, but she did care about Liza's feelings, despite what Liza might believe.

Their visit had not ended well, and once again, it was Ruth's fault. Three days was all Liza had asked. Three days of languishing in bed and lazy meals and glasses of wine. Ruth did not, as Liza thought, set out intentionally to spoil this lovely idyll. She did not start the fire down at the mansion, only responded to the moment and what it presented. They might have recovered from the bad start to Thanksgiving and Liza's anger over being left to take care of the turkey and stuffing, but then, on

Saturday night when they were eating leftovers, Liza asked when Ruth was coming home.

"I'm not sure," Ruth said.

"So it could be February or March?"

"Maybe." Ruth wanted to stay through the spring, but she did not think now was the time to reveal this.

Liza remained immobile for a moment, then raised the wine glass to her lips and took an angry sip.

Their goodbye the next morning was hasty, with only a perfunctory exchange of kisses, and the phone conversations since then had been no better. Liza said she could not get out of spending Christmas with her family. Maybe she could come for New Year's.

She would tell Liza then, when she came for New Year's, that she wanted to stay through the spring, maybe even the summer. Ruth reached up and set the opening on the enlarger lens. She wasn't rejecting Liza; she was embracing her true self. Okay, *true self* sounded ridiculously hokey, like something out of one of those idiotic self-help books. But this was how it felt, as though she had finally discovered who she was. If Liza loved her, she would understand. This project was as essential to Ruth as breathing.

She made three more prints and, when the last was in the hypo-wash, switched on the overhead light. She had felt hopeless about the idea of the visual diary when Liza visited. After she had printed the photos of the fire, the images seemed to take on the life they lacked before. The search for each day's photo was a part of the process as much as the time in the darkroom. The hours she devoted to one fed the other in a continuous loop that became magical, fueled by a force that existed outside her. She could not explain this to anyone; she could only say that she couldn't live without it.

She went to the kitchen and checked the clock. It was almost one, when she was due for lunch at Alice's. A light rain began to fall as she set off on the bicycle. Mist coated her face. Just once she wished her mother would get it. Was this asking too much? Just once she wanted her mother to say that she was proud of Ruth, that her work was wonderful (no, brilliant), her talent undeniable. Talent was not a word that meant much to her mother, though, unless it was a talent for baking casseroles or knowing where to find the best deal on shoes.

Ruth left her bike at the edge of the driveway and knocked on Alice's door. It opened instantly, as though Alice had been waiting on the other side. Ruth remembered, when she stepped inside, what her mother used to say about the house. It wasn't much more than a shack, with three rooms on the first floor and an unfinished attic where Alice and her brother slept. Alice's father, a quahogger, had drowned in a boating accident when she was nine years old. Her mother took over the store after that and, according to Ruth's mother, barely managed to put food on the table. The house, she said, was an embarrassment, even by island standards.

If this was the same place where Alice had grown up, a great deal had been done to it in the years since. The living room looked like any living room in America, with a couch and easy chairs and a large television in the corner, newspapers and magazines piled on a coffee table, and a book-case full of movies on videotape. Beyond were a dining area and kitchen, and past these rooms, a sun porch full of potted plants.

"Sorry you had to bike over in the rain," Alice said as she took Ruth's jacket. "I've got some soup to warm you up."

Alice gestured toward the table off the kitchen, which was set with two bright yellow placemats and silverware and napkins. Ruth took a seat and watched as Alice went to the kitchen and ladled soup into bowls.

"Chicken noodle," Alice said, bringing the bowls to the table. "Homemade." She gave Ruth an awkward smile, as though she needed to apologize for such an ordinary offering.

"It looks great," Ruth said.

Alice went back to the kitchen and returned with a plate of sliced white bread and another with a stick of butter. It was a meal, Ruth thought, out of her childhood.

"Brock's minding the store. I guess he can handle it. We're not too busy this time of year." Alice took the seat across from Ruth. "You've been taking lots of pictures, huh?"

"I've taken a photograph for every day I've been here so far. Well, I've taken more than that, but I'm assembling a collection with one for each day." Ruth swallowed a spoonful of soup, aware of the noise the spoon made scraping the china.

"You'll have to have an exhibit at the Improvement Center. We do that sometimes in the summer, have art exhibits. Sometimes people even buy the art."

Ruth wondered how the islanders would feel about her photographs.

"You've met my son, haven't you?" Alice said.

Ruth remembered her promise to Nick not to reveal that he had been by to visit. "I've seen him down at the dock."

"He came back to the island a few years ago. I don't know that it's the best place for him, being single and all." She stopped and dabbed at her mouth with a napkin. "He's never married."

This comment hung in the air between them. Ruth felt the urge to explain her status, in part for the satisfaction of shocking Alice, but also to put an end to any questions or suggestions. Before she could give in to this dubious impulse, Alice said, "He helps hang the art shows when we have them."

"He's a carpenter, huh?"

"Yes. Well, he's really an engineer, but he's not doing that anymore. He wanted to get out of the rat race. That's what he says anyway. It sounded like a pretty good life to me, what he was getting paid and all. He had a lot of money saved when he came back here. He built his own house on the other side of the island."

"Is he glad to be back on the island?" Ruth couldn't resist trying to get Alice to say more about Nick.

Alice drew her lips together as though giving careful consideration to what she would say. "Oh, I guess so. I don't know that he'd be terribly happy anywhere, between you and me."

Nick had not struck Ruth as unhappy. Restless, maybe, or a bit adrift, but he didn't seem depressed. "I bet the fire was hard on him."

"It was. He was the one who discovered it. That didn't help. He felt so responsible."

"He wasn't a suspect, was he?"

Alice gave her a startled look. "No."

"I just thought because he was the one to find it…I know he didn't have anything to do with it."

"The fire inspector questioned Nick just like everyone else, but he was never a suspect."

Alice folded her napkin and set it beside her bowl in a way that made Ruth regret what she had said. She was only fishing, trying to see what else Alice might reveal about Nick.

"Would you like some more soup?" Alice asked.

"No, thanks." Ruth set her spoon in the empty bowl.

"I've got some gingerbread for dessert. Then I'll show you that picture."

Alice went back to talking about the fire as she cleared the table. Everyone knew that those Hershel and Manning kids were involved, but they hadn't confessed. The fire inspector was supposed to come back to interview the boys and their parents. Typical of town officials from the mainland, he had missed two appointments now and had not rescheduled. They all hated coming to the island. They thought what happened on the island was the islanders' business, not theirs. As if the islanders didn't pay taxes like everyone else. "We help pay that fire inspector's salary," Alice said, "but he doesn't seem to remember that."

Alice brought two plates of gingerbread from the kitchen. "Sometimes I make cookies, but I felt like something substantial with this cold weather. Brock's supposed to be watching his weight. I have to hide stuff like this from him."

Ruth took a bite of the cake. "It's delicious. Really moist."

"Sour cream. That's what makes it moist. Use sour cream and any cake is delicious. Brock shouldn't be having that, either. He's got high cholesterol. But I can't resist every once in a while. When I was a girl we couldn't afford much. We had ice cream sometimes, and we'd get a cake for our birthdays. That was about it. We weren't allowed to eat the candy at the store. Eating up the profits, my mother said. She was right. You know, after that I just can't deny myself anything."

Alice finished her cake and left the table. Ruth could hear her opening and closing a drawer in the living room. She returned with a curled photograph of a young man in an Army uniform. With his big eyes, close-cropped hair, and cap perched on his head, he appeared to be barely out of childhood, a skinny teenager trying to play the part of a soldier.

"He looks so much like my mother," Ruth said.

"Well, they were twins. You must have seen other pictures of him."

"Just once or twice when I was a kid, at my grandmother's."

"People used to joke about it, how they looked so much alike but acted so different. Your mother was more outgoing. Pete was friendly, friendly to everyone, but he was a little more reserved. He loved the island. He wanted to come back here and be a quahogger."

"My mother's never talked about him much."

"They were close, even though they were so different. They left the island together when Pete enlisted. Lydia didn't want to stay behind without him."

Ruth fingered the cracked paper of the old photo. "How did you get this?"

"He sent it to me."

"It's funny that he loved the island when my mother couldn't stand it."

"I remember before he enlisted, he said he wished the war would end, and then he wouldn't have to go. He felt bad having such thoughts. He thought they were unpatriotic, but he couldn't help it. He didn't care about traveling and seeing faraway places and all of that."

"But my mother did. She should have been the soldier."

"She got as close to the action as she could. She was the only girl we knew who went off to the war."

"She always told those stories when I was a kid, how she was a Red Cross girl and baked donuts for the soldiers over in England. 'Those donuts won the war,' she said. She told us she got about ten marriage proposals a day."

Alice smiled. "Spirited. That's how we used to describe your mother. If it wasn't for her, I wouldn't have met Brock. We went down to the dance hall where the sailors hung out. Lydia told them we were eighteen."

"You weren't eighteen?"

"No, we were seventeen. The sailors wouldn't have given us beer if they thought we were seventeen."

"She never told me that story."

"Brock was there that night at the dance hall. Then after the war he came back and found me. We always said Lydia was the one to blame." Alice took the photograph from Ruth. "She was devastated when Pete died. Maybe she didn't want to talk about any of it."

Devastated was not a word Ruth would have used in connection with her mother, except maybe when a torn nail or stained blouse was involved. "I wish I'd known him," she said.

Alice held her gaze for a moment. "He was a wonderful man. Everyone loved him."

Ruth saw that she was not going to say more, though Alice's look suggested there was more to be said.

"Well, I better be getting back to the store," Alice said.

Ruth wanted to hear more about her uncle, but Alice stood, signaling that the visit was over. Ruth thanked her and pulled on her jacket. Alice walked her to the door and watched as Ruth climbed onto her bike.

"Stay dry," Alice called when Ruth pushed off.

She pedaled over the dirt road wondering what had just happened. Was Alice trying to tell her something about her uncle? Or just sharing memories? Ruth had never heard her mother talk about a romance between Alice and Pete. Lydia used to say, with a certain amusement and disdain, that Alice had one marriage offer, which she was lucky to get, and she took it.

Ruth stopped when she came to the foot of the hill. The road was empty in either direction; the sand stretching along the shore beyond the dock appeared silver in the overcast light. It was hard to imagine Alice as a teenager, harder still to imagine her being in love with Pete or anyone else. Ruth supposed she must have been in love with Brock once, though she didn't think you'd use the phrase to describe whatever went on now, at their age.

As she pedaled down the road toward the lighthouse, Ruth thought of her mother and Pete going off to the war. The stretch of rocky shoreline below her would have been the last view of the island they had before the ferry pulled out into the channel. She imagined the two of them on the deck together, watching the island grow smaller, the way she did when she went to the mainland for her shopping trips.

Chapter Twenty-three

She did not stop to speak with anyone. She drove the car off the ferry and kept going, across the parking lot and up to the road. In the gray light of December, the island had a more stark aspect than she remembered. Water the color of steel stretched into the distance, no longer an inviting sight.

She told herself she was ready for whatever she found out at the cove, but as she rounded the last bend, and the burned shell of the big house came into view, Nora realized how wrong she had been. Loss. The word itself mocked her. What had she lost? Something she didn't want, then or now. Something she was planning to destroy. Something that had never been hers.

She parked under the trees and sat there taking in the black swath of ground, the charred stone walls, and the cavernous space that used to be the house. It was a chilling sight. She didn't want to get out of the car.

The caretaker's cottage was untouched, Nick had told her on the phone, but he had not been inside. She needed to see that much, to determine if the place was still habitable. The smell hit her as soon as she opened the car door, a thick, acrid odor that made her feel nauseous. It was the smell not just of smoke but of annihilation, the smell of destruction, the smell of what could not be gotten back. She followed the path along the pines trees, as far away as possible from the burned grass that stretched like a pool of oil on all sides of what remained of the house.

She slipped the key into the lock and opened the cottage door. The smell was fainter here, but still present. Inside, everything was just as she had left it: dishes sitting in the drainer by the sink, her sketchpad on the table. The place was welcoming and cozy. She moved through the rooms cautiously, afraid that her initial impression would not hold. The bedrooms were compact and cheery, with the duvets and their flowered covers floating cloud-like over the beds, matching curtains at the windows, but the smell permeated everything. The flames may not have reached the cottage, but the fire had.

She would take all the bedding and the curtains to the mainland to be cleaned. She would give the couch and easy chairs away and get new ones. She would open the windows, on a warmer day, once the wreckage of the fire was carted off, and air the place out. She would hire Alice to clean the cottage again. She would return, no matter what Isabelle had to say about it.

She took down the curtains and piled them into a trash bag. As long as the big house had stood, even in its unfinished state, a piece of Gerald remained in the world, the exuberant Gerald who was full of grand plans. She wondered now if she would have been able to tear the place down when the time came. It had been done for her, in any case, but the destruction felt like a final death. Gerald was truly gone now.

She felt sorry not for herself but for him. The attempt to build the big house was the only great scheme he had pulled off, or almost pulled off. When she thought back on his life, what did it amount to? A string of parties and tennis matches, with a bit of education and travel thrown in. He had loved her, in his way, and spent time with his many friends, though the friendships never quite asked too much of him. He had adored his nieces and nephews, taken them on trips and bought them extravagant gifts. He played a good game of poker and was a generous host. This was, as far as she could tell, the sum total of his life. She supposed, when she stopped to think about it, no one's life amounted to all that much, or at least the lives of ordinary people did not. They had babies, went to work, ate and slept, acquired things and lost them, got sick and died. She knew what Gerald would say to this: He was not an ordinary person. But he was—just an ordinary person with money and a good deal of luck, until he boarded that train in Germany.

I'm sorry, Nora said to him. I don't know why I didn't finish the big house or why I wanted to tear it down. I should have completed it for you, but I couldn't. This was the only explanation she could offer. She simply could not finish building the big house after Gerald died. It was his place, not hers.

Nora cinched the trash bag closed and carried it outside. She was on her way to the car when she noticed someone coming down the road on a bike. The figure waved, and she realized it was the woman with the camera, Ruth, in her bulky down jacket. The hood was pushed back, so the short fringe of her brown hair showed. The cropped hair and lack of make-up and boyish clothes gave her an androgynous look that Nora found seductive. These days, it was often impossible to tell if young people were male or female. The moment of hesitation, when you weren't sure of their gender, was full of tantalizing confusion and possibility.

Ruth came riding over the rutted road and pulled up next to Nora's car. "I've been taking pictures," she said. "I hope you don't mind."

"Not if you show them to me."

"I'm sorry about the fire. It must have been a shock."

Nora opened the car door and set the trash bag in the back seat. "I was planning to tear the place down. I just don't like the idea of people prowling around out here. The cottage is full of smoke, but with a little cleaning up, I can move back in. Would you like to come see it? I can probably manage to make some tea."

"Tea would be good. I'm freezing."

"I don't wonder, riding around on that bike."

Ruth lowered the kickstand and gave her a small smile. "I'm dressed for it." She took the camera bag from the milk crate fixed to the back of the bike and slung it over her shoulder.

"Did you see the fire?" Nora asked as they followed the path around the edge of the burned grass.

"Not when it happened. I heard the sirens that night, but I didn't know what they meant. I came out the next morning."

"Was the fire out by then?"

"More or less. The men stayed out here for a couple of days to make sure it didn't flare up again."

"I wish I could repay them somehow."

"Get them a case of beer."

Nora laughed. "Beer? That's not much of a thank-you."

They reached the cottage, and Ruth followed her inside. "Does it smell very bad?" Nora asked.

Ruth sniffed the air. "It smells smoky. It's faint, but…"

"But still there." Nora went to the sink and filled the tea kettle with water. "I'll have to replace everything." She gestured toward the couch as she set the kettle on the stove.

Ruth draped her jacket over the back of the chair at the kitchen table.

"Where do you live when you're not on Snow Island?" Nora asked.

"New York, downtown, in Soho. My friend and I got a rent-controlled lease on a loft eight years ago, before everything went sky high. Now we can hardly afford a cup of coffee in our neighborhood."

"So you're starving artists."

As she took mugs to the sink to rinse them, Nora saw the look that went over Ruth's face and realized she had said the wrong thing.

"I do advertising photography," Ruth said. "My roommate's a graphic artist. We've got regular jobs, both of us. Not that regular jobs are enough in the city. My roommate wants to move to the island and open the inn."

"You'd be happy living here year-round?"

"I don't know. At first I loved it, but some days…"

"Some days it's too quiet, right?"

"Right."

"I think it's probably safe to sit in these chairs, smell-wise." Nora motioned toward the chairs at the kitchen table.

They sat across from each other and waited for the water to boil. Nora was reminded of those long-ago family dinners when silence suddenly fell over the table, as though she and her parents had become a gathering of strangers. After a few minutes, the tea kettle let out a shrill whistle, and she went to fill the cups.

"I'm afraid I don't have milk," Nora said as she returned to the table.

Ruth said she didn't take milk in her tea, and Nora wondered if she was simply saying this to be accommodating, though she didn't seem like the sort of woman to make such a gesture.

Nora wrapped her hands around the mug. "That would be a big change, to move from Soho to the island."

"That's what Liza wants. A big change. She's not my roommate, actually. She's my partner."

Nora gave an involuntary raise of her eyebrows and searched for a response. She could only come up with a faint, "Oh," and a half-hearted smile. Ruth was waiting, Nora realized, for her own acknowledgement to make the exchange of secrets equal. Perhaps this was how women behaved now, announcing brazenly that they were gay, but it was not Nora's style.

"So you've been together eight years?" Nora said after an awkward pause.

"Yes. Eight years. It's hard to believe."

"When you get to be my age, you'll believe it. Time speeds up. A year flies by."

"Why is that?"

"You don't fight things so much when you're older. You're more comfortable. Things don't matter the way they used to. One day blends into the next. Does that sound horrible?"

"Not really."

"Have you…" Nora paused and then plunged on. "Always been with women?"

"I had a couple of boyfriends in high school and college. It took me a while to figure it out. What about you?"

"I was married when I was twenty-one. That sounds young now, but it wasn't then. My husband died in his early thirties. I've been single ever since."

Ruth regarded her evenly, her gaze suggesting that she knew there was more to the story. Nora sipped the tea. She was not going to be made to feel dishonest by someone half her age who did not have the slightest idea what it was like to slink around queer bars in the 1950s.

She was trying to think of some way to change the topic that would not appear too clumsy when she was saved by a knock on the door. Startled, Nora rose from the table. She went to the porch and, through the blurred cover of plastic over the screen, made out the shape of a tall man. When she opened the door, she found Nick on the lawn, hands thrust into his jacket pockets.

"I thought that was your car," he said. "You should have called and let me know you were coming."

"I wasn't sure I could make the ferry until the last minute."

"I would have been here when you arrived."

"Yes. I thought of that. It was just as well I came by myself."

"How's the cottage?"

"A little smelly. Come on in. It's cold out there."

He followed her onto the porch, stopping to brush his shoes against the mat.

"Do you know each other?" Nora said with a gesture toward Ruth.

"We've met," Nick said.

Nora noticed that Ruth appeared momentarily taken aback, as though she were going to say something and then decided against it. Nick shifted his hands from his jacket pockets to the front pockets of his blue jeans.

No one spoke. Nick stood with his legs apart in that classic male stance. Ruth took a sip of her tea. Nora saw that the conversation was up to her.

"I want to thank you for everything," she said to Nick. "You and everyone else. I know you all put a lot of time into this."

"That's what the volunteer fire department is for."

"Ruth says I should treat you all to a case of beer to say thank you."

Nick smiled. "The guys wouldn't mind a case of beer."

"I'm going to meet with the fire inspector tomorrow, over in Barton. He says it looks like it was a cigarette dropped in the grass that started the fire. I know you don't smoke."

"No, I don't."

"I suppose those teenage boys don't smoke, either."

"Not that their parents know."

"No one's confessed to being out here smoking cigarettes?"

"Not so far."

"Do you think they're going to confess?"

"I don't know. I'd lay odds on it that sooner or later somebody's going to spill the beans, but it's hard to say."

Nick darted a look at Ruth, as if to suggest he did not want to be more explicit with her present. Nora recognized that there must be camps of people on the island: those with inside knowledge, and those on the outside. Ruth, like her, was clearly an outsider, though by virtue of the fire Nora had been brought inside, at least temporarily. She changed the subject and asked Nick if he knew anyone who would be interested in the sofa and chairs. With a little work, somebody might be able to get the smell out. He said he would ask around. She told him she would be in touch later that week about hiring someone in Barton to clean up the mess left by the fire.

Nora exchanged a few more words with Nick out on the lawn and returned to find Ruth standing by the table.

"I should be going," Ruth said. "Thanks for the tea."

"Thanks for the company. I didn't know what would be waiting for me when I got here."

"If you need a place to stay until you get this place fixed up, there's plenty of room at the inn."

"That's sweet of you. I'm going back to the mainland today, but maybe I'll take you up on that when I come back."

Nora watched through the bedroom window as Ruth jumped on the bike and rode off down the road. She envied Ruth her casual ease about being gay. In Nora's day, when the police used to raid the gay bars, being open about it could get a person carted off to jail. It was the men they arrested; the women were largely invisible. Still, even for the women, every encounter was laced with fear and its ever-present cousin, shame.

She tried to imagine another life, one in which she had been free from the start. She would never have put up with Isabelle. This might have been better for all of them—healthier, to use a word that got tossed around so much these days. But would she change any of it, if she had the choice? No, she didn't think she would.

Chapter Twenty-four

The call came from Isabelle's son Burt when she was back from the island. He delivered the news curtly and hung up. Nora walked through the rooms of her house asking herself if she felt different. She didn't. If anything, she felt less certain of what the future might hold.

When she arrived at the church three days later, Burt placed a hand under her elbow and escorted her up the aisle. She was aware of rows of mourners stiffly facing forward. Isabelle sat in the front pew beside her daughter, son-in-law, and grandchildren. Nora took a seat behind Isabelle and stared at the back of her head. Every hair lay neatly in place, the black jacket of her suit fit snugly, and a folded tissue sat in her lap. Isabelle's daughter Heather leaned over the back of the pew and whispered hello.

Isabelle turned to face Nora. "You're here," she said.

As if, Nora thought, she expected me to be somewhere else this morning. She took Isabelle's hand. Tears filled Isabelle's eyes, and she turned to face forward. In the cavernous hush of the church, Nora was left staring at the back of Isabelle's head again. Better that, she mused, than gazing at the massive casket in front of the altar rail.

Burt took the seat on the other side of Isabelle. Heather's children, two boys still in elementary school, squirmed at the end of the pew. The organ sounded the first notes, deep and ponderous, and everyone stood, hymnals in hand. The words rang out, tremulous at first but then clear: "A mighty fortress is our God, a bulwark never failing." Nora could not remember the last time she had sung the hymn, or the last time she had been in church for that matter, but the words came back in an instant, called up from the sure well of memory. Once the hymn concluded and the minister said, "The Lord be with you," the response sprang to her lips automatically, its cadence like the rocks lining the shore at Gooseneck Cove, worn and familiar, the smooth surfaces comforting.

The minister concluded the prayers and motioned for the congregation to be seated. The rattle of kneelers pushed into place rippled through the church, along with a smattering of cleared throats, but otherwise an expectant silence filled the space. Nora let the sound of the minister's voice roll over her. She caught the gist of his sermon without latching onto the particulars. Jesus had died for their sins. The hope of the resurrection made this loss bearable. Henry's long and distinguished life, his work as a banker, his service to his church and community, his devotion as a father and husband, were exemplary. And forty-four years of marriage was an accomplishment to be emulated. Isabelle did not move; her neck remained rigid, her eyes set on the minister's face.

The service proceeded exactly as dictated in the Book of Common Prayer. There would be no folksy sharing of reminiscences, no unscripted moments. Henry would have approved. He abhorred the tacky.

As the congregation sang "Ye Watchers and Ye Holy Ones," Burt, Heather's husband, and some other younger men gathered on either side of the casket and wheeled it down the aisle. Isabelle, Heather, and the children followed as the organist played a slow postlude. When the family had disappeared through the church doors, people spilled silently out of the pews, the expressions on their faces fixed, everyone, it seemed, fearful of saying or doing the wrong thing.

Outside, Nora watched Burt, Heather, and Isabelle climb into the black limousine. She found her car, started the engine and, when the sound of classical music suddenly came blaring from the radio speakers, lowered the volume. She joined the procession of cars which moved onto the avenue, the long bullet of the limousine in the lead. Within minutes, the procession passed through the wrought-iron gates of the cemetery and wound along a maze of paved lanes. As she pulled her coat around her and stepped from the car, Nora spotted old neighbors of Isabelle and Henry's, friends who had visited in Maine for weekends, and the couple who used to come over on Friday nights to play bridge, people she hadn't seen in years. How much their lives, and hers, had narrowed in recent years, without dinner parties and overnight guests.

Nora tottered across the grass in her heels, expecting Isabelle to turn and motion her to come forward, but she did not. The minister opened the prayer book and glanced from one side of the circled crowd to the other, as though pulling them in with his gaze. He intoned the words of the burial service in a deep voice. Nora found herself staring at the bright green squares of carpet laid on either side of the casket to hide the grave. Everything about the arrangement took on a glaringly artificial aspect, when what they were doing, lowering a coffin into the ground, was as old and basic an act as any. She did not want something like this. She would be cremated and have her ashes scattered somewhere. But where? And who would do the scattering?

The grandchildren placed single roses on the casket, the minister said a final prayer, and Burt led Isabelle back to the limousine. As she passed Nora, she said, "He loved roses."

Nora remembered the rose bushes in Maine that Henry fussed over and pruned. She nodded. Isabelle's eyes stared blankly ahead. Nora wasn't sure Isabelle knew what she had just said or to whom she had spoken.

From the cemetery, the procession returned to the church. Nora turned on the radio and listened to the noon news broadcast. Bush has issued a statement, the announcer reported, that he will abide by the resolution passed by the United Nations Security Council, giving the Iraqis until mid-January to leave Kuwait, but if Hussein does not withdraw by then, the United States will take military action. War again. It did not seem possible, after the great hope of the fall of the Berlin Wall and the end of the Cold War. Just a year ago, Nora reflected, we were swept up in the belief that there would be no more reasons for war. The bloody nightmare of the twentieth century was supposed to be over.

People gathered in small groups in the parking lot back at the church. Their faces took on a more relaxed air as they entered the parish hall, where long tables were covered with bowls of pasta salad and platters of sandwiches and fruit. Nora recognized Isabelle's touch, plentiful but not too lavish, tasteful without being extravagant. Isabelle stood with the other family members in a receiving line just inside the door. When Heather spotted Nora, she left the line and came over to shake Nora's hand.

"How's she doing?" Nora gestured toward Isabelle.

"I think she's still in shock a bit."

"It wasn't a surprise really."

"No. There's just a lot of feelings left over."

Nora was not sure if she meant left over after the years in the nursing home and the ravaging of Alzheimer's, or left over from other things.

"It will take time," Nora said, realizing her words were a cliché.

Heather returned to her place next to Burt. Nora ducked out of the line of people waiting to speak to Isabelle and went to sit at a table.

Nora had spent the days since Burt's call uncertain whether she should go to see Isabelle. Finally she brought Chinese food over for dinner. She and Isabelle were alone for only the briefest of moments, just long enough to link hands and exchange a quiet look. Now, Nora saw, the last of the line of friends and distant relatives had finished speaking with Isabelle, and she was headed toward Nora's table.

"The family eats first," Heather said as she set her coat over the back of the chair beside Nora's. "Come on."

"Like at a wedding, when the bride and groom eat first?" Nora said.

"Right."

Isabelle went through the food line with Burt at her side. Heather and her family followed. Nora came along behind them, suddenly aware of a ravenous hunger. All that standing and singing hymns and keeping her face composed had taken every bit of her strength.

"The food is good, isn't it?" Isabelle said when they were all seated at the table.

"Delicious," Heather's husband Rob said. "Great caterer. Everything looks really nice."

Isabelle gave him a grateful glance. "It's so hard to tell when all you have to go by is the menu."

As they ate, one person after another stopped by the table and hov-ered next to Isabelle's chair, speaking in hushed tones. Many of them were shockingly old. Nora wondered if she looked that wrinkled and feeble.

"Who are all these people?" Heather said. She leaned in, so she was speaking only to Nora. "I didn't know Dad had so many friends."

"People he worked with, people he knew from church and golf and bridge," Nora said. "They add up."

Heather gave her a pained look, as though the idea of her father having friends was not one she had considered before, and turned away to tell Todd, her son, to stop playing with the pasta salad.

Finished eating, Nora tried to catch Isabelle's eye across the table. If Isabelle was not talking to a well wisher, she was in conversation with Burt, her head and eyes lowered, grasping Burt's arm as though it was an anchor keeping her afloat.

When most of the people had gone, and the caterer was circulating, ready to scoop up the linen tablecloths and napkins, Nora gathered her coat and purse and stood to go.

"You're coming back to the house, aren't you?" Heather asked.

"No. I'm a little tired, like everyone else. You all need some time to yourselves."

"All right, I'll walk you out to the car."

Nora circled the table and tapped Isabelle on the shoulder. Isabelle turned with the bereaved widow expression firmly in place. "It's me," Nora said softly.

Isabelle's features relaxed. She reached up and took Nora's hand. "Thank you."

"For?"

"Everything."

Nora leaned down and gave her a quick hug. "I'll call you later."

She and Heather made their way through the parish hall and out to the parking lot in silence. When they were almost to the car, Heather said, "I saw you once. You and Mom. When I was twelve or so."

"You saw us?"

"In the bedroom. I was walking past, and the door was ajar. It was just a moment, but you had your arms around each other, and then you kissed. I didn't think anything of it then. It was a few years later, when I was older, that I realized what I had seen. It was odd, really, like the memory had been waiting there for me, until I was old enough to understand it."

"What you saw was two friends being affectionate with each other."

"No. I saw lovers having a secret kiss."

They were standing beside the car now. Nora fixed her gaze on the silver half-circle of the door handle.

"I hated you for a long time," Heather said. "I thought you had stolen my mother. Stolen her from my father and stolen her from us."

Nora kept her eyes lowered.

"You did steal her, didn't you, a part of her anyway? There was a part of her that was always missing. That's how it felt. She was there, but she wasn't there."

This, Nora reflected, was precisely how it had felt to her, too, that Isabelle was never fully present when they were together.

"I actually used to think of you as a house wrecker," Heather went on. "You became this great big bogey man, or woman, the cause of everything that was wrong in our family."

Nora raised her head and met Heather's look. "Do you still think of me that way?"

"Sometimes."

"I'm sorry."

Heather waved her hand in the air, as though brushing away the need for explanation or apology. "My father was a difficult man. He didn't give Mom much. Money, of course, and a nice house and vacations. He wasn't cheap. But he didn't give her a lot of love. Even when I was little, I saw it. There was this constant chilliness about him."

Tears brimmed in Heather's eyes. "When I was very little, I worshipped him, but then when I got older, I couldn't stand the way he treated Mom. It made me so angry sometimes, I could hardly look at him. You remember those days. When you came to visit, the house seemed a little lighter. You made us laugh. Remember when we used to go play miniature golf? Dad would never do things like that with us. It was always you and Mom. Except then when I was a teenager, I hated you, too. I hated him, and I hated you. It was very confusing."

"I didn't think you had any idea."

"You were so careful. I don't think I even heard the word lesbian until I went to college. It was certainly never uttered in our house."

"Your mother doesn't think of herself that way, as a lesbian."

Heather brushed the tears from her eyes and smiled ruefully. "Well, that's a relief."

"That's not what I—"

"I know. But does it make any difference what you call it if you two had an affair that went on for forty years under my father's nose?"

"Have you talked to your mother about this?"

"No."

"Maybe you should. It wasn't quite the way you are describing."

"Not quite?"

"No, not quite."

"You aren't denying it."

"I'm not denying it, but what you're saying is not entirely accurate, and I'm saying maybe you should be having this conversation with Isabelle."

Heather's eyes welled up again. "We don't exactly talk about stuff like this."

"When you were children, you and Burt, there was nothing going on. That time you saw us wasn't what you thought. We weren't together. I didn't want to come between your mother and you, any of that."

"So you weren't together then, but you were later? I'm not sure it matters much one way or the other."

"I understand that to you it doesn't. I just want you to know that I was not entirely insensitive to your feelings, yours and Burt's and your father's."

"Not entirely insensitive? That's so big of you."

Nora placed her fingers around the door handle. "You need to talk to your mother about this."

"But you were always the one I could talk to, that's the thing. Until I hated you and Mom and Dad so much. I thought you were the hugest bunch of hypocrites I'd ever met."

"Of course we were hypocrites. Once you reach a certain age, everyone becomes a hypocrite. It's inevitable."

"I don't believe that. It's too cynical."

Nora attempted to open the door, but Heather grabbed her arm.

"I want my mother to be happy," Heather said.

Nora recognized these words as a dubious gift, gave Heather's arm a squeeze, and yanked open the door. She slid behind the wheel and pulled the door closed. Heather held her gaze through the window for a moment, before turning and threading her way around the parked cars back to the parish hall.

Chapter Twenty-five

Nick sank into the couch cushions and pressed the power button on the remote control. The television leapt to life, and, assaulted by a breakfast cereal ad making impossible claims about losing weight and improving health, he pushed the mute button and surfed the channels. When he had signed up for the satellite connection, he had imagined the island would no longer feel so isolated—the world would come to him. But the joke he made about three thousand channels with nothing on any of them was true.

He watched a confusing assortment of images click past and told himself he should be reading a book or listening to music instead of killing time so mindlessly, but he didn't have the patience for reading or even music right now. He didn't have the patience for much these days. He shut off the television, grabbed his coat, and stepped outside. The waves broke on the rocks below with a soft hiss. Under the black sky, the geese were just visible across the lawn, huddled together beneath the bushes.

The men were all over at Cliff's, playing poker, but he had no plans to meet Rachel. He had not spoken to her since the day she stopped by the Lundborns'. Two days later, he had picked up the first installment of the wood order for the schoolhouse over on the mainland and brought it back on the ferry. He waited until after dark, when he knew she would be gone, to deliver it. He left the wood in a huge pile on the lawn by the schoolhouse. He would go stack it on the weekend.

Nick drove past the quonset hut. The single streetlight above the dock cast a small circle of yellow on the pavement. The perfect stillness of that spot of light, with the store and dock beyond, had the feel of an Edward Hopper painting. Hopper's images made him want to shake the solitary figures in their contained landscapes free, but at the same time, he recognized the truth in them. Sometimes life did feel as empty as those paintings.

Nick pulled up next to the inn and climbed out of the truck. Light shone through the front windows, though he could not see Ruth inside. He rapped on the door. No answer. He rapped more loudly. After another wait, he opened the door, stuck his head inside, and called, "Hello?"

A muffled voice answered him, and he heard a door open. "I'm in the darkroom," she called. "Who is it?"

"Nick."

He thought of simply retreating, going out the door and quietly closing it behind him, but then she appeared in the hallway.

"This isn't a good time," he said.

"No, it's okay. I just have to finish this print."

He stepped inside and stood there hesitantly.

"Come on down to the darkroom," she said.

He left his jacket on a chair and followed her around the corner, down another hall, and through a door at the end. It took a moment for his eyes to adjust to the hazy red light, but then he could make out a claw-footed tub with a board set on top of it and metal trays on top of that. The bathroom was spacious, big enough for a dresser in one corner and a basket full of magazines in another. She shut the door behind them.

"You're sure I'm not in the way?" he said.

"No. Stand over there." She pointed toward the dresser. "This will just take a few minutes."

The enlarger was set on a small table by the tub. She slid a piece of paper into a holder and flipped a switch. Light shone from the enlarger onto the paper. As his eyes adjusted further to the strange half-light, he could make out other prints floating in the metal trays.

"I've never been in a darkroom before," he said.

"This one is pretty makeshift, but it works. Come over here. You can watch it develop."

She took the sheet of paper and set it in the first tray. He peered down into the clear fluid. Gradually a black-and-white image took shape on the flat surface of the paper. He made out what looked like rocks. A pungent smell came up from the trays.

"This stuff isn't good for you, is it, these chemicals?"

"No. I'm probably killing brain cells like crazy."

"You don't worry about that?"

She shrugged. "I've got some to spare. I try not to stay in here too long, and I open the window when I'm done. I use the tongs so I don't get the chemicals on my hands."

She leaned over the tray to examine the print. He couldn't tell how she could see much of anything in the red light.

"I'd go blind doing this," he said.

"You get used to the safe lights."

"So that's a picture of rocks?"

She glanced up. "Right. On the beach down by the store. I love the different shapes and the tones. This is one of what I call my abstractions." She picked up the print with metal tongs and moved it to the next tray.

"I hear you've been going over to visit my mother," he said.

"She had me over for lunch. She wanted to show me a picture of my uncle. Pete, my mother's twin brother. He died in World War II."

"I don't think I've ever seen that."

"Your mother's never showed it to you?"

"No."

"He's in his Army uniform. I guess they were good friends. All three of them, Pete and my mother, and Alice."

"There weren't many kids on the island then. Just like there aren't now."

"Were there more when you were growing up?"

"Not really."

She went and lifted the print into the next tray.

"I should be going. I don't want to interrupt you," he said.

"I'm done now. You can have one of those beers you left last time."

"You didn't drink them?"

"No. I'm more of a wine drinker."

She moved the photo into a large plastic tray filled with other sheets of paper. She slid the piece of plywood back, so it rested over the edge of the tub, and set the plastic tray beneath the faucet. Then she turned the faucet on full, sending the water gushing into the tray and making the prints bob up and down.

"Okay, lights on," she said as she flipped the switch on the wall and gestured toward the photo on top of the pile beneath the running water. "You like it?"

"Sure. Beautiful rocks."

She laughed. "They are beautiful, even if you don't think so."

"I wasn't being sarcastic."

"All right. You want one of those beers?"

"Sounds good." He followed her back to the living room. She went to the kitchen and returned with an open bottle in one hand and a glass of red wine in the other.

"Nobody was at the quonset hut tonight, huh?" she said as she handed him the beer.

"They're all playing poker over at Cliff's."

"I was going to ask you to take me to the hut some night."

She sat on the couch, and he took the chair across from her.

"I'll take you if you want," he said. "You shoot pool?"

"Not since I was a kid."

"That's mostly what goes on at the hut. So, have you got a boyfriend back there in New York?"

She gave him a quick look, as though he had asked an overly personal question. He felt instantly that he had made some sort of mistake.

"No. Have you got a girlfriend?"

"Not really." He took a long gulp of beer and avoided her gaze. "I'm a klutz with women."

"Most men are."

"What's that supposed to mean?"

"Just that a lot of men don't know what to do with women."

"Are you talking about physically or emotionally?"

"Both."

He shrugged. "I suppose you're right."

She brought the glass to her lips and took a sip of wine. "I heard you on the radio. Jolly Roger of the bay—that's you, right?"

He raised his eyebrows. "I don't know anything about a pirate radio station."

"Why shouldn't you have a station on the island? You can hardly pull in anything from the mainland."

"Yeah, the reception stinks half the time."

"You came in loud and clear."

"It's illegal, of course."

"But nobody's going to bust you, right?"

"Nobody has so far. I guess the FCC doesn't care as long as I don't horn in on another station."

She drank the rest of the wine and went back for another glass. "You want another beer?" she called from the kitchen.

"Sure." He downed what was left in the bottle he was drinking. One beer didn't make a dent, even if he drank it fast. After two, he might get a vague buzz.

She returned and handed him the cold bottle.

"I've got a thousand albums and a lot of stuff on cassette," he said. "I wasn't planning on having a radio station, but the guys at the hut were always bugging me about it. You've got all that music, why not, they said. Finally I decided they were right. I used to take radios apart, so I know something about it. I don't broadcast that often. Three times a week maybe."

She leaned back into the lumpy couch cushions and sipped the wine. He tried to make out something of her body beneath the bulky sweatshirt. Small breasts, and a little bit of a waist, though she couldn't be called fat. She seemed jumpy and easily distracted, but at the same time, highly observant. He felt that she was watching him, searching for clues.

They sat in silence until she said, "Your mother never talked about my uncle?"

"Not that I can remember."

"It seemed like he was somebody special to her."

"Special like a sweetheart?"

"Maybe."

"The story I always heard was she met my father when he was stationed at the Navy base. Then he shipped out, and she thought she might never see him again. When the war was over, he came walking off the ferry one day. She was standing on the porch of the store, and she nearly fainted. She thought maybe he was dead. They were married a couple of months later. She was twenty years old. He was her first love."

"That's pretty much the story I heard. My mother said it was lucky there was a Navy base here, otherwise your mother never would have met Brock. How's your back?"

"All right. I get these spasms. They come and go. You want to walk on it?"

They both laughed at the strange suggestiveness of the question.

"Really," he said. "Your feet are the greatest."

She slipped off her shoes and waited as he set the bottle on the table and positioned himself on the rug. The cracking began as soon as she stepped onto his back. He had to stifle the urge to moan, it felt so good. Her feet were small and compact, not much bigger than a pair of hands moving up and down his spine. His muscles unkinked as she inched soundlessly back and forth. He was anchored to the floor but floating at the same time. He remained completely still, turned away from her, his cheek pressed into the worn carpet. The rug smelled of dust and onions fried in oil.

When she stepped from his back, he rolled over and reached for her hand. She gave him a confused look, but let him pull her down beside him. He wrapped his hand around her neck and guided her toward him. Her lips, thin and precise, parted for his tongue. He felt himself getting hard. She returned the kiss for one slow moment, then jerked away.

"I told you I was a klutz with women," he said.

"Don't say that. You're not a klutz. I am."

"No, you're not. Not at all."

He reached for her hand again, but she moved away.

"Sorry," she said. "I can't do this."

"Can't or don't want to?"

She gave him an annoyed glance. "I think it's the same thing."

He sat up, hoping the bulge in his pants was not too noticeable. "I'm the one who should say I'm sorry."

"No, it's not your fault. It's mine."

He got to his feet. She was standing a ways from him, with the backs of her legs pressed against the edge of the couch.

"Still friends?" he said.

She nodded yes.

"All right then, why don't you come over for dinner some night? I'll behave myself. You can watch my TV with three thousand channels."

This time the smile was small and tight, but she said, "Okay."

"I haven't blown it totally, have I?"

"No."

He made his way to the hall and retrieved his jacket. He was about to reach for the door when she grabbed his hand and squeezed it. He decided it was best to keep on going. He wasn't about to attempt another kiss.

He stared at the sky as he started up the truck. A glittering cover of stars stretched from one horizon to the other. He glanced back, but there was no sign of Ruth through the living room window. It was then, as he pulled away, that it occurred to him she might be into women. The short-cropped hair, the bulky clothes that were neither feminine nor masculine, the distant air she gave off—he should have seen it earlier. He felt like an idiot.

Grabbing her was an impulse of the moment. He couldn't say why he had done it, but she had not rebuffed him, not entirely. He rolled down the window with the hope that the cold air might clear his head and sweep the memory of her tongue in his mouth off into the night.

Chapter Twenty-six

Ruth was seated at the dining room table, her finished bowl of cereal in front of her, when a truck flashed past out on the road, a shiny Nissan driven by Nick, his block-like profile behind the wheel. She jumped up and pulled on her jacket. Outside, she tugged at the zipper as she climbed onto the bike. The ferry only came and went twice a day. If she wanted to run into Nick down at the dock, this was her chance.

She pedaled quickly, aware that her hair was a mess and would be in worse shape by the time she reached the dock. She recognized what she was doing as stupid, even juvenile. This did not make her stop. If any-thing, it made her pedal faster.

Ruth reached the store just as the ferry was pulling in. Nick's truck was parked in its usual place. He stood beneath the store's porch, his arm propped on the railing as if he owned everything in sight. He reminded her of one of those lanky Marlboro men in the advertisements. The idea that she had any interest in this guy made her lightheaded with disbelief and fear.

She braked cautiously down the hill, hoping not to hit a rock and spill over the handlebars. It seemed that everyone in the parking lot turned to look at her, everyone except Nick that is, and that they all somehow knew why she had come. She told herself she was imagining the sly and vaguely pitying looks on their faces.

After dismounting, she lowered the kickstand and climbed the porch steps. Nick was talking to an older woman Ruth hadn't met. He glanced up. Their eyes locked for one charged moment, and then she was pulling open the door. She managed enter the store, she felt certain, looking nonchalantly cool and unperturbed by the fact that he had not spoken to her. Once inside, it occurred to her she needed a reason for being there. Brock was behind the counter, engaged in conversation with Silas, who occupied his place in the chair by the stove. She said hello and wandered down the first aisle.

She watched Nick outside, still talking to the woman, through the clouded surface of the window smeared with dirt. It was difficult to see much beyond the large shape of his head, though it seemed his mouth opened in a laugh, and she wondered, in a weirdly possessive way, what had elicited this response.

Ruth carried a can of green beans and a jar of applesauce to the counter.

"Stocking up, huh?" Brock said.

"Yes." She saw by Brock's expression that he had meant the comment as a joke. "I don't need too much today."

"You sure you're eating enough over there at the inn?"

"I'm eating enough."

"Alice said she fed you some soup last week."

"Yeah, I came over for lunch."

"She makes a mean pot of chicken soup."

"She does."

Brock rattled on about what a great cook Alice was, as anyone could see from his waistline, and took forever to make change and set the cans in a small paper bag. Ruth caught a glimpse of Nick moving away from the porch. The ferry's horn sounded, signaling its departure.

By the time she freed herself from the conversation with Brock and made her way outside, Nick was starting up his truck. She set the paper bag in the milk crate on her bike and willed herself not to look up. She would not let him know that she cared one way or the other whether he was present, though if she hurried, she could get on the bike and reach the road just as he did.

Ruth pushed the bike over the rocks up the steep hill. She heard Nick behind her. He stopped at the crest of the hill. The window on the driver's side was rolled down.

"Hey," he said. "You in a hurry or something?"

"No."

"How's the photo biz?"

"Okay. How's the building biz?"

"All right."

They remained there in silence for a moment. "See you later," he said, turning down the road. Ruth rode off in the opposite direction, wondering whether he had said *see you later* as if he meant it, as a promise of sorts, or just as an automatic response. She couldn't decide.

The phone was ringing when she stepped through the door at the inn. She dropped her coat on a chair and hurried across the living room. Maybe it was him, back at his house already.

"Ruth? Is that you?" a woman's voice said.

"Yes."

"God, this connection really stinks. It's Joan. Listen, I just talked to Mom. What's this about you not coming for Christmas?"

"I told Mom you all could come here. She said forget it."

"I really didn't believe you were serious about staying on the island. I thought you'd be bored to tears in about a week."

Ruth did not respond for a moment. "I'm not bored."

"God, I would kill myself, staying on that island all alone."

Yes, Ruth thought, you would.

"Can you get a newspaper or anything?"

"The *New York Times* comes a day late."

"So that's it, that's your complete contact with the outside world, a day-old copy of the *Times*?"

"It seems like plenty to me."

"Mom says you're doing something with taking a photo every day, so you can't leave the island."

"That's right."

"But it's Christmas. It's one day. What's the big deal?"

"I'm making a visual diary. I have to be here every day."

"That's a great idea. I love it. But honestly, who's going to know if you miss a day?"

"I will."

"So what am I supposed to tell the kids?"

"Tell them I'm very sorry to miss the holidays, but I'm working on a big project. I'll send their presents. And I'll be there next year."

After an awkward silence, Joan switched topics. "We're starting the renovation next week."

Ruth had forgotten about the impending construction work.

"So we're not going to have Christmas here," Joan said. "It'll be at Mom and Dad's."

"How long is the renovation going to take?"

"A couple months at least. The place will be crawling with workers. But it's worth it for a mud room and a new bathroom and new windows. And we're putting a deck on the back with a hot tub, did I tell you?"

"No."

"We got a hot tub that fits six. It's going to be hot tub party central around here."

"Great. With bathing suits or without?"

"With bathing suits. Really, Ruth, I'm not inviting the neighbors over to get naked."

Joan went on about choosing tile for the bathroom. It was a lot more complicated than you would think.

Ruth nodded absently. Choosing tile and renovating a bathroom sounded deadly.

"Well, I better go," Joan said. "We'll miss you."

"Yeah, I'll miss you, too."

They hung up without any discussion of selling the inn. This was a first. Joan had finally gotten the message. For now, the topic was closed.

Ruth wandered down the hall to the darkroom and stared at the photos hanging to dry. She could not think what she would find to shoot that day. She seemed to have exhausted the island's possibilities. Why, she asked herself, had she insisted to Joan that she could not come for Christmas? The entire idea of the visual diary was nothing but a pretty illusion, or delusion. She wondered sometimes if she was coming unhinged, spending so much time in the darkroom. Certainly her perfectly idiotic crush on Nick, if it was indeed a crush, signaled a serious imbalance. Even the word "crush" seemed to give whatever was going on too much legitimacy. Her infatuation was more in the nature of a passing illness, a case of strep throat or the flu.

She pulled on a sweatshirt over her sweater and retrieved her coat and camera bag. When she didn't believe in the photographs, the best response was to get out the door and force herself to take more of them. In the back of her mind, the suggestion lingered: Maybe she would run into Nick, though this was not why she was venturing out. She was a photographer going in search of images. If she just happened to bump into him (he was constantly driving from one side of the island to the other), it would be an interesting coincidence, not something she had gone out seeking.

She rode up the Broadway hill in a standing position, her feet pushing hard on the pedals and her arms straining against the handlebars. Near the top, she feared she would fall over, but she gave a couple more strong pushes and made it. A ways before the schoolhouse, she turned onto a dirt lane that disappeared into the trees, and came to a field covered with the junked hulks of old cars. Model Ts with their doors missing, a Chevy truck from the forties, a boat-like car with fins from the fifties—they were strewn about with no regard to age or make or condition. Ruth climbed from the bike and lowered the kickstand. She circled the cars a few times before bringing the camera to her eye. Under the clouded sky, the rusted bodies took on sculptural forms, the dulled paint giving them the look of mud or stone. Black-and-white film would only intensify the effect.

It had been nearly a week since Nick came by, and she had not seen him other than down at the dock. He had to be avoiding her. She should not care one way or the other, except that she did care, though she could not begin to say why. She kept telling herself she was not attracted to him because first of all, she was not attracted to men, and second of all, if she were, he was about as far from her type as you could get. Nick was far too big, with his huge shoulders and oversized hands. The few men she had slept with were all slight in build, their slim bodies and narrow hips almost girl-like. She didn't know why she had let Nick kiss her or why she had taken his hand. Too much time alone, maybe, or too much time lost in the world of the island, where the twin poles of male and female ruled. She was not looking for a lover; she already had one. As she often reflected, she would not leave Liza for another woman—or, God forbid, a man—she would leave her to be on her own. The idea of being unencumbered was the real temptation.

She had not slept with a man since art school. Oren Schwartz, tall and skinny and Jewish, with his hawkish face and black eyes, painted wild canvases that were, in the vocabulary of the art workshop, charged with energy. When he worked in the studio, he became blind to anything but the blank surface before him and painted with an intense brooding. The rest of the time, he joked constantly, making fun of himself and others. She loved the way he could skewer anyone with his sarcasm. Their relationship, or affair, or whatever you wanted to call it, lasted a short six months, but when she thought of being with a man, she always imagined Oren with his slender hands and quick laugh. They made love once in the art studio at four a.m. She went home with a smear of green oil paint across her buttocks.

Ruth threaded through the cars, clicking the shutter as if on automatic pilot, though after a few minutes, she experienced the familiar sense that nothing existed but what she saw through the lens. The cars were beautiful and ugly at the same time. The close-ups of a door hanging by one hinge and a battered car seat had the same haunted quality as the other images she had made recently of the fire and the quonset huts.

The times she had been with men, the sex was good enough, but she had not been able to shake the feeling that something was missing. She used to imagine a woman's body and face when she made love with Oren, a strategy that left her resentful and confused afterwards, ready to blame him for what she saw as an awkward game. Over time, her relationship with Oren and the other encounters with men came to seem like a necessary but misguided piece of her life, rites of passage she needed to endure in order to reach the real thing. So what was she doing following big old Nick McGarrell around the island?

Ruth took one last photo, with her hands going numb, and tugged on her gloves. She set the camera in the bag and wove off down the dirt lane on the bike. As she came to the road, she saw a deer bent over the brush. She stopped and took out the camera, slowly and carefully. This was not, she suspected, a photo she would end up using, but she couldn't resist taking it. The deer raised its head, as though posing, the black pools of its eyes overflowing. In some other language, it seemed, they spoke to each other, before the deer bounded off into the woods. She felt an ache of sadness for the animal and her own confused self as she climbed back onto the bike.

When she reached the inn, Ruth spotted a white piece of paper stuck beneath the door. With a quick tug, she released the piece of paper. In precise lettering, it read: "Ruth, Want to go by the hut tonight? I'll pick you up after seven. Okay? Call me if not. – Nick." Beneath the message was a neatly printed phone number.

She clutched the piece of paper between her fingers, annoyed that she had missed him. She would have imagined messier handwriting from Nick, but then she remembered that he was an engineer. She stepped inside, went down the hall to the bathroom, and fished the rolls of film from her pockets. Maybe she could find an excuse for not going to the hut. It struck her now as a perfectly insane idea with trouble written all over it.

Chapter Twenty-seven

Nick set his tools in the toolbox, snapped the lid shit, and heaved it up into the truck. He left the Lundborn cottage with the heat turned up full blast in the cab. When he reached the Danks' house, he turned down a long driveway lined with trees. He could see Mary Lou through the window, her white hair standing up from her head. Their eyes met as he climbed out of the truck.

He crossed the lawn, nearly frozen ground now, and rapped on the door. It took a long time before she answered.

"Nick McGarrell," she said. "What can I do for you?"

She was wearing a worn bathrobe that hung on her plump body like an old bathmat, the cloth so thin you could see through to her jelly-like thighs. Nick was not sure she was wearing anything underneath.

"I'd appreciate it if you'd stop feeding the geese."

"The geese? I don't really feed them. Just a few little bits of stale bread, that's all. It won't hurt them."

"I'm not worried about hurting them. I don't want them to get used to this place and stay. You're encouraging them to stay."

"I'm not encouraging those birds to do anything."

"Yes, you are."

"Honestly, do you really think I have some sort of control over those geese?"

"If you keep feeding them."

"They're the most harmless things. I don't know why you're obsessed with getting rid of them."

Nick was so incensed by her use of the word obsessed that he could not formulate a response. In the time he stood there, searching for words, her husband emerged from a room at the back of the house and came shuffling to the door in a pair of sweatpants and slippers.

"Got a visitor here?" he said.

"Yes," Mary Lou answered. "He doesn't want me to feed the birds."

Stu Danks remained beside his wife a moment and shuffled back out of sight.

"If you come onto my property again, I'm filing trespassing charges," Nick said.

"Fine. I'll feed them when they cross the road." Her doughy face was full of determination.

Nick walked quickly to the truck, his hands shaking. She was still standing in the doorway, staring at him defiantly, as he drove off. He pushed play on the tape deck and blasted the music full volume. He drove along by the marsh until he came to his house. The geese were not scattered over the lawn, their necks elongated like periscopes, as they usually were. They huddled together by the brush, bedded down against the wind. Wait till January, he thought. Maybe then you'll go, when the wind comes tunneling off the bay at thirty miles an hour.

Inside, he went straight to the answering machine on the kitchen counter. No little flashing red light, which meant she hadn't called, and they were on for a night at the quonset hut. Nick didn't care what the guys had to say when he showed up with Ruth. On a Saturday night, the place would be full anyway, and his arrival with Ruth less noticeable.

He flopped on the couch, pulled the bag of pot from his pocket, and rolled a joint. By the second toke, he felt the tension in his shoulders give way. He turned on the TV and stared at the jerking images without registering what they conveyed. He thought of Mary Lou Danks in that ratty old robe and laughed. The woman was crazy and always had been. *Do you think I can control those geese?* No, he didn't think anyone could *control* the geese. He did think it was possible to train them, though.

He pinched the end of the joint and dropped it in the ashtray. Nick flipped through the channels until he came to a ballroom dance compe-tition. The music stank for the most part, and the costumes were absurd, but the spectacle was mildly entertaining. He left the TV on while he heated up a can of ravioli and returned to the couch to eat. He consid-ered smoking another half joint, but decided he had enough of a buzz. The dancers struck exaggerated poses, lifting their legs in the air and tossing their heads back. Such drama for such a stupid sport, if you could call it that. He left the tomato-smeared plate in the sink and shut off the television. In the bathroom upstairs, he ran a comb through his hair and stared absently at his fingernails, trying to think why he was doing so. He grabbed a six-pack from the refrigerator on his way out the door.

The clouded sky had a murky look. He scanned the low cover of clouds as he pulled in front of the inn. Ruth answered the door almost as soon as he knocked. She was wearing a close-fitting pair of blue jeans instead of the usual cargo pants, and a gray turtleneck sweater. No make-up, of course, but he had not expected make-up.

"Come on in," she said.

Nick remained just inside the door while she went to the kitchen and returned with a bottle of wine.

"I thought I should bring something," she said self-consciously.

"Sure. That's how it works at the hut. B.Y.O.B." Nick couldn't remember the last time someone had showed up with a bottle of wine.

She stood there as if she expected him to do something, maybe go into the living room, maybe lean down and kiss her (or was he imagining this?). He was determined not to fall for those big eyes now. Better, he thought, to go straight to the hut.

"Ready?" he said.

She pulled on a down jacket with puffy sleeves and said, "Ready."

Nick decided against opening the passenger door of the truck for her. He didn't want to be accused of being a paternalistic chauvinist. He swung up into the cab and waited for her to get settled and close the door.

"I wasn't sure you'd be up for this," he said.

"Going to the hut? Or going to the hut with you?"

"Either. Or both."

She turned to look at him, arching her eyebrows somewhat mischievously, and he had the sense that they were going to be all right. However this shook out, she wasn't going to make it too awkward.

"I need to get out of the darkroom every once in a while," she said.

"Before you turn into a mole?"

"Right." She gave him that faintly amused look again.

"So we're okay, huh?" He moved his hand back and forth in the space between them. "Just friends."

He thought that she looked disappointed and told himself he was an idiot for saying anything, but then she nodded and said, "Yeah, I've got a girlfriend back in the city. I should have told you that."

She did not meet his look, though she said the word *girlfriend* in a bold tone, as though daring him to be shocked or repulsed.

"I thought it might be something like that," he said. Any further comment he could imagine ("It's fine with me if you're a lesbian") struck him as too ignorant or patronizing.

They went past the dock and then he turned in at the hut. It looked like the whole island had turned out, there were so many cars scattered over the lawn. When he shut off the engine, she reached over and placed her hand on his.

"I'm sorry," she said.

"For what?"

"I should have told you about my girlfriend."

He shrugged. "It's okay."

"We've been having some problems actually. I'm not sure what's going to happen with us."

She left her hand on his. Was she telling him that things were over with her girlfriend, and she was now available to him? This was new territory. He had no idea how to respond, beyond feeling wariness mingled with a small thrill at the idea of enticing a lesbian into bed.

"Relationships are tough," he said. His voice sounded wooden to him, the comment vacuous.

"Yeah, it's no picnic."

"How long have you been together?"

"Eight years."

"That's a long time."

He kept his gaze fixed on the windshield. She still had her hand on top of his. He was searching for something more to say, perhaps a question about what was going on between her and her girlfriend, though he wasn't sure he wanted to get into the details, but then a car pulled up beside them. He slid his hand from beneath Ruth's and gave a quick wave to Ian, who stepped from the car and slammed the door.

Nick waited until Ian was inside the hut and said, "Guess we should go in."

"Anything I should know?"

"About what?" Nick thought for a moment that she had heard about Rachel.

"I don't know, what goes on at the hut."

"Nah. It's just a bunch of bored islanders. You'll see."

He climbed from the cab, anxious to get inside before someone else saw the two of them. She hesitated before following him. Maybe she did want to get into his pants. He was about as confused as he'd ever been with a woman. He had convinced himself it wasn't even close to a possibility.

He took the lead, six-pack in hand, and held the door to the hut for her, which he figured was an okay gesture here. Music came blasting at them, followed by fumes of cigarette smoke. The haze made it difficult to see much other than the shapes of bodies, lots of them, ranged around the pool table and standing in corners. Ruth placed a hand on his arm. "I didn't bring a corkscrew," she said. "You think they've got one?"

"Maybe. I'll ask Gary."

Gary was already heading toward them. Nick spotted Rachel on the other side of the pool table talking to Ian. She rarely showed up at the hut, even on the weekends. He wondered if she had come on purpose, to let him know she was keeping tabs on him. Eddie was nearby, with a pool cue in hand, his gut hanging over the belt cinched round his jeans. No uniform tonight. Not that this would fool anyone. Eddie was never off duty.

Rachel scanned the crowd, her gaze moving slowly and methodically. He could tell she had noted his presence, but she did not allow their eyes to meet. He considered turning around and leaving immediately, until he remembered Ruth.

"Welcome to the hut," Gary said. "I'm Gary." He extended his hand for Ruth to shake as though they were meeting in a bar in Boston or New York.

Ruth introduced herself and said, "Nice neon sign collection."

"It's been what, twenty years that I've been collecting these?"

Gary looked at Nick for confirmation. Nick shrugged. He didn't know how long Gary had been accumulating the signs. He tried not to glance in Rachel's direction, but it seemed impossible to avoid. Wherever he turned, she was in his line of view. Why had he smoked that joint? He imagined she could see it in his eyes, even across the domed space of the hut.

Ruth held up the bottle of wine. "Have you got a corkscrew?"

Gary did his best to conceal a smile. "A corkscrew? Hmmm. Cliff's probably got one on his jackknife."

Gary called over the din, "Hey, Cliff. Got a lady here who needs a corkscrew. You got one on that jackknife of yours?"

Ruth flinched at the word "lady." Cliff came sauntering over with a pool cue in hand and, without introducing himself, took the wine bottle and screwed the tiny spiral of metal into the cork.

Rachel remained on the other side of the pool table. Their awareness of each other darted across the room like a silent conversation. She was clearly taking in every move he made, every move Ruth made, while appearing to pay no attention to them.

Cliff freed the cork with an elaborate flourish and handed the bottle to Ruth.

"You got any glasses?" Nick said to Gary.

"Yeah, shot glasses."

"That'll do."

Gary went over to shelves lining one side of the hut and returned with a couple of shot glasses.

"I'm not sure I've ever done shots of wine," Ruth said.

"Yeah, well, drink up." Gary handed one glass to Ruth and the other to Nick.

"I'm not drinking wine," Nick said.

"Hell, I'll do a shot." Gary grabbed the wine bottle and poured two shots.

Gary's hand was less than steady already. Nick thought he was going to pour the wine right over onto the floor, but he stopped short. He watched Gary and Ruth tip the glasses to their lips and realized sweat was running down the back of his neck. "What is it, ninety degrees in here?" he asked Gary.

"I got the stove cranking. Cold as a witch's tit out there tonight."

"You think this is cold? Wait another month."

"Yeah, we're all crazy to be living on this island." Gary addressed these words to Ruth. "Certifiable. You freeze your ass off from November to April. How's it over at the inn?"

Nick went to the refrigerator. The pot hit him all at once, suddenly kicking in, so he felt too loose, rickety even. He seemed to be watching himself from above, a camera hanging on the ceiling, just waiting to see what mistake he was going to make. He took a bottle from the six-pack before setting it in the refrigerator and left his coat in a pile of others on a nearby chair. Ruth was laughing at something Gary said, and then Gary was pouring them both another shot of wine. Nick moved off, around the pool table, convinced Ruth could take care of herself. He went to stand by Brad, who was waiting for his turn in the game. Rachel remained in the opposite corner, behind the pool table, darting glances in his direction.

"Got a friend with you, huh?" Brad said.

"She wanted to check out the hut."

"It's a happening place, the hut."

"Tonight it is. We've even got the police chief here."

"So are you two an item?" Brad jerked his head toward Ruth, who was lifting another full shot to her lips.

"Not exactly. Her mother and my mother are old friends."

"Oh, you're family then?" Brad raised his eyebrows.

"Sort of."

"I heard she's from New York. Funny the people who turn up on Snow Island. You never know."

"No, you don't."

"Hey, did that fire inspector ever come back?"

"Nope. He said he was coming over a week ago, and then he never showed. They don't really care who set the fire as long as it's out. It's our problem, not theirs."

"Seemed like he was determined to get to the bottom of it."

"They can't be bothered with what goes on over here. Out of sight, out of mind."

"Hey, Brad," Cliff called. "Your shot."

Nick looked for someone else to talk to, but the men were all leaning in around the pool table. He was about to return to Ruth and Gary when Rachel made her way toward him.

"How's your photographer friend like the hut?" she said. She kept her voice low and her gaze on the pool table.

"She seems to be having a good time."

"She's downing those shots of wine."

"What are you drinking?"

"Beer."

"That's the drink for an island girl."

She flashed him a barbed look and said, "Sorry to be so boring."

Words tumbled through Nick's mind, words he could not catch hold of. It was too hot in the hut, and he was either too buzzed or not buzzed enough, he couldn't tell which. He searched for a retort that would land a quick blow, but his tongue went thick in his mouth. She was wearing a tight, scoop-necked sweater that showed off the smooth skin over her chest. He wanted to grab the beer in her hand, drain it, and sweep her off to someplace where they were alone, truly alone. Then he remembered he was angry with her, that they weren't speaking, though they had so little contact under the best circumstances, it hardly made a difference. Before he could say anything, Eddie came over.

"They wiped me out." Eddie gestured toward his pants pockets.

"They play every night, you know," Rachel said.

"I should have known better, you mean?"

"I'm just pointing out they get more practice than you do."

"You think I should be over here more often?"

"Not unless you want to become a pool shark."

Eddie turned toward Nick. "How's that kitchen coming?"

"All right. Anyone need a refill?" He raised his empty beer.

"Not at the moment," Eddie said.

Nick caught Rachel's eye as he moved off. He thought he saw a flicker of apology in her look, but he couldn't be bothered to read her signals tonight. She made him more tired than he could say.

He brushed past Cliff and Ian without stopping. He could hear Ruth saying something about being an advertising photographer as he came alongside Gary. He waited for Gary to be distracted by the pool game and leaned down. "I've gotta get out of here," he said to Ruth.

She looked surprised. "Oh."

Nick did not give her a chance to leave with him. He said he would see her later and grabbed his coat, waiting until he was outside, encircled by the cold air, to ease his arms into the sleeves. He managed to clear the door without meeting Rachel's look again. The night air stilled his mind in a swift instant. He was not high or drunk, just tired, tired of the people and the place, of the stupid music Gary played and the fruitless search for action on a Saturday night. If he'd been on the mainland, he would have climbed into the truck and gone driving for hours with his own kind of music blasting, eating up road for the sake of eating up road. On the island there was nowhere to go. He started up the truck and headed out to Gooseneck Cove.

Chapter Twenty-eight

When he woke the next morning, Nick knew he had to get off the island. He left on the second of the morning ferries and, on the other side, drove the truck off the boat and up Church Street. Within minutes, he had passed through Barton and was making his way north. The towns that lined the bay went by, one after another, though it was difficult to say where one town ended and another began. The string of malls made for a continuous stream of supermarkets and discount clothing stores and fast food restaurants. Whatever character the towns once had was obliterated.

Nick slipped onto the highway and got the truck doing eighty. He marveled when he made this trip how easy it was to leave the island behind. The ride to Boston was not that long, though on the island the city felt hundreds of miles away. He lost himself in the sense that he was going somewhere.

He found a parking space near Kenmore Square, a rare occurrence, and toured the record stores. They were still called record stores, though they didn't sell many records anymore. "Compact disc store" did not have the same grungy air of romance. He searched the used bins for treasures on vinyl and cursed the fact that he could not get anything he wanted on tape. It was CDs or nothing now.

He went down the street from the record store to a diner where he had eaten once before. It was hot and noisy inside and the place smelled of grease. Not a bad smell, Nick thought. A little grease never hurt anyone. He took a seat at the counter.

"I'll be with you in a minute," the waitress said as she went past with a stack of dirty plates balanced on her arm.

Nick nodded and reached for a newspaper someone had left on the counter. Across the front page, the headline read "Bush Sends New Units to Gulf to Provide Offensive Option, U.S. Force Could Reach 380,000." *Offensive option*—that was a nice euphemism. He flipped to the cartoons and read those until the waitress returned, and he ordered a hamburger.

"You want ketchup with that, doll?" the waitress asked as she set the plate in front of him.

"Sure."

She went sashaying down the counter and slid a bottle to him. Nick slapped the bottom with the flat of his hand and dipped the fries in the ketchup pooled on the plate. They were just the way he liked them, crispy on the outside, fluffy and hot on the inside. He was starting on the hamburger when a man came in and took the stool next to him. "You done with that paper?" the man asked.

"Yeah. It's not mine. You can have it."

The man scanned the front page. "Looks like we're headed for war."

Nick took a bite of the hamburger and wiped his fingers on a napkin. "Maybe, if it's not just a lot of talk."

"That kind of talk always goes someplace."

The man went back to studying the headlines for a moment and then looked up. "That's where I know you from," he said. "The vet center. You were in that group."

Nick did not remember him from the veteran's group he had attended when he lived in Boston, and with his neat haircut and pressed pants, the man did not look like all the aging hippies with graying pony-tails at the center.

"I only came a couple times," the man said. "You were in 'Nam, right?"

Nick nodded.

"So was I. Second battalion, twelfth infantry, 1970 to '71. We were based at Dau Tieng."

The waitress stopped in front of them and wiped down the counter with a rag that might have been white once. "What are you having?" she said.

"The cheese omelet with hash browns."

"Cheese omelet coming up. You want coffee with that?"

"Okay."

She whipped around to fetch a cup and the coffee pot. When she had moved off, Nick said, "I was there 1966 to '67. First battalion, fiftieth infantry."

"You served your whole time?"

"The whole tour."

"Me, too. Lucky suckers, huh? I used to lie around praying to get injured so I could get out of there, but no such luck."

"You still go to the vet center?"

"No."

In the silence that followed, Nick knew they were both thinking of the men at the center and their impassioned rants. When he was living in Boston, he went to the center once a week and took his place in the circle of orange plastic chairs, under florescent lights that made everyone look pale. He couldn't tell the story he had to tell beneath the flickering white light. He went for a few months and then stopped. The other men were on such short fuses he thought one of them was going to strangle somebody. They were angry and nasty and incoherent and full of the worst kind of self-pity. He didn't see himself in them.

The man sipped his coffee. "You ever been to the wall in D.C.?"

"No."

"You should go. I know some guys don't want to go there, but it's pretty incredible."

Nick had seen plenty of photos of the Vietnam Memorial. He didn't need to see all those names etched in granite for himself. He pushed his plate to the edge of the counter and reached for the check.

"You live around here?" the man asked.

"No. I live down in Rhode Island, near Providence."

"I'm Doug." The man extended his hand.

"Nick." They shook hands, and Nick slid off the stool. "Good talking to you."

The man nodded. "See you around."

For a moment Nick thought he was going to add the word *brother*, but to his relief, he glanced down at the paper and said no more.

Outside the wind sent leaves scuttling along the sidewalk. Nick went to the truck and started it up. Beyond the standard exchange of where you served in Vietnam and when, there was not much to say, and he hated the darting looks they gave each other, both of them trying to figure out if this was one of the seriously damaged, seriously crazy ones, or just a guy like the rest, wounded but still standing.

He drove out of the city. The sky was darkening, with a few snowflakes swirling in the air. When he reached Barton, snow was falling lightly over the bay, the thin flakes disappearing into the expanse of gray water. The ferry would not leave for another hour. He parked by the dock and walked up Church Street and around the corner to the Priscilla Alden. The cavernous lobby of the hotel looked even emptier than the last time he had been there, with its bare floor and the absence of furniture. The grayed paint on the walls was peeling. There was no one at the front desk and no sign that there might be anyone in the back. The doors to the old dining room stood ajar, but the tables and chairs were gone.

Nick took the stairs to the second floor and went down the hall. He heard the sound of a television on the other side of the door when he knocked and then a raspy voice telling him to come in.

George Tibbits was seated in a chair by the window in his usual outfit of warm-up pants, sweater, and slippers. The television blared an ad for a sunroom you could attach to your house. George turned his head when Nick stepped through the door and stared at him. "Oh, it's you," he said finally.

Nick crossed to the TV and, after some searching, found the volume knob and turned it down. "How are you, George?"

George gazed back at him through eyes clouded by cataracts. "A little tired."

"A little tired, that's all?"

George held his hands out, palms up, as if to say he wasn't the one to answer this question. "I don't like the cold. It gets to my bones more than it used to."

"Are you getting your meals?"

"Sure. Those meals on wheels people come. Lunch and dinner. Two meals a day."

"And you eat what they bring you?"

"I have some of this and some of that. They take away what I don't eat. You know, when you get to be ninety, your appetite isn't what it used to be."

"I've heard that." Nick went to the bed, the only other seat in the room, and perched on the edge. "I brought you the log to look at."

George took a pair of glasses from his sweater pocket and settled them shakily on his nose. He flipped slowly through the pages of the notepad, reading over the dates and notes as though searching for clues. He reached the last page of notes and left the pad open, so it dangled from his hand. "I don't know if I can come over again until the spring."

"That's probably a good idea. Wait for the warmer weather. I'll take care of the places until then."

George gave him an anxious look and glanced down at the notepad as if it could tell him more.

"Have you heard anything about what's going on with the hotel?" Nick asked.

George shook his head. "They say it could be sold any time, but they don't say when. They keep taking everything away. The lobby's empty."

"I noticed. Did you hear from the people at town hall, the housing authority?"

"I got a letter." George gestured in the direction of the dresser. "I'm on a waiting list."

This answer was not reassuring. Nick tried to imagine what would happen to George when the sale of the hotel went through, if he had not been assigned an apartment in the senior citizen housing yet. He supposed they would have to bring him over to the island and find someone to take him in.

"Did you go look at the senior citizen apartments?"

"They came with a van. They took me over. It has a kitchen. I don't need a kitchen."

"No, but you need a place to live."

"I have a place to live. Right here. I've lived here twenty-one years. Other people come, other people go, but I'm always here. Here or the island. I don't need another place to live."

"The hotel is being sold, George. They're going to knock down the walls and make condominiums." And sell them for obscene amounts of money, he added to himself.

"Well, the day they knock the wall down, I go. Until then I stay."

George had said the same things, in almost exactly the same sequence, the last time Nick visited. There was not much he could do besides call the woman at the housing authority, which he had already done repeatedly. The waiting list was the waiting list. She could not be swayed.

"They didn't give you any idea at the housing authority? How long the list is or anything?"

"They just said I'm on a list."

"I'm going to call them again, see if I can find out anything."

George flipped the notepad closed. "I don't want to move."

"I know. But you can't stay here."

"People think it's strange, but this is my home."

Nick gently pried the notepad from George's hand. He had never heard George comment before on what other people might think of him. As odd as he had always been, a fact that registered on everyone who came in contact with George, he had never shown the slightest awareness of his own peculiarities, or any concern for how they appeared to others.

"George, when it's time for you to move, we'll come over and help. My mother and I. We'll be here."

"Alice? I'd like to see Alice."

"She'll be here when it's time for you to move."

"Alice was always a help to everybody."

"I've got to catch the ferry, George. I'll stop by next week and see how you're doing."

George nodded. "Tell Alice I say hello."

Nick took in the room as he made his way to the door: the square of rug covered with stains, the single bed with its worn spread, the small black-and-white TV on the dresser. He thought, as he always did, that he could not leave George here with so little to occupy his days, and then reminded himself that George had clearly chosen this solitary life for himself and did not want his pity or anyone else's. Nick stopped to turn up the volume on the TV on his way out.

Downstairs, the front desk was still deserted. The teenagers they hired to mind the place didn't know anything in any case. The imminent sale of the hotel had been rumored for more than a year, but one thing after another kept holding it up—developers backing out, financing falling through. Word was that the current deal would happen. This time they'd found a developer with deep pockets who had the time and patience to, as he put it in a quote in the newspaper, "transform Barton into a fashionable destination."

Nick hurried down Front Street and headed to the dock. It took George Tibbits a while to process things, but his mind was intact. If it weren't for the sale of the hotel, he could go on living as he always had. When he had first moved into the Priscilla Alden, there were a few other long-term residents, but in recent years he had been the only one. The hotel was so run-down, no one stayed there besides islanders who had missed the last ferry. George Tibbits lived in a ghost hotel, something of a ghost himself.

Nick had heard stories about George Tibbits from the old timers, people like Miss Weeden, who had been gone a long time now. They said George was an ordinary boy growing up, but when he came back from the First World War he hardly seemed to remember anyone. He returned to the island once a year and kept to himself, barely acknowledging the people he encountered. Nobody could say if it was the war or the deaths of his aunts while he was gone, but one thing was clear: he wasn't the same.

Nick had met vets, like the one at the diner, who put on a good show, but he could see through the façade. He knew their hands shook when they woke in the middle of the night, too. It was no different for a veteran of World War I. All the talk about Vietnam, all the books and articles, amounted to a pile of words. The Vietnam vets he met at the center liked to think their war was the worst, that they had seen things far more horrific than the vets of the other wars who marched in pressed uniforms in the parades, but Nick couldn't see turning it into a contest.

He found his truck in the ferry parking lot and drove onto the boat. He was still in the cab, waiting for the ferry to pull out, when Rachel's car drove onto the deck behind him. He considered pretending he was not even aware that she was on the boat, but when the ferry's horn sounded, and it became apparent that they were the only passengers for the crossing, he realized this was not an option. She got out of her car and went into the passenger cabin. He waited a moment and followed her.

She was seated on the metal bench in the overheated cabin, which smelled of stale popcorn. He sat beside her and said, "I didn't know you were over on the mainland."

"I took the early ferry."

They gazed at each other, as though trying to determine how friendly they were going to be.

"They're closing the state home, where my brother was," she said. "I went to say goodbye to some of the people. The same nurses who took care of him are still there. Some of them have been there forty years. Kind of amazing."

"Where will they go now?"

"They'll just retire, most of them."

"And the people in the state home?"

"They'll go to group homes, the ones who are left. There were hardly any patients left. They've been closing the place down for years."

Rachel did not mention her brother often, though everyone on the island knew the story. He was born with Down syndrome in the 1930s and sent to live in the state home, where he spent his whole life. When he was still alive, Rachel went to visit him every few weeks, something her father and mother had never done. Nick had heard that the brother was so impaired he couldn't talk.

"You didn't stay long at the hut last night," she said.

"No. That music Gary plays drives me crazy."

"Kind of left your date in the lurch, didn't you?"

"She wasn't my date."

Rachel was about to speak when Captain Otis came swinging through the door.

"Looks like that storm's going to hold off for a while," Otis said.

"Yeah, it's not really accumulating," Nick said.

"We'll have to see about the morning run. If the wind kicks up too bad, we could have to cancel. But you'll be on the island by then." Otis took the bills they each handed him and gave them their change. "We'll have you over there in another twenty-five minutes."

They sat in silence after he was gone. "So are you seeing that photographer woman?" Rachel finally asked.

"No. She's a lesbian actually."

Rachel raised her eyebrows.

Nick glanced out the window to make sure there was no sign of Otis or his assistant on the deck, then placed his hand over hers. She shot him a look which he could not read, surprise at his touch, maybe gratitude. He drew his hand away.

"Nora Venable's gone back to the mainland," he said.

"I heard."

"A death in the family or something. I'm not sure when she'll be back, if she's coming back at all."

"Are you telling me this for a reason?"

"Just wanted to make sure you knew."

She held his look. "I'd be lying if I said I didn't miss you."

"That makes two of us."

He thought that she was going to smile, but she bit her lip and turned away.

"This is too hard, Nick."

"I never asked you to leave Eddie."

"Maybe that's part of the problem."

"Do you want to leave him?"

When she glanced up, there were tears in her eyes. "It's not a question of wanting or not wanting. It's a question of what's possible."

"Anything's possible."

"You're ready to move off the island?" she said. "That's what it would mean. I'd have to quit my job, and we'd have to leave. We couldn't stay."

He shrugged. "I don't know about that."

"There's no way I could stay on the island with Eddie still there. I couldn't do it."

He had fantasized about having this conversation more than once in the past, but now that it was happening, he found himself simply longing for it to be over.

"Yeah, I can see that," he said.

"You can see what?"

"That you couldn't stay on the island."

"And you could?"

"It would be different for me."

They sat without speaking after that. When the island came into view through the small square of window, Rachel took his hand and brought it to her lips, planting a brief kiss.

He wanted to carry her to the truck. She was his. She had always been his.

"I'll be out at the cottage, unless Nora Venable comes back," he said.

She bit her lip again and turned away. The ferry's horn gave a deep blast overhead. He could see people gathered by the store. They were that close to the island. He waited a moment longer, but she said nothing. He squeezed her hand, rose from the bench, and went out onto the deck.

Chapter Twenty-nine

The gulls circled overhead making their raucous calls. Alice followed the arc of their flight, wings dipping as they rode the air. How precise they were and how steady, as though the course of their journeys had been marked in advance, stamped on the sky. She slipped the key in the lock and unlatched the door. The familiar smell of coffee and damp wood, and underneath something vaguely ancient and musty, met her inside the store.

The cat came sauntering from the back room, where he slept in a cardboard box curled with an old towel. He stretched his front legs, flexing his paws against the floor and arching his back. Alice stooped down to pet him as he rubbed against her legs. He followed her to the back room, where she fed him before turning to her other tasks—dumping the old coffee grounds in the trash and rinsing out the pot, scooping the fresh coffee from the bag, straightening the piles of newspaper, nudging the cans of soup and beans and tuna fish back into neat rows.

She heard footsteps out on the porch and glanced at the clock behind the counter. Seven-thirty. Silas Wardell came shuffling through the door as he did every morning at this time. He wore an old plaid wool jacket and an orange hunter's cap and walked unsteadily, hands sunk in the pockets of a ragged pair of jeans. "Morning, Alice," he said as he fell into the easy chair by the stove. He rubbed his hands together and glanced at the stove. "No fire?"

"I'm getting to it."

"How'd you sleep?"

Alice gave a noncommittal shrug. "Not great."

Silas shook his head. "I was up half the night. It's a curse."

Alice poured a cup of coffee, added milk, and carried it over to Silas. He grasped the cup in both hands, bracing his elbows against the arms of the chair.

"Without this stuff, I wouldn't know if I was coming or going," he said.

Alice knelt by the stove. Brock had laid the wood the night before. She only needed to add some wadded newspaper and light it. She left the door to the stove open a crack to give the fire as much air as possible. After a few moments, the flames leapt up, lapping at the wood.

"They say you don't need as much sleep when you get old, but I don't know about that," Silas said. "Some days I feel like a walking zombie. It doesn't get any better, I can tell you that. I sleep for two hours and then I'm sitting straight up in bed, staring out the window. Ain't much to see, that's for sure, just that old light swinging round."

Once the fire was going, Alice opened the cash drawer and checked to see that she had enough singles and change, then did an inventory of the cigarettes behind the counter. By the time she had finished her tally, Silas was slumped back in the chair with his eyes closed. She took the coffee cup from his hand and set it on the table beside him.

She was seated behind the counter sorting through her order forms when Fred Hershel opened the door and stepped hesitantly inside. He was early this morning, well before the time when he drove the children over to the schoolhouse. He approached the counter with a wool cap in his hands. He glanced at Silas and turned the hat in a slow circle between his fingers. She couldn't tell if he wanted Silas to hear what he had to say or wanted to make sure he was asleep.

"Looks like it's cleared," Fred said.

"Yes. It might even warm up."

"I'm not quite ready for winter."

"Neither am I."

Fred cleared his throat. "The boys told us something last night. They did start the fire. It wasn't intentional, of course. They were fooling around with matches. They didn't mean for anything to happen. We're going to make sure they understand just how serious this is. They're very sorry, and they know they should have told the truth right away." He paused to run his tongue over his lips. "This is hard for us, that they didn't tell the truth. We've raised them to be honest."

Alice tried to conceal her amusement. Fred seemed to be stunned by the revelation that children, his in particular, were capable of lying.

"I'm going to call the inspector over in Barton and Mrs. Venable. The kids will do whatever they have to do. They'll work to pay off any expenses. I guess, well, if you could say there's a silver lining, it's that this has brought us closer together."

Alice thought he was talking about the Hershels and the Mannings becoming closer to the islanders, but then he added, "Us and the children. They've learned some lessons."

"I imagine it wasn't easy for them to tell you," Alice said.

"No, but they should have 'fessed up right away. They understand that now."

Alice wondered if they had been made to understand with the slap of a hand or a belt. Fred struck her as the sort of man who would be capable of making his point with force.

"There's just one thing," Fred went on. He looked at Silas, whose eyes were still closed. "It's why I came to you first. The boys say your son's truck was parked out by the mansion that night. Nick said all along that he wasn't there. They're sure he was."

"Did they see him?"

"No. Just the truck. They noticed it as they were leaving."

Fred held her gaze, and she saw behind his studied politeness a hint of satisfaction, even triumph. He wouldn't have revealed the boys' confession, she felt sure, if he hadn't been able to implicate Nick at the same time. She ran through the possibilities in her mind and could find none that fit. If Nick had lied about being out at the mansion, he had a reason for doing so, but she could not think what it would be.

Alice did not say anything, just continued to meet the challenge in Fred's look.

"I'll be telling the inspector this," he said. "He'll probably have some questions for Nick."

"I'm sure he'll be able to answer them." She met the evenness of his tone with a calmness of her own, though she wanted to order him out of her store.

"I'm sure he will."

Fred smiled in that condescending way of his. Alice looked down at the order forms and willed herself not to respond as he made his way to the door.

Mrs. Venable had left the island, so there was nothing out of order with Nick going out to check on the place, but he had concealed the fact that he was there, if the boys were in fact telling the truth. She supposed they could be lying about this, too. Fred Hershel would not let go of it, though, until someone other than his children paid a price.

Nick had seemed moodier and more preoccupied to her lately. She accused herself of watching him too closely and being too quick to pick up on the slightest sign that anything might be wrong, but he was always vaguely uneasy, even when it was just the two of them drinking a cup of coffee together. She remembered how steady and reliable he was as a teenager. She leaned on him then more than she should have, in the years when she and Brock seemed to be constantly at odds. Without quite articulating it, she had thought of Nick as a better version of his father, the man she wished Brock would become.

Alice gazed at the order forms, unable to recall where she had been before Fred came into the store. Silas stirred but did not open his eyes as Brock came lumbering up the porch steps and through the door.

"It ain't getting any warmer out there," he said. "I thought the forecast said it would get up to forty."

"So did I."

"Crazy weathermen. You might as well just stick your head out the door. I made some pancakes. You eat breakfast?"

"No. I just had some juice."

"Go on up to the house. I'll watch this place."

Alice gathered the order forms. "Silas went right out after a couple of sips of coffee."

"That stuff puts him to sleep instead of waking him up."

She nodded, an automatic gesture that was not connected to her thoughts, only to the recognition that he had spoken. She pulled on her coat, told Brock she would be back in a bit, and climbed the hill to the house. When she got there, she slid behind the wheel of the old Chevy and started up the car. If she drove the long way around the island, past the lighthouse and the inn, Brock would not see her go by.

Alice took the main road along the water until she came to the turn for Broadway, as the road that cut across the center of the island was called. It was marked by a small hand-lettered wooden sign attached to a utility pole. The summer people made jokes about the street name, letting out guffawed laughs, as though the comparison between this Broadway and the real one was too ridiculous. For all they knew, the island's Broadway could be the original one. Snow had been settled in the 1600s by some of the first pilgrims, who used the island as a place to graze their sheep.

She drove past the schoolhouse and went on to Snow Park, then swung around to the road that bordered the marsh. She could not remember the last time she had been inside Nick's house. She felt nervous about arriving unannounced, but she needed to tell him right away, before Fred or someone else caught him off guard.

His truck was in the driveway. She pulled in behind it and skirted the mob of geese that surrounded her car. She saw Nick through the window as she climbed the steps. He came and met her at the door.

"Hey there," he said, looking puzzled and concerned. "Is everything okay?"

She did not want to have this conversation with him. She wanted to let the whole thing slide back into confusion and doubt, where it had been before Fred came into the store. She followed Nick inside. Dirty dishes were piled on the kitchen counter, and wadded up tee shirts and sweatshirts covered the couch. Outside, a cardinal made a chirping call.

"Fred Hershel came into the store," she said. "The boys have confessed to starting the fire."

"It's about time."

"They say you were out at the mansion that night. They saw your truck."

"They saw my truck?"

"When they were leaving. That's what Fred says."

He shoved one hand into the front pocket of his pants and began fingering some loose change.

"Were you there?" she asked.

He let out a long exhale. "Yeah, I was." He stared back at her with a whiff of defiance, as if to say he did not owe her or anyone else an explanation.

"Fred's going to call the inspector."

"I bet he is." Nick rattled the change in his pocket. "I was broadcasting at the cottage. I had all my equipment set up. I figured it was safer, in case I got caught. I saw the kids, but I didn't want to come out of the cottage and have everyone ask what I was doing."

He spoke quickly, keeping his eyes on something beyond her shoulder. She had the distinct sense that he was making the story up as he went along, barely grasping the word he would utter next.

"If I came out with the kids there, I'd get busted," he went on. "It'd be the end of the radio show. I guess it's over now anyway, if Fred and the inspector are going to come snooping around. The place would have burned down anyway. There was nothing I could do."

"Except stop the boys before it got started."

His expression remained defiant. "Yeah, but I didn't think they were going to start a fire. I didn't think they were that stupid. By the time I realized what was happening, it was too late. Did you tell Dad?"

"No. I came here first. He's back at the store."

"Everybody will hear about it by tonight. Fred will make sure of that. No more radio show."

"I'm sorry."

He took his hand from his pocket and crossed his arms over his chest.

She didn't want to accuse him. If anyone was in the wrong, it was the boys and their parents, but Nick's story did not quite make sense.

"As long as we're airing the laundry, I've got a question for you,"

Nick said. "What went on between you and Pete Giberson?"

Alice didn't think she had ever mentioned Pete's name to Nick. The question struck her as grossly inappropriate, even impertinent. She was tempted to tell him it was none of his business.

"Ruth over at the inn said you showed her a picture of him," he said.

"He was her uncle. I thought she'd like to see the picture."

"Would you have married him if he hadn't died?"

Hearing Nick say the words catapulted her back to the day when the letter arrived informing her of Pete's death, and she was consumed by the hollow sense that her life had just ended, too. "That was our plan."

"You were engaged then."

"In a way. We never told anyone. There was no ring."

"And Dad didn't know about this."

"No, I never saw any reason to tell your father. It would only hurt him."

"I didn't figure you for having a secret love in the past."

Alice pulled her coat closed and fastened the top button. His words struck her as cruel, reductive and dismissive, as though Pete had been some distant figure, like a movie star, on whom she had a schoolgirl crush.

"Pete dying—well, that was horrible," she said as she fastened the rest of the buttons. "But then your father came to the island and..." She tried to think of a way to finish the sentence. To say that Brock's arrival made everything fine would be a lie, one Nick would recognize as a lie.

"I better be getting back to the store," she said.

He followed her to the door and held it for her. "Thanks for the warning about Fred."

She made her way down the front steps, uncertain whether she was too angry to speak or too confused. As she pulled out of the driveway, she saw the white oval of his face and dark hair framed by the window. She thought of all the times she had watched him go—off to school in the morning when he was a boy, boarding the ferry for trips to the mainland when he was older. She never knew, in those years after he came back from the war, if he would return in a day or a week or a month. He had always been the one in control, a puppet master pulling the strings of her emotions.

Alice drove past the schoolhouse and made the turn onto Bay Avenue, dipping down toward the water. She had shown the photo to Ruth because Pete was alive for a minute when Ruth held the photo in her hand. She longed to hear his name spoken, and Ruth gave her the excuse to talk about Pete, to call him out of the empty air.

Alice took the turn up the hill to her house. Inside, she reheated the pancakes and watched the juncos hopping about on the ground through the kitchen window. She was sure that Nick did not mean to be so brusque. He didn't realize how distant he could seem, how judgmental.

There had been times when she had come close to telling him and his sisters about the baby she had given up for adoption. That secret weighed on her, but she saw now that she had been right to keep it. Even Brock did not know. Besides Mrs. Santos at the Priscilla Alden, who had provided Alice with an alibi during the months of the pregnancy, her mother and Pete were the only people who had ever known about the baby, and they were both gone now. If Pete had been the father, she would have married him when he was home on leave and kept the baby, but she and Pete had done no more than kiss during that strange night before he shipped out. Ethan Cunningham, the father of her baby, was dead now, too. No one could tell her story.

Alice poured syrup over the pancakes and carried the plate to the table. She wasn't sure what she would say to Brock about Nick's account of the night of the fire. Maybe he had not been alone out at the cottage. She remembered the sheets she had found on the bed when she cleaned the place. So Nick had his secrets just as she had hers. It must have been Ruth who was out there with him. She had to smile at the thought, unlikely as it seemed. She wished she could pick up the phone and call Lydia, but she had not heard from Lydia in fifteen years, maybe longer, and the news, if it was news, wasn't hers to report.

Chapter Thirty

Nora reached for the phone, but stopped herself. She had already left two messages that day. The phone would ring and ring, the tinny sound mocking her, before the answering machine clicked on, and Henry's clipped voice sounded, as though he were at the bank. "You have reached the Whittets. We are unable to take your call right now. Leave a message after the beep and we will get back to you."

If she had not been so anxious to reach Isabelle, she would not have listened to the message more than once. When Henry was in the nursing home, having his voice still on the answering machine seemed simply odd. Now it was downright spooky.

Nora had been telling herself for three days that she would have to get in the car and drive over to Isabelle's. She stood by the kitchen counter staring at the phone a moment longer and scooped up the car keys. The pale sky had the thin look of snow.

She drove through the winding streets of the neighborhood mechanically, registering the presence of cars on either side of her without imagining the people they contained. Today she did not listen to the radio. She could not tolerate anything but silence. On the news that morning, the reporters said Bush would not go into Iraq before Christmas. He would wait until the deadline imposed by the U.N. resolution passed. Though she applauded this moment of restraint, it seemed monstrously strange to have a war tastefully timed not to spoil anyone's Christmas.

Nora took the highway into Boston, exited at Copley Square, and parked in the garage. A dank scent followed her into the stairwell and down two flights, until she reached the corridor that connected the garage with the mall. Two teenage girls snapping gum and talking in screechy voices walked in front of her, oblivious to the fact that they had nearly bumped into her. "She's a slut," one girl said. "I told him that like a million times. She's just a fucking slut."

Nora caught this much of the exchange before the girls disappeared into the stream of shoppers thronging the mall. Weren't they supposed to be in school? she wondered. And did it even cross their minds that using such language at top volume in public showed at best a pathetic lack of imagination and at worst a shocking disregard for those around them?

A muzak version of "God Rest Ye Merry, Gentleman" played over the loudspeakers, and a fake silver Christmas tree covered with white lights decorated one shop window. Nora unbuttoned her wool coat and threaded through the crowded corridors until she came to the toy store. Heather's children were nine and eleven now, too old for the stuffed animals she had sent in the past. She studied the selection of books, but decided in the end on a board game. She hoped Heather would see it as a peace offering.

She paid for the game and left the store. She had not gone far when she felt a hand on her arm.

"Ma'am?" a male voice said.

She turned to find an older man with graying hair holding a suede glove in his hand. After a startled moment, in which she checked to make sure her purse was still safely hanging from her shoulder, she realized the glove was hers.

"You dropped your glove," he said.

"Oh, thank you. Thank you very much." Nora took the glove from him.

His features had a gentle look. He was not in a rush, eyes glazed over, like all the other shoppers. He gave her a small smile that seemed to be poking fun at both of them and the swirl of motion around them, and said, "Merry Christmas."

Nora was further startled by this. People didn't say "Merry Christmas" anymore. It was politically incorrect. "Yes," she responded. "Merry Christmas."

The man nodded, still smiling, and moved on. Nora followed the maze of the mall to a clothing store. Here she picked out a scarf for Heather and a cashmere cardigan for herself in a soft gray with pearl buttons. Not that she needed another sweater. She had enough clothes in her closet to last the rest of her life, even if she lived to a hundred, but the soft feel of the sweater seemed at that moment to be the answer to the gnawing dread inside her. She was on her way to the checkout when she turned back and chose one for Isabelle, too, in a muted shade of rose.

Taking her shopping bags into a café, Nora ordered a cappuccino and sat at a table in a chair with spindly legs. She watched the shoppers stream past as she listened to the numbing repetition of piped-in carols. For many years, she had spent Christmas with Stephanie, Gerald's niece, the one member of his family she genuinely liked, but now Stephanie was divorced and living in Arizona. They had not been in touch for a year at least.

Nora finished the cappuccino and made her way to the garage with the oversized shopping bags flapping against her legs. She thought of the cottage on the island and the quiet view of the cove. Maybe she really did belong there more than she did here in the cold glitter of the city.

Small flakes of snow were falling when she pulled out of the parking garage. She made her way to the highway only to inch along in stop and go traffic. Rush hour started earlier and earlier, by two in the afternoon some days. She tuned in to the classical station, which was playing Brahms' third symphony. When the mournful second movement started up, she reached for the dial, but then stopped. The music was achingly sad, but beautiful, too.

She followed the route to Isabelle's without thinking, as though this had been her plan all along. She pulled in behind Isabelle's car. The snow was still falling lightly, but it did not look like it would add up to much.

She rapped on the door and waited. After a moment, Isabelle appeared in one of her long jersey skirts. She showed no surprise at seeing Nora on the other side of the glass.

Nora gave Isabelle a quick kiss on the cheek. Isabelle accepted the gesture without responding.

"I've brought you something," Nora said. She handed the shopping bag to Isabelle with a flourish. "An early Christmas present."

Isabelle took the bag, but did not move as Nora draped her coat over a chair.

"Well? Aren't you going to open it?"

"You told Heather," Isabelle said.

"Told Heather what?"

"About us."

"No," Nora said. "I did not tell Heather about us. She brought it up. She guessed. Did she say that I told her?"

"Not exactly."

"What did she say?"

"That you more or less confirmed it."

"I told her to talk to you, that's what I did. I told her it wasn't the way she thought."

"Well, that's the same thing as telling her, isn't it?"

"She cornered me in the parking lot."

"I'm not going to do this," Isabelle said.

"Not going to do what?"

"I'm not going to go parading around being a lesbian with you now just because Henry is dead."

"Christ, I don't want you to parade around with me."

They stood staring at each other, as though aghast at the people they had both become. Nora could not think how they had reached the point where this conversation was occurring.

"I can't just go dancing off into the sunset with you," Isabelle said, her voice quieter.

"Is that what you think I want?"

"Yes."

Nora supposed she was right; this was what she wanted, or at least a version of it. "I know you need time," she said. "I understand that."

"No, that's the thing. You just think I need time to come around. But it's more than that."

"More than what?" Nora felt, as she had in the past with Isabelle, that she was waiting patiently for an inarticulate child to say what she meant.

Isabelle pulled at the hem of her blouse. "I'm going out to Chicago. I'm leaving on Tuesday. I'm going to stay with Heather through January, maybe longer."

Nora thought of several bland responses she could make. *It will be good for you to get away I'm sure. Heather and the kids will love having you there.* She rejected all of these studied observations.

Isabelle continued to twist the hem of her blouse between her fingers. "I need something different right now."

"Different." Nora heard the blank tone of her own voice and wondered what she had just said. Her mind was leapfrogging forward, into a future without Isabelle.

"You know what I mean."

No, Nora did not know what she meant, but she suspected it was better not to ask. "You need to be with Heather and the kids. I can see that."

Isabelle stepped forward and wrapped her arms around Nora. They exchanged a chaste kiss. Nora felt how thin Isabelle's arms were and wondered if she had been eating.

"Oh, it's almost four." Isabelle stepped back and glanced at the clock on the wall. "I've got yoga at four-thirty. Do you want to wait here? I'll be back by six."

"No. I'll go on."

They stood in silence a moment, then Isabelle hugged her again and planted a kiss on Nora's cheek. "I'll call you later."

Nora retrieved her coat. As she pulled the door to, she saw the shopping bag still sitting on the chair, unopened.

Chapter Thirty-one

The cover of clouds made the dark nearly impenetrable. Not even a hint of moon showed. Nick peered ahead, trying to discern more than the suggestion of a path, but the ground was a study in gray. He felt his way along with the equipment heavy in his arms. The sharp air hit his face as he rounded the cottage, turning into the wind. He was awake suddenly, and more certain. She would hear him on the radio. She would come.

He set the pile of equipment inside the porch and unlocked the door. The place still smelled faintly of smoke. He saw the fire again, the flames jumping at the sky as though alive, and quickly switched on the light. The room was pretty much as they had left it that night, except for the missing curtains and a couple of sheets of drawing paper on the table. He pushed the drawings aside, charcoals of the burned ruins of the mansion. Kind of macabre, but kind of beautiful, too. He wouldn't have figured Nora Venable, in her perfectly tailored clothes, for an artist.

Nick set up the transmitter, attaching it to the line he had run through the window to the antenna, and put the turntable and tuner in place. He went back to the truck for a crate of albums. When it was all assembled, he switched on the mike and pulled it close. "Good evening," he said. "You're listening to WBAY, Jolly Roger radio, the music of the bay. It's a cold one out there tonight, so let's listen to some warm music. Here's Luther Allison doing 'Part Time Love' off his album *Luther's Blues*, which came out in 1974. I'm playing this for you on the original vinyl. I bought this in a record shop in Boston the day the album was released."

He set the record on the turntable and lowered the needle. He thought he heard a noise out on the porch. Had she seen his truck go past and followed him? He sat still, listening, but there was only the wind at the window. It was a risk to broadcast again, now that he had given the radio show as his excuse for being out at the mansion during the fire, but it was one worth taking. He didn't think Fred Hershel would attempt to make more trouble than he already had.

He put on another cut by Allison, slipped a bottle of beer from his jacket pocket, and propped his legs on the table as he took a couple of long pulls. He hadn't smoked a joint since before noon. He had scrubbed his fingers raw with a little brush his mother gave him for cleaning vegetables until he couldn't detect the scent of pot. Rachel would have no reason to reproach him tonight. A single beer was acceptable.

He flipped through the albums. The covers contained entire years of his life. Each one evoked a time, a place, a mood. They seemed to know him better than any person ever had. Nick drained the beer and set the empty back in his pocket. He considered going to the truck for another, then thought better of it and checked his watch. It was after eight. She was usually there by seven-thirty at the latest. Eddie was over at Cliff's playing poker with the rest of the boys; Nick had seen his truck parked at Cliff's when he drove out to the cove. Maybe she hadn't tuned in yet and had missed the sound of him going by. He imagined her stepping through the door, unbuttoning her shirt, unhooking her bra, with her hair silver in the half-light. He loved the way it brushed her bare shoulder, and the slowness of the look she gave him, as if they had all the time in the world, though they both knew they had no time at all.

He turned the mike on and said, "Hello, folks. Hope you're all doing well tonight. I'm curled up here in the studio bringing you a mix of blues and soul, a little something to keep you company, maybe get you up on your feet. That was Luther Allison doing 'Someday Pretty Baby.' Up next is Sonny Terry's 'I Got a Woman.'"

The music filled the room, Terry's version of the song a little too light and happy. When Rachel showed up, he would put on something slower, sexier. He played a few more Sonny Terry cuts and followed them with some James Brown. He kept the records spinning for another half an hour, forty-five minutes, and still she wasn't there. He could drive to her house and take her on the floor of that kitchen Eddie wanted to redo. He saw the whole scene in his mind, knowing that it would never happen. Eddie packed in the poker game early sometimes. There was no predicting when he might return.

It was too late for her to come now, even if she tuned in and heard him. When the song came to an end, he lifted the needle and switched on the mike. "This is Jolly Roger signing off. You've been listening to WBAY, the music of the bay. Goodnight, everyone."

He packed up the equipment and carried it to the truck. Chances were he wouldn't broadcast again, but there was no sense in a goodbye. He took the road away from the mansion with only the barest awareness that he was driving. When he reached the Brovellis', he slowed down. Eddie's truck was not there, but her car was, and beyond the outline of the vehicle, the yellow squares of the downstairs windows shone. She was seated at the kitchen table, bent over something, her profile clearly visible. She didn't raise her head or give any sign that she heard him out on the road. So it was intentional. She knew he was out at the cottage, waiting for her, and she didn't come. The realization took hold, coiled inside him, a sickness waiting to strike.

When he came to the fork, Nick headed toward the store instead of home. Cliff's place was blazing, every window washed in light. He felt a wave of hatred for those men with their big guts and dopey grins. He thought of how they looked away when he approached, as though they were sharing some private joke. He had always been on the outside of their closed circle. Not that he wanted to enter that circle. He didn't. He had placed himself outside it with good reason, because he chose to be outside, because he wanted something else. What exactly? He couldn't say, he just knew it wasn't what they wanted.

He passed the store and went on toward the inn. He saw Ruth through the front windows when he got out of the truck, lying on the couch in a boyish posture, her chin tilted and short hair falling over her brow, a book propped on her chest. He thought for a moment that he was making a mistake, until she raised her eyes and let the book fall to the floor. Her face did not look boyish then as she tugged at her sweater, adjusting what must be a bra underneath.

She met him at the door, her eyes wary and, if he was reading it right, a tiny bit eager.

"Hi," she said, making the single syllable sound like a question.

"I brought you some more beer. In case you're running out."

"How thoughtful." She took the six-pack from him with a smile and led him into the living room. "You want a glass?"

"Nah. The bottle's okay."

She handed him a bottle and took one for herself.

"I thought you didn't like that stuff," he said.

She shrugged. "Cold night like this, a beer might taste good."

He sank onto the couch, fatigue running through him. He didn't have the patience for this sort of give and take, not now. He didn't know why he had come.

She sat in the armchair across from him and gave him an expectant look.

"How's the photo biz?" he said.

"Okay. How's the carpentry biz?"

"'Bout the same."

"You don't like it, do you?"

"No. I like it fine. It beats working for somebody else. I call the shots. That suits me now."

"I heard you on the radio tonight. You haven't been on in a while."

"Yeah, I had to shelve the broadcast."

"Did something happen?"

"Sort of."

"You got caught?"

"Not exactly. People got wind of it. People who might turn me in, but so far nothing's happened. The FCC probably couldn't find the island anyway. Hey, I'm sorry about leaving the hut like that. I didn't mean to leave you in the lurch. I just had to get out of there."

She nodded. "Gary kind of looked out for me, but when I saw I was going to be the only woman left, I decided it was time to go."

"You're safe at the hut. Those guys aren't as bad as they look."

She nodded again, though she did not appear particularly convinced. She drank her beer in long gulps. Maybe, he thought, she was trying to get drunk.

The single floor lamp by the couch was too bright. Either they needed to skip the small talk and go straight to the bedroom, or he needed to leave. This awareness flitted through his mind, but Nick remained where he was, slumped into the soft cushions of the couch with his back shooting little pained darts of protest.

"Are you going home for Christmas?" he asked.

"No."

This answer surprised him. "Not into the holidays, huh?"

"I don't want to leave my photography project."

"That's dedication."

"Dedication or insanity. There's a fine line."

"Why is that, that so many artists are crazy? It's practically a cliché."

"I don't think artists are that much crazier than anyone else, you just hear more about them." She set her empty bottle on the table. "Do I seem crazy?"

"No. Not really."

"You want to see some new photos? Then you can decide."

"Sure." When he stood up, he noticed how cold it was. The room felt like an icebox. "You got any heat in this place?" he said as he followed her down the hall.

She glanced back with a smile. "I keep it on sixty."

"Feels colder than that."

"There's a few chinks in the walls. And some broken window panes."

"I could fix that for you."

"Right, if I had any money to pay you."

She led him to a cell-like bedroom at the end of the hall. She took a portfolio case from the floor and arranged the photos on the bed. They were all black and white, the tones muted, shots of the old Navy base and the abandoned cars in the lot behind the schoolhouse. A little moody for his taste, but the kind of stuff that looked professional, that you might see on a greeting card.

"Nice," he said.

She gazed up at him, waiting for more. He felt too tall, a giant looming over her.

"You ever take pictures on sunny days?" he asked.

"I don't like sunny days."

He laughed. "Don't like them or don't like photographing them?"

"Don't like photographing them."

"I guess we don't have too many sunny days this time of year anyway."

"I'm not trying to make New England postcards."

"I know." He put his hand on her arm. "You're funny."

"What do you mean?"

"You act like you don't care what anyone thinks, but it's pretty easy to get you riled up." He ruffled the short ends of her hair with his fingers. It wasn't the right move, but it was the one that came most easily.

"I'm not riled up." Her tone was a combination of annoyance and pleasure.

"Your pictures are great. You don't need me to tell you."

She ducked her head and mumbled what he took to be "thanks." He moved closer and pulled her to him. Her head barely reached his chest. He leaned down to kiss her with no idea why he was doing it, except that it seemed to be the inevitable next step. She returned the kiss, hesitant at first, then willing.

"You got any beds around here that aren't covered with pictures?" he said.

She took him by the hand and led him across the hall to a room with a double bed. He noticed a tee shirt and pair of underpants draped over the back of a chair as he fell onto the bed beside her. Her hand was on his belt buckle, undoing it. Bold, he thought. He wondered if she had ever been with a man. He needed to get this right. Take it easy, he told himself.

The only light came from out in the hall. He couldn't make out her face until he raised himself on one elbow. He slid his other hand along the waistband of her pants. She was wearing bikini underwear or nothing at all, another surprise. He leaned down to kiss her and felt himself go limp. He probed her mouth with his tongue, trying to will a response, though he knew none of the old tricks would work.

Her hand was inside his pants, but he remained pathetically flaccid. He didn't have the motivation it would take to get out of his clothes. The thought of her seeing him in a baggy pair of undershorts made him tired. He sat up and swung his legs over the side of the bed.

She put her hand on his back in a gesture that felt almost maternal. "What's wrong?"

"I shouldn't be doing this," he said. "I'm sorry. I just broke up with someone. I'm on the rebound. I don't know what I'm doing." He recognized how inadequate his explanation must sound. He got to his feet and re-fastened the belt buckle. "I like you. I just don't think…I don't know. This isn't right."

She looked even more boyish, or girlish, with her clothes all rumpled, her shirttail showing beneath her sweater. He was passing up a real opportunity, but he just wanted to escape, fast. He thought of saying "thanks," a pretty lame impulse under the circumstances. Instead he said, "I'll come by sometime when I'm not so messed up."

She remained on the bed, her big eyes fixed on him, accusing him, laughing at him. He went down the hall. The empty beer bottles greeted him in the living room, and they, too, seemed to be snickering. He got out of the inn and into his truck with not much else registering besides the need to go home and get into his own bed and burrow under the blankets.

He went the long way around the island, hoping to avoid anyone leaving the poker game. When he came to the turn at Broadway, he kept going down to the old Navy base. He realized, in a sudden burst of insight, that he never should have brought up the possibility that Rachel would leave Eddie. As soon as he had uttered the words that day on the ferry, he knew they were a mistake. The next step hung before them, undeniable. The contained bubble burst.

Nick slammed his fist against the steering wheel. He could have left it alone. He could have sworn to Rachel he would never smoke pot again, and they could have taken up where they had left off, but no, he had to point out just how magnanimous he was, letting her stay married. Sometimes he couldn't believe what a moron he was.

When he reached the gate, Nick shut off the engine and the lights, and waited for his eyes to adjust to the murky scene before him. After a few moments he made out three deer close together, heads low to the ground, their bodies lean and graceful, their legs like sturdy twigs. These deer had escaped the annual hunt held a few weeks earlier. They would make it to spring.

He reached behind the seat for a beer and opened it. "Here's to making it to spring," he said as he raised the bottle to his lips.

Chapter Thirty-two

The sound of a truck carried from out on the road, a distant hum that grew closer as she watched through the schoolhouse window. When Nick parked on the grass and came striding through the door, she was not surprised. It seemed to take him a long time to cross the open space of the bare floor and make his way through the maze of desks. Rachel remained in her seat, a pencil poised between her fingers.

He stood in front of the desk as though he were one of her students again and said, "Cliff's going to take the job here."

She wished they were in the kitchen, where she could do something—make tea, flip through the accounts book. The schoolroom felt cavernous all of a sudden, the overhead light so bright it made her eyes hurt.

"Cliff's a decent plumber, better than I am," he said. "Maybe he could fix that faucet in the bathroom. He'll stack you a neater woodpile, too."

"The woodpile's fine."

He looked at her then, his expression so hard and dismissive, she wanted to crawl into the cubby hole beneath the desk. She glanced away, at the worn leather belt threaded through the loops of his jeans, but that was no better. She settled on a spot over his shoulder, the red sheets of construction paper tacked to the wall with the leaves the children had collected glued to them.

He wasn't asking for her permission or her approval to quit the job. He was simply informing her. She grasped this, but not what would come next.

"Cliff's a good worker. Lousy poker player but a good worker," he said.

"As good a worker as you?"

"Don't fuck with me, Rachel."

He jammed his hands in his front pockets. She had never been scared of Nick before, but she felt fear now, and a sadness so deep she did not know how she would climb out of it. She wanted to defend herself, though she saw there was no point. She waited a moment, then said simply, "I'm sure Cliff will do a good job."

He moved rapidly toward the door, his work boots echoing on the floorboards. He paused with one hand on the doorknob and turned to look at her. "I wasn't in love with you when I came back to the island."

"I know," she said.

His back was broad, his shoulders squared off in the tightly-fitting jacket. That was his goodbye—the sight of his tensed back and the slam of the door, the sound of the truck starting up and the spew of gravel as he pulled away too fast. Rachel closed the roll book and walked carefully toward the girls' bathroom, where she went into one of the stalls and began sobbing like a child. How very, very stupid she had been to think that she could toy with him and with herself, to believe that the simple pleasure of sex was enough, to ignore the fact that it would end this way. She had entered some parallel universe where nothing that she knew to be right remained true. How had she let this happen?

She was not a strong person, that much was clear, not strong enough to resist something ultimately so juvenile. She couldn't think of another word for it. They had both gone back to those charged months in the schoolroom and become eighteen together. Idiotic. Idiotic and beautiful, idiotic and irresistible. If she was luckier than she had any right to be, Eddie would never know.

From the day when she first became aware of his suggestive look in the schoolroom all those years ago, she had loved Nick, even when she could not admit it to herself. She had given in to that love at last because, in her blind selfishness, she couldn't say no to the loveliness of his eyes and the drunken wonder of his hands on her body. Rachel blew her nose on a wad of toilet paper and emerged from the stall to find her face in the mirror, a patchwork of red. She splashed cold water over her puffy eyes and patted them with a scratchy paper towel. Maybe Eddie wouldn't be home yet, or she could slip past him without scrutiny.

Out in the schoolroom, she collected the canvas bag full of papers to be graded and closed and locked the door behind her. She checked the clock on the dashboard as she started up the car. Four-thirty. Eddie might still be down at the dock.

Rachel circled the island and made the turn out to the cove. Nick's truck was not parked at his house, and she did not pass him on the road. He must have gone down to the dock with everyone else. That's how it would be now. She would see him from a distance, standing in the parking lot. She would wave at him when he passed on the road just like anyone else. The thought of this was so wrong it seemed obscene.

She pulled into the driveway, relieved to find that Eddie wasn't home yet. The house was filled with a silence that seemed to contain whispered accusations, as if the couch and chairs were judging her. I'm not that woman anymore, she wanted to tell them. She set her tote bag on the coffee table and went upstairs to change into her running clothes. She added an extra sweatshirt and pulled on a hat and gloves before heading out the door. The light was already draining from the sky.

She listened to the crunch of the hard ground beneath her feet as she fell into the rhythm of the run. The accusation of Nick's last words seemed to follow her down the road. He had not been in love with her when he returned to the island. She set a trap and made him fall in love with her again. God knows this might have been true, though she didn't see it that way. The thing unfolded with a life of its own, as if in free fall, one look leading to another, one hint of desire building on the next. She had never planned or schemed any of it, or thought beyond the next moment, and in doing so, she had come very close to throwing away her life.

Rachel picked up speed, making the turn onto the paved stretch of road, with the sense that she had narrowly escaped a lethal accident. She woke up now like the survivor of that accident, amazed to find herself still here, safe in the cocoon of her life. She didn't want to leave the island or Eddie, and by some miracle, it appeared, she was going to get to stay.

The ferry was gone, the parking lot by the dock empty. Eddie must have driven the other way around the island or stopped by to see Silas. Her feet felt numb in her sneakers. She pushed herself on, all the way to the old Navy base, knowing that when she turned around, the wind would be at her back.

She wished she could transform Nick into the teenage boy she remembered, the one who did love her, though she had dismissed his interest then as nothing more than a schoolboy crush. She thought of the day when she had tried to persuade Nick to apply to college so he could avoid the draft. She had climbed into the jeep beside him during the lunch break at the schoolhouse while the children ran across the lawn. He slid his hand over her thigh; she felt his fingers, firm, ready for more, through her wool skirt and stockings. She pushed his hand away and stepped from the jeep. For the rest of the year, she made certain they were never alone together, and in June, just after graduation, he went off to basic training.

Rachel had always felt that Nick went to Vietnam as much to spite her as for any of the other reasons he gave (he didn't want to go to college, he was ready to serve his country if he was called to serve). She blamed herself for everything that followed—the years when Nick wandered around with his engineering jobs, sullen and moody on his visits back to the island; the fact that he had never married; the pot smoking. The affair had been her way of trying to atone, though this was as stupid an excuse as any, and probably far from the truth, whatever the truth might be. If only she could have returned Nick's affection back then, when they might have been able to make it work, at least once he graduated from the schoolhouse—but she had to recognize that even this was a fiction. They could not have run off together, the schoolteacher and the eighteen-year-old.

At the gate to the Navy base, Rachel came to a stop. In the lowering light, she spotted a deer, head raised, eyes alert to her presence. They stared at each other for a moment before the animal bounded off. She saw the flash of white tail as it disappeared, swallowed by the dark. She turned and resumed her run back down the length of the island.

Rachel kept her eyes on the ground, watching for potholes and loose gravel. It was so dark now that she could see little. The lights on the mainland were barely visible through a cloudy haze. If she still went to church, she would go to confession, though she recognized the impulse as pure hypocrisy. It would be too convenient to return to the Catholic fold now, only when she needed it—and besides, she didn't deserve absolution. What she had done to Eddie was unforgiveable. She would not do such a monstrous thing again. She would be content with what she had; no, more than content. She would embrace her incredible luck at being loved, at having a companion and a family, at getting up each day knowing what to expect.

She ran past the dock and on toward the dump. She glanced up the hill when she reached the quonset hut. Cars were already parked outside. A quick scan revealed Nick's truck among them. She wondered if he had brought the lesbian again. Probably not.

When Rachel made the turn into her driveway and slowed to a walk, she saw that Eddie was home, his truck pulled in behind her car. She found him ensconced in his chair, legs elevated, the remote in his hand, watching the news. She crossed the room and leaned down to give him a brief kiss.

"What's for dinner, hon?" he asked.

"I made some chili in the crock pot."

He nodded approvingly.

Rachel went to the kitchen, raised the lid of the pot, and stirred the chili. She would throw together a salad to go with it.

Upstairs, she stripped off her sweaty clothes and stepped into the shower. The water ran over her face and down her arms as the steam slowly rose around her. She thought about how wonderful it was to take a simple shower, and then to pull on pajamas and spend a night in front of the television, with a gratitude that brought tears to her eyes again. She bit her lip, pushing back the tears, and reached for the worn bar of soap on the edge of the tub.

Chapter Thirty-three

Ruth sat propped on pillows, the covers piled around her, and sipped from a coffee mug, happy to be alone on Christmas morning. Thank God, she thought, nothing more had happened with Nick. She had learned her lesson. What in the world had tempted her to try a man again? Now she remembered, only too well, why she had given men up. They messed with your head for the pure fun it, like cats toying with mice. They turned on and off, human light switches, one minute there, the next—gone.

Men were another species entirely, emotionless clods with no awareness of the people around them. Taking responsibility for their own actions was a concept that did not exist in the universe where they lived. They went blithely on their way, puffed up with their own importance, satisfied to serve their needs and run roughshod over everyone else's. Ruth had wished at times that she could borrow some of that arrogance, but in the end, she was glad to be a little quieter and less assertive, someone who at least tried to act like she cared. She wouldn't want to carry one of those oversized male egos around with her.

What she felt now more than anything was embarrassment at her own silliness, though it was worth pointing out that she was not the one who had started this particular interlude of weirdness. Nick was the one who kissed her that first time on the floor of the living room, not the other way around. A girl might get ideas from something like that. She should not have gotten ideas, of course, but what could she say? Winter was coming, and she was just a tiny bit lonely, and on the island she felt cut off from everything she knew, and then Liza was being so pissy on the phone. None of this added up to any sort of a rational justification, she had to admit, but as a collection of reasons, well, she thought most people could see how it might have happened, even if Nick's appeal escaped them (as it certainly did her now). She could not imagine what she had seen in him. She had fallen under the spell of an old cliché, the Marlboro man reeling her in with his remote dispassion.

Ruth drank the last of the coffee and kicked off the blankets. The light shone on a coating of snow out the window. A white Christmas. She felt exultant, the way she had when she was a child and the first snow fell.

She dressed quickly, pulling on long johns topped by a turtleneck and sweater, and took the path behind the inn down to the beach. She knew now why she had stayed. When she brought the camera to her eye, one shot after another took shape instantly, as though the clean compositions just waited to be discovered. A dark line of rocks dusted in white, the gray horizon beyond. The lighthouse against the snow, white on white. A mound of sand like human skin against a blanket.

Only a couple of inches had fallen. It would melt by the end of the day, or sooner if the sun shone. She would have to work quickly. Ruth fired off a few more shots and went to get the bike. She knew the scenes she wanted to capture, the stretches of beach and marsh she needed to visit again. She pedaled into the wind, glad to be out so early, when the island remained in the thrall of absolute silence and emptiness. The sky lay above the water like a flat, gray hand.

She wondered as she rode along what Nick was doing to mark the day. He would no doubt be going over to his mother's, if he was not there already. They might pass on the road. She would not expect him to stop. He had not come by again, as he'd promised (or was that threatened?). Their encounters down at the dock were brief and mostly wordless. Once he said hello and asked how she was, then made an innocuous comment about the weather. He threw out that little lifeline, as though not entirely willing to leave her stranded, drowning in her own silence, and said goodbye with a curt nod of his head. He was a jerk. That was the long and the short of it. She should have trusted her first instincts and stayed away from him.

There were no signs of life at the store when she rode by now. She could tell her mother that for once Alice had closed the place. The wind stung her face, but she pulled the hood of her jacket tight and pushed on, to the fork past the Improvement Center and the dump. By the marsh out toward the west side, she stopped. The sky rewarded her, full of billowing clouds with the early light shot through them.

"Film is cheaper than shoe leather," one of her professors in art school used to say. "Don't skimp on film. Take five shots instead of one." She had followed the advice ever since, but now she was on the verge of running out of film. If she was careful, she could make it to New Year's, when Liza would arrive with more.

Ruth went back the way she had come. At the turn to Gooseneck Cove, she pedaled out toward the sandy beach. She followed the path through the brush, which was thinner now than when she had arrived on the island. The snow reached partway down the beach. Closer to the water, the dark wet mark of the retreating tide took over. She knelt on the thin layer of snow and zoomed in on the sand. From this angle, the view telescoped into narrow bands of snow, sand, and water. She held her breath as she snapped the shutter. She imagined this abstraction alongside the earlier photos, an even colder and starker image. Like Chinese ink paintings, her photographs would capture the island in minimal strokes of dark and light full of quiet drama.

She was still kneeling in the wet sand when she heard a voice behind her calling hello. She turned to find Nora coming toward her in one of those bulky shearling coats and a pair of fitted leather boots.

"Merry Christmas," Nora called.

Ruth got to her feet feeling that she had stepped into a surreal play. "Merry Christmas."

They stood staring at each other, as though trying to account for their presence in this surprising place at dawn on Christmas morning. Ruth laughed. She couldn't stop herself. How liberating it was to have cast off the trappings of the rest of the world.

Nora smiled uncertainly.

"I didn't expect to run into anyone here this morning," Ruth said.

"Neither did I."

"Shouldn't we be opening Christmas stockings somewhere?"

"I was never a big fan of Christmas stockings."

"I agree. Too many little bars of soap."

"So you're on your own today?"

"Yes. And you?"

Nora nodded. "My friend—the one you met—her husband died. She's gone to be with her children."

Ruth noted the way she used the phrase "my friend." She had used the same phrase in the same way countless times herself, but Nora's friend had a husband.

"I'm sorry," Ruth said.

"Don't be. He had Alzheimer's and was in a nursing home. It was a blessing, really."

"I'm missing Christmas with my family for the first time in my life."

"You sound quite happy about it."

"I am."

Nora gave her a playful smile, and Ruth felt that this woman understood why she was kneeling in the snow on a beach instead of sitting by a Christmas tree in her pajamas. She wanted to go back to shooting while the light was still muted, the snow fresh, but now that they had stumbled on each other, two refugees from Christmas, it seemed they would have to do something to observe the occasion together.

"Have you had breakfast?" Ruth asked.

"No. I saw the snow and headed straight out."

"So did I."

They gazed at each other with the surprised satisfaction of two people who have found a kindred spirit when they least expected it. Ruth had always disdained older lesbians, who struck her as cardboard cutouts, either overly butch gym teachers or closeted librarians, but maybe she had misread this woman.

"Would you like to come over for breakfast?" Ruth said. "I can make an omelet."

"Sounds heavenly."

Her voice carried that tinge of sarcasm that always seemed to be at least faintly present, but Ruth saw by the look on Nora's face that she meant it.

"I'll walk back to my place and drive over," Nora said. "Does that give you enough time?"

"I think so. I'll take a few more photos and bike back."

"I didn't expect you would be here over the holidays."

"I didn't expect you would, either."

They exchanged a friendly and conspiratorial glance. Nora said she would see Ruth in a bit and turned back to the path.

The sky remained clouded, but behind the cover of gray, light shone through. The sun might appear by the end of the day. Ruth went down to the water and shot a few close-ups of wet rocks and strands of seaweed. Everything looked somehow sharper today, the whites more white, the grays more gray.

She rode the bike to the inn, the wind at her back now. She saw no cars or people, not even a deer, as she pedaled along Bay Avenue. When she reached the inn, Ruth turned up the heat inside. Today she would splurge.

She took eggs from the refrigerator and cracked them into a bowl. She was slicing a red pepper when she heard the knock on the door. She went to the hallway and waved Nora inside.

"I thought I should bring you something," Nora said. She held out a bottle of olive oil, good olive oil, with a red ribbon tied around the neck. "This is all I could find for a Christmas present."

"That's a great present." Ruth set the bottle on the table and took Nora's coat. She had always wanted one of those shearling coats, but could never justify spending the money on one, not when a down jacket was a fraction of the price and kept her just as warm.

"What a wonderful place," Nora said. "Did your family run it as an inn?"

"My grandmother did."

"It has character."

"Is that a nice way of saying it's run down?"

"No, not at all." Nora glanced into the living room and down the hall toward the bedrooms with an appraising eye. "Looks like you've got plenty of space."

"There are five bedrooms downstairs and ten upstairs, but it's a bit old-fashioned. I mean, it's a real inn, not a hotel. Anyone who stayed here would get to know their next-door neighbors pretty quickly."

"Some people like that."

It did not sound like Nora would include herself in this group. Ruth went to the kitchen, turned on a burner, and dropped two pieces of butter into the frying pan.

"Is there anything I can do?" Nora asked.

"Sit down and get out of the way. That's what my mother always used to say. She wasn't one for sharing the kitchen."

"And you take after her?"

"No, actually, I don't. Not at all. You can make the toast if you want."

Nora went to the other end of the counter and put two pieces of bread in the toaster. "I didn't take after my mother, either."

They exchanged a quick glance as Ruth placed the sliced peppers in the frying pan. She knew what Nora meant. Lesbians never took after their mothers, or rarely did.

"She disapproved of you?" Ruth asked.

"Not when I was married. That was fine. After my husband died. She wanted me to get remarried, but I didn't of course. There were plenty of other conflicts. Even as a girl, I was known for being a bit wild. I was never the prim little girl my mother wanted."

"Neither was I. Fortunately my older sister wanted to wear dresses and patent leather shoes. She made my mother happy."

"And you refused to wear patent leather shoes?"

"Whenever I could. Growing up in the sixties was really like growing up in the fifties, in Connecticut at least. Everybody was still wearing those bouffant hairdos. We went to church every Sunday in our little dresses with the smocking across the front. I actually had a pair of white gloves for Easter."

"My mother was still wearing a corset when I was a girl. She couldn't vote until women got the right when she was in her thirties."

Ruth added the eggs and cheese to the frying pan and watched as bubbles formed across the top of the yellow liquid. "We've come a long way, baby, huh?"

"Yes and no. Do you want the toast buttered?"

"Sure." Ruth slid the plate of butter down the counter.

Nora opened cupboards until she found a plate for the toast. "I envy women like you," she said. "You can do anything. It wasn't like that for us."

"What would you have done?"

"I don't know. Become an airplane pilot. Run a business."

"You can still do those things."

Nora carried the toast to the table and shook her head. "I'm too old."

"Have you been painting?" Ruth flipped the omelets.

"Not since the fire, but I'll start again now. I finally got the smell out of the cottage."

Ruth let the omelet cook another couple of minutes, then served it onto two plates and brought it to the table. "Are you going to stay all winter?"

"I don't know. I'm at a crossroads of sorts."

Ruth took a seat across from Nora and reached for her fork. Ruth said, "What kind of a crossroads?"

Nora paused with the fork poised over her plate. "I've spent my life waiting for someone, it seems, I shouldn't have waited for. Foolish, I guess." She flashed a smile. "And you? Are you staying through the winter?"

"I'm not sure. I'd like to stay as long as the photos are going well."

"They're going well, I take it?"

"At the moment, yes."

"You promised you would show them to me."

Ruth nodded as she reached for a piece of toast. The sound of her chewing seemed suddenly too loud. She wanted to ask Nora about her friend, the one she had waited for, but she sensed Nora was not willing to say more.

"It's funny, the two of us ending up on this island," Ruth said.

Nora took a piece of toast without meeting her gaze. "We're not the sort of people you'd expect to find here?"

"No."

Nora, eyebrows raised, gave her a look that said, all right, I admit it, you've found me out. "It's one of the stranger places I've ever been."

"Yes, and one of the more beautiful."

Ruth reached for her juice glass and raised it in a toast. Nora clinked her glass against Ruth's.

"Alice has invited me to her Christmas party this afternoon," Ruth said. "I'm sure she wouldn't mind if you came."

"Oh, no, I couldn't do that—"

"It's a sort of open house. She invites everyone on the island. You should come, really."

"Well, if you don't think I'd be crashing."

"No. Everyone goes."

"Alice has spent her whole life on Snow, hasn't she?"

"Yes. She's a true islander. Her mother and my mother were friends when they were teenagers."

"And she's always run the store?"

"Since she was ten or so, when her mother bought the place. Well, her mother ran it, then Alice took the place over when she and Brock got married. But my mother always used to say that Alice was the brains behind the operation."

"She seems to be the brains behind everything—the post office, the store. Don't you wonder what she might have done if she hadn't lived her whole life on an island?"

Ruth considered the other ways Alice could have spent her life, but she could not imagine her anywhere else. She was about to say that Alice appeared happy enough, then stopped herself. She wasn't sure this was an accurate representation of Alice, or of anyone for that matter.

They sat in silence, empty plates in front of them. They should move on, it seemed, to the next step, either in the day or in their knowing of each other, but whatever might be about to unfold remained unclear.

"I'll do the dishes," Nora said as she rose from the chair.

Ruth watched her gather the dishes and carry them to the sink, grateful for the help and the company. This was not a day to be spent alone, she had to admit, despite what she might have thought.

Chapter Thirty-four

She knelt over him, her long hair brushing his face. He struggled to make out her features, and then he recognized her as one of the girls from the whorehouse in the village. He reached up to touch her, confused. I never did this, he thought. I never paid for any of those girls. She was remarkably beautiful, her fingers floating above him, bird-like. He took her hand and guided it over his chest, down to his groin. Her robe opened, revealing breasts much larger and fuller than he had expected. She leaned down to kiss him, and he felt her hands at his throat, cutting off the air. He thrashed from side to side, but her legs remained clamped in place, holding him down. Then he saw that the person was not a woman, but a man in uniform. The woman's hands weren't big enough to strangle him, but the soldier's were. He grabbed the soldier by the wrists, wrenched free, and woke gulping air.

When he opened his eyes, Nick felt his heart rattling in his chest and saw the miniature Christmas tree across the room, lights winking on and off. He wanted to seize the thing and toss it out into the snow. He forced himself to breathe slowly, one panicked gasp at a time, and pressed his damp palms against the thick cloth of his jeans. He had not intended to fall asleep. He meant just to listen to some jazz, an antidote to the endless syrup of Christmas music, and read the newspaper, which he found now on the floor beside the couch, the pages unfurled like paper flags.

Nick went to the kitchen and leaned on the counter. The clock over the sink told him it was three. He was due back at his parents' in half an hour for the party. He had never slept with any of the Vietnamese girls. They were too child-like, and besides, it was too risky. They had strains of clap over there that left you close to dead. He used to go to the village near the base and buy a soda at the whorehouse, and sit out front with the girls. He would give them money just for sitting there, being company, but that was all. He couldn't remember the last time he thought of those girls with their stick-thin bodies and iridescent hair hanging down their backs. He knew the soldier in the dream, of course—his old friend, the lieutenant.

Snow still dusted the ground outside. The hand-sized tracks of the geese led off to the marsh. He opened the refrigerator, grabbed a beer, and took a drink. The summer when he came back from Vietnam, before he went off to college, he had brought one of the waitresses from the diner home one night. They lay on the back porch of the triple decker on an old mattress, naked at four in the morning, the heat bathing them in sweat. She reminded him of the Vietnamese girls, thin as a boy, with pointy little breasts that poked up from her chest in an almost comical fashion. He had not seen many women naked and didn't know what to expect. He remembered the surprise of discovering how quirky and unique an actual body could be. She was nothing like the fantasy women in the magazines. They fumbled their way through sex, both of them hesitant and clumsy, and when it was over, he told her in a whisper that he had just returned from Vietnam. He could no longer remember her name, but he could still see the repulsion and fear in her eyes as she pulled away from him.

She wrapped the sheet around her, as though she no longer wanted to be naked in front of him. "Did you kill anyone?" she said.

No, he said, he didn't kill anyone, but as soon as the words left his mouth to hang in the humid air, he knew they were a lie. In that moment, when the woman stepped from the mattress and pulled on her clothes, he understood. He had killed the lieutenant, though no court would convict him of the crime. He lived in a haze of music and marijuana those first months back from Vietnam, but with her question, so direct and unexpected, the waitress pointed a finger at the heart of the story. He could not claim he had never killed a man.

She was the first person to ask the question, but not the last. People seemed to think they had a right to know. For the guys at the hut, it was a matter of how many gooks he got. For his mother, who asked the question when he came home the first time, and grasped his hand while tears ran down her face, it was a need to make certain he was still the same. For the nameless waitress at the diner, who never spoke to him again after that night, it was an accusation. He quickly learned there was no right answer.

Ten of them went into the village that morning with the lieutenant. As soon as the chopper lifted off, taking the lieutenant away, it was over. They returned to base and went to eat in the mess tent. "That was some strange shit," one of the guys said as they shuffled down the chow line.

"Yeah, it was," Nick responded.

Those were the only words he had ever spoken about what happened.

The official story boiled it down to a few palatable essentials. They were surrounded by guerillas, and Jankins stepped on a mine in the confusion. The men fought off the guerillas and bravely got the lieutenant out. That's how the Army reported it. There had been times over the years when Nick had considered trying to track down the lieutenant's family. If he told them the truth, maybe the lieutenant would leave him alone.

He drank the beer fast, downing the bottle. The hammering action of his heart slowed, and the ringing in his ears lessened. He thought of smoking a joint, but decided that was not a good idea, not with the Christmas party looming.

Once he had gone to the library on the mainland and searched through a collection of Oklahoma phonebooks, but he had found no listing for Jankins, and the more he thought about it, the less sure he was that he had the lieutenant's hometown, or even the state, right. He played the scene over in his mind: the initial phone call, the drive to a house out on the prairie in a rented car, the looks on the faces of the bereaved parents when he told them that their son died kicking a rigged Coke can like an idiot while the men stood by and watched. A fragging, for all intents and purposes. Jankins wasn't the first officer to be killed, intentionally or otherwise, by his men, and he certainly wasn't the last. After a while, the idea of telling Jankins' family the truth struck Nick as just another cliché. He wasn't able, in the end, to convince himself it would make any difference. What was the point of doing something so cruel? Let the parents believe their son died in some noble way, for some noble cause.

He set the beer bottle by the sink. His mother had asked him to come early, so he would be there to greet the guests. As if such formalities mattered on the island. But it was a day when even the islanders put on a little show of knowing how to observe special occasions. He took another beer from the refrigerator for the ride and headed out.

The geese stretched out their long necks and swiveled their heads back and forth. The buttons of their black eyes, fixed on him, made him nervous, but after a few squawks, they settled back down by the bushes. If they noticed the snow beneath them, they gave no sign.

It had looked like it might clear earlier, but now the sky had that flat hue again. He uncapped the beer and chugged half the bottle as he steered the truck over the rutted road. When he reached his parents' house, he chugged the rest before going inside.

"Nick, is that you?" his mother called from the kitchen.

The house felt uncomfortably warm already. "Silent Night" was playing on the boom box. The Bing Crosby version was so canned and corny it sounded fresh somehow.

"Put your coat in the downstairs bedroom," his mother called.

Nick did as he was told. Before he reached the kitchen, he met his very pregnant sister carrying a plate of sliced turkey to the table.

"I see you dressed," Ellen said.

Nick glanced down at his jeans and rumpled shirt. "Yeah, these are my dress jeans."

She arched her eyebrows. "Nice."

He went to the kitchen, determined to ignore Ellen, who did nothing but criticize no matter what he did. He found his mother wearing an apron splattered with what looked like blueberry juice, an anxious expression on her face.

"This pie should be done," she muttered as she leaned down to open the oven door.

"I can get it," Nick said.

He took the pot holders from her and slid the pie out of the oven and onto the counter. Alice eyed it suspiciously.

"It looks done," he said.

"Yes, I'm just afraid it's too runny."

"Why'd you make a pie?"

"I've got so many frozen blueberries. I made a cake, and there's plenty of cookies, but then I thought it didn't look like enough."

The counter was covered with plates of food—sliced bread, deviled eggs, frosted Christmas cookies. Beads of sweat lined the skin above Alice's lips. He didn't know why she insisted on throwing this party year after year, but he could imagine what she would say if he questioned her. It's a tradition, and what would people like Silas Wardell do on Christmas if they didn't come to her party?

"Looks like you've outdone yourself, Mom," he said.

She glanced at the clock and untied the apron. "People will be here any minute." She raised her hands to her head, as if trying to tame the hair that stood out in frizzy wisps. "Your father's still asleep. Could you wake him?"

Nick was all too happy to leave the overheated kitchen to his sister and mother. He climbed the stairs to the second floor and heard his father's snoring down the hall. He stood in the doorway of the bedroom, reluctant to go in. Brock lay on his back on the double bed in his clothes, his belly rising and falling, his mouth hanging open.

His mother's flannel nightgown was draped next to a pair of his father's green work pants on a straight chair beside the bed. He looked away from what seemed suddenly like an intimate scene. He couldn't say when he had last entered his parents' bedroom.

Nick sat down on the edge of the bed with the hope that this would rouse his father. Presents they had opened that morning sat in a pile in one corner—a gardening book for his mother, a flannel shirt for his father, a bottle of fancy hand lotion with a box of soaps in a matching scent. The pile of objects seemed to be rebuking him, accusing him of thinking less of his parents and their small lives than they deserved.

He thought of the conversation with his mother about Pete Giberson and felt ashamed. He only put her on the spot like that to draw attention away from what he might have been doing out at the mansion when the fire started. He had no right to question her about Pete or to judge her. Maybe it would be an overstatement to claim that his parents had a happy marriage (he wasn't sure such a thing existed), but they were content enough, friends who knew each other well and could live with where they had ended up. When he was younger, he would have found such a relationship, with its lack of mystery and romance, appalling. Now he understood that it was an achievement. If his mother still carried a small flame for Pete Giberson, she was entitled to it.

Nick placed his hand on his father's shoulder and shook him gently. "Dad, wake up."

Brock turned his head from side to side like a startled deer. "What?" he said loudly.

"The party, Dad. It's time for the party."

"I didn't mean to sleep so long," Brock said as he swung his legs over the side of the bed.

"Yeah, I fell asleep myself."

"Wears a person right out, Christmas, doesn't it?" Brock ran his hands through his thinning hair and smiled. "I'll be down in a minute. Your mother's in a lather, isn't she?"

Nick nodded. "She's made twice as much food as she needed to."

"That's your mother."

"You think we could ever talk her out of doing this party?"

"No. She'll be throwing this party when she's ninety."

Nick suspected his father was right. He reached down, took Brock by the elbow, and helped him to his feet.

"Guess I better make myself presentable, huh?" Brock said.

Nick nodded and made his way out of the room. When he glanced back, he saw his father pulling up a pair of suspenders to keep his pants in place. They weren't the faded green ones he usually wore, but a special pair in a bright red plaid.

Downstairs a knock sounded on the front door. The party had begun, on cue. He met Alex, Ellen's husband, emerging from the bathroom.

"Merry Christmas," Nick said in a sardonic tone.

Alex smiled. "Be nice."

Nick found Mary Lou Danks and her husband downstairs, bundled in their winter coats and hats and gloves. It hadn't occurred to him that they would show up. Mary Lou gave him a brusque hello and pushed past him. Stu regarded him with a tired and confused look before surrendering his coat. Nick answered the repeated knocks on the door and carried coats to the front bedroom, and watched his mother greet the guests and bustle back and forth to the kitchen. She did not appear frazzled now. She was calm, almost radiant.

Silas Wardell, who had walked from his place near the dump, shook the remnants of snow from his boots and lumbered across the living room trailing pools of water. The room was close to full when Nick opened the door to find Rachel and Eddie and their son and daughter on the stoop. Eddie took care of the awkward moment, as he so often did, by slapping Nick on the back. "Ho, ho, ho," he boomed.

Nick exchanged a quick glance with Rachel. "He's the original Santa," the daughter said, rolling her eyes.

They all piled their coats in Nick's arms. He avoided meeting Rachel's gaze again. He felt like the hired help, an afterthought, as he carried the coats into the bedroom. He was dumping the coats on the bed, thinking he could just slip out the kitchen door right now without saying a word to anyone, when he sensed someone behind him.

"Nick," Rachel said, her voice low.

She was wearing a bright red sweater dotted with white snowflakes that made her look like an old lady.

"How are you?" she said.

"Fine."

"We miss you at the schoolhouse."

We? Who was she including, the Hershel and Manning kids? He

didn't think they missed him.

"It's…not the same," she said.

She gazed up at him, like she was giving him some sort of gift. Are you insane? he thought.

"I'm pretty busy with my other jobs," he said in a tone that sounded wooden even to him.

"It's good you've got work, with the economy so bad and everything."

"Yeah, well, the summer people have still got some money to spend."

"I'm glad."

He thought that she was going to reach out to him, take his hand or give him a hug, but the moment passed. She held his look, her eyes full of words that would not be spoken, and turned away. He remained there by the bed until she was swallowed up by the nervous chatter of the party in the other room.

Chapter Thirty-five

"We could walk," Ruth said. "It's not that cold."

"No, it's not. The air is quite nice," Nora said.

"Oh, I almost forgot. The cookies."

Ruth went to the kitchen and returned with one of those blue tins of butter cookies that were stacked by the checkout in the supermarkets this time of year. She pulled on her puffy down jacket and a hat that hugged her head, so only a couple of strands of hair showed, plastered to her forehead. She reminded Nora of Mary Martin playing Peter Pan.

The water stretched beyond the beach, placid and devoid of color. It was hard to remember the reflective blue of its sparkling surface earlier in the fall. Nora had dreaded this day, afraid of being alone and missing Isabelle more than she could say, but it had turned into an adventure of sorts thanks to Ruth.

"So where's your girlfriend today?" Nora asked as they walked down the road.

Ruth gave her a sidelong glance, as though surprised to hear her use the word. Nora was uncertain whether she had said the right thing (was partner, which sounded so clinical, the preferred term?).

"With her family. She'll be here for New Year's. We've never spent Christmas together."

"Would you like to?"

"Of course. I'd like to get married, too, but that's not going to happen."

"You mean because it can't happen?"

"Right."

Ruth gazed off at the water. Nora understood her resentment and anger, even shared it in a vague way, though she could not imagine walking down the aisle with another woman. Such gestures struck her as unnecessary, even dangerous. It was enough for two women to find each other and carve out a little peace and privacy if they could.

"Does your family know?" Nora said.

"You mean about me and Liza? Yes, but my mother pretends she doesn't. I told her I was gay a long time ago. I don't think it computed. She just couldn't accept it. We've never talked about it again. She refers to Liza as my roommate. My sister is fine with it, but with my parents, we avoid the whole thing."

"That's a challenge."

"Everything about my mother is a challenge. My father just tries not to stir up any trouble."

Nora imagined having a conversation with her own mother about being a lesbian. It was inconceivable. Though of course her mother must have known that such people existed, they did not exist in her circles. Her mother went to her grave convinced, Nora was certain, that she had never known anyone who was gay. But what did it mean to be "gay," beyond the mechanics of sex? When her mother was alive, Nora would not have described herself as a lesbian, even though she had slept with women. As a category, it barely registered in her mind, either.

"Things have changed so much," Nora said. "At least you could tell your mother, even if she couldn't accept it. I couldn't tell anyone."

The words were out before Nora realized what she had said. This time, Ruth simply nodded her head, as though she had just been waiting for the spoken confirmation of what she already knew. There was no need, she seemed to be saying, for a reaction. Nora felt quietly grateful.

"Things have changed," Ruth said. "But not enough."

Now it was Nora's turn to nod in mute acknowledgment.

They reached the dock and turned up the hill to Alice's house, past the white church that stood out against the darkening sky. Nora wished that they were not going to the party. She steeled herself for the prospect of being with people, too many of them.

The house was nondescript, like countless others on the island, a small box-like place with wings that had been added haphazardly, giving it a thrown together look. They knocked and waited outside the door. Nick appeared after a moment on the other side. He was clearly startled to see them, or at least to see Nora standing behind Ruth.

"I brought a friend," Ruth said. "I hope that's okay."

"The more, the merrier," he said.

They remained in their places, Nick on one side of the door, Ruth and Nora on the other. She could not read the look that darted between Nick and Ruth. They both appeared nervous. Something, she thought, has gone on between these two.

Ruth handed the cookie tin to Nick. "Merry Christmas."

He looked down at the tin as if he couldn't think what he was supposed to do with it, then ushered them inside and took their coats. The room was crowded with people standing in twos and threes, cups and plates in their hands; an assortment of children wandered among the adults. A Christmas tree festooned with old-fashioned flashing bulbs and gobs of fake tinsel stood in the corner. It was exactly what Nora had expected, an overdone thing in the worst of taste.

"It's a bit of a madhouse," Nick said. "Help yourselves to some food."

He nodded in the direction of a table covered in platters and disappeared with their coats. They stood by the door, hesitating, but then Alice threaded through the throng.

"Mrs. Venable," she said, obviously flustered. "I'm so glad you came."

"We ran into each other on the beach this morning," Ruth said. "I invited her."

"Good," Alice said, without much conviction.

Nora thanked Alice, hardly aware of the automatic words she was speaking, and added something about how festive the house looked.

Alice smiled bashfully, almost girl-like despite the gray hair in a braid down her back. "I love Christmas. It's my favorite holiday."

"I can tell," Nora said, taking in the Santa figurine on top of a bookcase and another tableau of little china snowmen.

Nick returned with the cookie tin and handed it to Alice. "Ruth brought these."

"Oh, thank you," Alice said to Ruth. "How nice. I'll put them right out."

Alice bustled off with the tin, but Nick remained beside them. The three of them stood in silence, looking not at each other but at the people ranged before them. Nora thought how parties were the same everywhere, no matter how tasteful, or distasteful, the decorations. People stood awkwardly, searching for something to say until they could bear it no longer and moved on in the hope of finding a better fit with someone else.

Ruth was the one to break the quiet. "It was nice to get a white Christmas."

"Yeah, we don't get much snow out here, surrounded by the water," Nick said.

"You've got your own micro-climate," Nora said.

"Something like that."

Behind them came the sound of a rap on the door.

"Duty calls," Nick said, and left them alone at the edge of the crowd.

Nora followed Ruth to the food tables and surveyed the array of offerings. The cookies appeared to be homemade. The tin Ruth had brought was not in evidence. "What's that?" she said, pointing to the punch bowl.

"I think it's mulled cider," Ruth said.

Mulled cider. How quaint. Everything about this gathering was quaint, and vaguely tacky. It was, Nora told herself, rather wonderful in its way. She thought of Gerald, who would not have been able to attend a party like this. He could hire the islanders, but he could not socialize with them. She was glad that the world, or at least her corner of it, was more democratic now. People like Gerald still held power, but not as absolutely. Millions of Americans, who lived perfectly legitimate and even vital lives, had never seen the inside of a country club and could care less if they ever did. Perhaps this represented some sort of progress.

Nora helped herself to a cup of mulled cider and frosted cookies in the shape of stars, which tasted like something from her childhood, rich with butter and gritty with sugar. She searched the room but did not see Fred Hershel or his family. That, at least, was over. The boys had apologized and were doing odd jobs to raise money to repay her for all the things she had to replace in the cottage.

Alice's husband, a tall man with a big gut, came over and wished them a Merry Christmas. Clearly the politically correct prohibition on this greeting did not exist on the island. Nora supposed Snow Island had never been home to many Jews.

"You still planning on building a house down there where the mansion was?" Brock asked Nora.

He towered over her in his bright red flannel shirt and plaid suspenders like a lumberjack. Nora had to step back to take him in. "I'm thinking about it. Maybe in the spring."

"And what about you?" Brock turned toward Ruth. "Are you going to get the inn open again?"

"I don't know. I need to win the lottery or rob a bank."

"Yeah, that place ain't been touched in a long time. She was a sweet woman, your aunt, but she wasn't much for maintenance."

"No, she wasn't," Ruth agreed.

Ruth and Brock continued to talk about Ruth's aunt and the condition of the inn. Nora sipped her cider, feeling absurdly self-conscious in her calf-length wool skirt and heeled boots. She had intentionally dressed down, but she stood out nonetheless among all the women wearing blue jeans and bulky sweatshirts.

When Brock had moved off, Ruth said, "We don't have to stay long."

"No, I'm having a good time." Nora was aware that her assertion did not sound particularly convincing, though she did truly believe she was better off standing here drinking mulled cider than back at the cottage by herself. She took another cookie and attempted to eat it without spilling powered sugar on her sweater.

A number of people stopped to introduce themselves and to ask how Nora was getting on. After some head-shaking over the fire, and a few awkward pauses, they moved on. Nora felt that she and Ruth were marooned in the middle of the crowd, marked off like an exhibit of freaks in the circus. She tried to be friendly, but there seemed to be little she could do to dispel the discomfort she clearly elicited.

After another cup of cider and a piece of pumpkin bread, Nora turned to Ruth and said, "Had enough?"

Ruth nodded.

Others had already left, back to their family celebrations or whatever it was the islanders did with the holiday. They found the bedroom where the coats were piled without bothering Nick again and said their good-byes to Alice and Brock. They stepped outside into a darkness deeper than Nora thought she had ever known. With the cover of clouds, no moon or stars were visible; not even the winking lights of the mainland shone tonight.

They went down the hill in silence, casting off the noise and heat of the party. Nora pulled the scarf tight around her neck. The wind came off the water with a biting force.

"I didn't know you were thinking of opening the inn," Nora said as they turned onto Bay Avenue.

"I'm not sure I am. The place needs so much work, and my sister wants to sell it. I may have to buy her out."

"What will that cost?"

"Nobody has any idea what the place is worth. There aren't exactly a lot of properties to compare it with. Maybe two hundred thousand."

Nora could only assume that Ruth did not have access to such resources. "That's a lot of money."

"For a 'sentimental attachment,' as my sister puts it, yes."

"Maybe it's a good investment."

"Maybe, but I'll have to buy my sister out and come up with the money to renovate the place."

"And you'd do all that for a sentimental attachment?"

"I love the place."

They walked on a ways before Nora spoke again. "I can see why."

When they reached the inn, Nora declined Ruth's invitation to come inside. She wanted, with a sudden ferocity, to be alone. The lighthouse beam swung over the road as she drove away. She could just make out the water beyond the shore.

Chapter Thirty-six

Mornings were her best time, when she set off for a walk to the beach, and then returned to spend a couple of hours painting. In the afternoons and evenings, she lost the thread of her new life. She found herself making one cup of tea after another and listlessly paging through books she did not want to read. Today, she decided, the hours would unfold differently. Once she returned from her walk, she would make some calls to the mainland and set up appointments. She was ready to start on the plans for the new house.

The sun shone on the water, crisp and bright. Nora wrapped the scarf around her neck and set off on the path she had cleared through the snow. The white expanse hurt her eyes, but she was glad for the snowfall that had, at last, concealed the black ground and the debris from the fire. The cottage was surrounded by a clean slate that seemed to beg for the construction of something new.

She strode quickly down the road, welcoming the feel of the cold air on her face. She had almost reached the turn-off to the beach when she saw a car approaching. She stepped to the edge of the road to let the car pass, but then she realized she knew the car and the familiar features of the person behind the wheel. Nora remained fixed at the side of the road. This unannounced arrival had the character of a dream.

Isabelle brought the car to a stop and rolled down the window. "I thought I'd find you here."

"Here on the island or here at the beach?"

"Both, actually."

Without saying more, Isabelle pulled the car into the turn-off. Nora met her there.

They stood on the sandy path just beyond the car, neither of them speaking for a moment. Nora was not at all sure how she was supposed to respond. As if understanding this, Isabelle reached out and linked her arm through Nora's. "Should we continue your walk?" she said.

They moved on down the path to the beach. When the water came into view, Nora said, "When did you get back?"

"Yesterday."

"I thought you were staying until February."

"I changed my mind. I thought it would be nice to spend New Year's on a deserted island."

Isabelle gave her a mischievous smile, which only made Nora angry, though she tried not to show it.

"Heather didn't mind your leaving?" Nora said.

"No. In fact, she encouraged me to go. She said I was getting to be a mopey old grandmother mooning around the house. She and the kids would rather have me breeze in for a week and breeze out."

"You didn't like Chicago?"

"I liked Chicago fine, but I missed you."

They came to the edge of the water. Isabelle kept her arm linked through Nora's and pulled her in close.

Isabelle had made the pronouncement about missing Nora as though she should be congratulated for it, but Nora was in no mood to do so. After a couple of silent minutes, though, she softened. "I missed you, too," she said.

Isabelle turned, wrapped her arms around Nora, and kissed her. It was, Nora realized, the first time they had ever kissed in public, out in the open air, under the sun.

"I'm going to put the house on the market," Isabelle said when they broke apart. "Are you still looking for a roommate?"

Nora smiled. "No. I'm looking for a wife."

Isabelle leaned forward and gave her an affectionate peck on the lips.

They made their way back up the beach, arms linked, and got into the car. Isabelle rattled on about the grandchildren and the weather in Chicago, one monstrous snowstorm after another. She was determined, it was clear, to show Nora that she had changed. She was breezy and cheerful and apparently unconcerned about all the things that in the past had loomed as such obstacles. When they reached the cottage, she produced bags of groceries from the trunk of the car.

"You've got enough food for a month it looks like," Nora said.

"Then we can stay for a month if we like."

Nora took two of the bags and made her way along the path, uncertain whether she was ready for this new Isabelle.

As they stood side by side at the table inside the cottage, taking cans of soup and cartons of milk and juice from the paper bags, Nora was consumed by one wave of resentment after another. Was she simply going to let Isabelle waltz back onto the stage as if nothing had happened?

Isabelle took charge of the groceries that needed to be refrigerated while Nora set the rest of the purchases in the cupboard. It was only then, when they had finished this task, that Nora noticed Isabelle was wearing the cashmere sweater she had given her the last time they were together. She wasn't sure that the sweater, like a flag Isabelle silently waved, constituted enough of an apology.

"How about some tea?" Isabelle said.

Nora motioned toward the cupboard to indicate where the tea bags were kept. Isabelle fluttered about the small room, filling the tea kettle and setting it on the stove, taking down the china teapot and two cups. Nora remained standing, a still point in the center of Isabelle's happy rush of movement, until the kettle began to whistle. She went to the stove and turned off the burner.

"Sit," Isabelle said. "I'll pour the tea."

Isabelle placed her hand on Nora's shoulder and guided her to the chair, as though, Nora thought, she had become an invalid in Isabelle's absence. She had to admit that this was not far from the truth. She was ready to be taken care of, even pampered.

Isabelle washed out the teapot with warm water at the sink. Nora had to smile as she watched her go through the careful ritual of making tea the correct way, with the pot warmed in advance and the boiling water poured over the tea bags. She never bothered with such details; she rarely used the teapot, in fact, but Isabelle took the same amount of time with the preparation whether she was making tea for herself or for a crowd. Nora recognized, with a pang of mingled hurt and hope, that she loved Isabelle for this.

When Isabelle was seated, the teapot and sugar bowl and creamer arranged just so, she reached across the table and placed her hand on top of Nora's. "I wanted to surprise you."

"You succeeded."

"Good. You're not easy to surprise, you know."

Nora supposed she had made a point throughout her life of surprising others and seeing that they could not surprise her, though Gerald had, of anyone, been the most capable of taking her on in this game. She often thought of his death as his last unpredictable act.

"Is that tiresome, not being able to surprise me?" Nora said.

"No. It's endearing. And a little bit of a challenge."

Isabelle poured the tea and sat there swirling the spoon back and forth in her cup. Nora studied her with the sense that her entire life had collapsed into this moment. In the tilt of Isabelle's head and the precise movement of her hand, in the lined skin of her face and wispy hair, it was all present: Gerald and then his loss, Henry and the children, the card games and swims in Maine, the years when she and Isabelle had their fleeting times together and the years when they did not, the dinners for ten around candlelit tables, the cigarettes smoked behind the bushes in the backyard. How unbelievable it all seemed now, including the long deceit of their relationship. It couldn't, she saw, have been otherwise.

"So when can we start building the new house?" Isabelle asked.

"I was planning to make some calls today, see about finding an architect. Nick gave me a few names. It will be a couple of months probably before they can start."

"Maybe the house could be done by the fall."

"Maybe."

"It's beautiful here in the fall."

"Yes, but it's beautiful all year. Even in winter." Nora gestured toward the window. "It snowed on Christmas. I spent the day with the photographer at the inn. Her girlfriend is coming over New Year's. Or partner. I guess that's what they say."

Isabelle took a sip of tea. "Is that what we have to call each other? 'My partner'?"

"I think Nora and Isabelle will work fine."

"I detest that term. It's not a business we're talking about."

"No, no one would run a business this way."

Isabelle laughed. "You mean so capriciously?"

"Something like that."

"Maybe it will be different now." The wistful tone in Isabelle's voice suggested she wasn't quite sure.

"You miss Henry, don't you?" Nora said.

Isabelle raised her eyes to meet Nora's. "I've missed him for a long time, since he got sick. He wasn't really there these last years."

Nora took a drink of her tea. It seemed she should say more, but at the same time, there was nothing more to be said. Isabelle rose from the table and took the cups and teapot to the sink. When she had finished doing the dishes, she turned with that brisk look on her face again and said, "Where are the numbers for those architects?"

"In the bedroom. I'll get them."

Nora stepped over Isabelle's suitcase and rummaged among the piles of paper on the dresser. She held the list of phone numbers in her hand, staring at the numbers and names down the page as though reading an account of someone else's life, though maybe it had been her life all along.

Chapter Thirty-seven

"They moved the lighthouse," Ruth said. "When I was fourteen. Joan and I carved our initials in the wet concrete."

She unfurled the blanket and set it by the base of the lighthouse. Liza waited until the blanket was arranged, then placed the champagne bottle and two glasses on it.

"They're still here." Ruth traced the scratched sets of initials with her fingertip.

The beam of light moved over their heads in a slow circle. Liza sat beside Ruth, her back pressed against the base of the lighthouse.

"We used to go clamming here, on the other side of the point," Ruth said. The tide was high now, the rocks along the shore covered, but she saw it the way she remembered, at low tide, with her mother and father and sister bent over the muck pulling up clams with mud-covered hands. "The tide's wrong now."

"Wrong?" Liza said.

"For clamming. At low tide, it's a big mudflat. You drop a rock and look for the spurt the clam makes. Then you take them home and steam them up and dip them in melted butter. The best food I've ever eaten. If we got the big ones, the quahogs, we'd stuff them."

"They're kind of slimy."

"Not if you cook them right. And you have to soak them long enough to get the sand out."

"What time is it?"

Ruth peered at her watch in the dim light. "Quarter of."

"You're waiting until midnight to open that champagne?"

"Yes." She had gone to the mainland on the ferry and walked a mile to the liquor store, then spent the rest of the week rehearsing this moment, when she would pop the cork and make her announcement. Liza was not cooperating, though. She had been sullenly silent all through dinner.

"Nora came over the other night," Ruth said.

"Again? What's going on between you two?"

Ruth laughed. "She's seventy. Nothing. I think she's intrigued. She keeps asking me questions about the two of us."

"It's good of you to take her education in hand."

"Apparently she's had some long-standing affair with a woman who was married."

"That sounds promising."

"The woman's husband just died. She's pretty tight-lipped about the whole thing. I can't get much out of her."

"Getting involved with the married ones never works."

"I feel bad for her."

"I don't. That's just asking for trouble."

Ruth thought Liza could show a little more sympathy for Nora. She was ready to spill the news right now, certain it would jolt Liza out of her torpor, but she glanced at her watch and vowed she would stick to her plan. Not until midnight.

"Is there a women's dance tonight?" Ruth said.

"Yeah, Suzie and a bunch of other people rented a loft downtown. 'Womyn Ring in the New Year' or something like that they're calling it."

"Womyn with a y?"

"Of course."

"Is Lillie the DJ?"

"Probably. She's doing the whole shoe-polish hair and black finger-nails thing now. Kind of scary. She and Martie broke up."

"They broke up? God, you didn't tell me. When?"

"Last month sometime. I ran into her on Prince Street, and she told me she moved. I wouldn't have known otherwise. I don't think they're broadcasting it around."

"They were always so…"

"Butch?"

"Well, yes, but also inseparable. You never saw one without the other."

Ruth waited for Liza to say more, but she continued to stare out at the flat surface of the water as if she were having a conversation with the ocean.

They sat in silence after that, hunched against the lighthouse. Ruth clenched her fingers inside her gloves, trying to will some warmth into them. She wondered if she had miscalculated everything somehow. She made herself sit there and listen to the hiss of the waves breaking without saying more.

When Ruth checked her watch again, it was five minutes to midnight. She peeled the wrapping from the top of the champagne bottle and kept an eye on the second hand inching around the watch dial. Three minutes, then two. She imagined that at the stroke of midnight, they might see fireworks over on the mainland, or hear someone on the island ringing bells and shouting into the cold air, but the moment came in complete silence. Thousands of people were crammed into Times Square raucously celebrating; on Snow Island the new year arrived with no notice other than the rush of water over sand.

Ruth turned and gave Liza a long kiss before popping the cork from the bottle. Liza held the glasses to catch the foaming liquid.

"To 1991," Ruth said as she lifted her glass and clinked it against Liza's. "The year when we open the Snow Inn."

Liza lifted her glass to her lips and drank. "I didn't think you wanted to stay on the island."

"The place has kind of grown on me. Nora says she'll lend us the money."

"You're kidding."

"Apparently she's loaded."

"How much money are you talking about?"

"We didn't get into details. She just said she could loan me enough to repair the roof and do some of the renovations if we want to open the inn."

"What about your sister?"

"Maybe we can get her to give us a couple of years, see if we can get the inn going, then buy her out."

"You're serious. You want to do this." Liza took a drink of the champagne, still gazing out at the water.

"This is what you wanted," Ruth said.

"Yeah, but I've got to tell you something."

Ruth waited through the long pause until Liza spoke again.

"I fooled around with Melissa." Liza took a gulp of champagne. "It was totally stupid. I'm sorry."

"Fooled around? What exactly does that mean?"

"It was after the dance two weeks ago. We were both drunk. She asked me to walk her home, and I said okay, and…neither of us were planning it or anything."

"You slept with her."

"No. We just made out. She tried to get me to stay, but I didn't."

Just made out. Ruth was not sure *just* was the appropriate word choice, though at the same time, she felt an uneasy sense of relief. "So how was it?"

Liza did not answer.

"I mean it. How was it? Is she a good kisser?"

"I was drunk."

"So?"

"I don't know. I don't remember." Liza's face was set in pained defiance. "I'm not interested in Melissa, and she's not interested in me."

"Then why did you make out with her?"

"It was just one of those stupid things in the moment. I thought you'd at least appreciate the fact I told you."

Later Ruth might appreciate Liza's honesty, but for now she would have preferred not knowing. "What the hell were you drinking?"

"Tequila shots."

"Tequila shots. That's very mature."

"Martie started it. I don't know what I was thinking. It was like we were all back in high school."

"And Melissa was the cheerleader you couldn't resist?"

Liza rested her head on her knees and did not answer.

"So how hot is she?"

Liza remained with her head down. "You're the one who went away. You're the one who decided to stay here without even consulting me."

Ruth was ready to respond that this didn't give Liza a license to cheat on her, but she stopped herself. Instead, she put her arm around Liza, who received the gesture with a stiff indifference, and said, "I guess I should tell you that I let that Nick guy kiss me."

Liza lifted her head. "He kissed you?"

"He came over, and I walked on his back, and he kissed me." Ruth didn't see any point in mentioning the other encounter when she groped in his pants, and he bolted out the door.

"What do you mean, you walked on his back?"

"He has back problems. He asked me to walk on his back."

"That is really weird. Are you attracted to him?"

"Are you attracted to Melissa?"

There was a pause before Liza answered, "No, not really."

"I'm not really attracted to Nick, either."

"There's kind of an important difference." Liza downed some champagne. "Melissa's a woman."

"Which makes it okay for you to fool around with her?"

"Maybe I could understand you being attracted to another woman. I can't understand how you could be attracted to a man."

Ruth held Liza's gaze. "I don't think it matters whether it's a man or a woman."

"Really? You might fall in love with a man tomorrow just as easily as a woman?"

"Theoretically, but that's probably not going to happen."

"Because?"

"Because I'm in love with you."

Tears pooled at the corners of Liza's eyes. "Jesus, this is quite a night for revelations. How could you have kissed that guy? He's like a con-struction worker or something."

"Yeah, it was strange. And like you said—stupid."

"You better pour me some more." Liza held out her glass.

When Ruth tipped the bottle, the champagne glowed as it filled the glass, bubbling with luminescence. She filled her own glass and raised it.

Liza brushed away the tears with the flat of her hand. "So we're going to open a dyke inn on Snow Island."

"Looks like it."

They drained their glasses and got to their feet. The path was a white swath cut through the dark. Ruth draped the blanket over her shoulder and gripped the glass by its stem while Liza retrieved the bottle. They made their way unsteadily back to the inn, shoulders knocking against each other. Above them, the beam from the lighthouse circled, so low it seemed to brush the tops of their heads.

EPILOGUE
January

Rachel opened the door, stepped into the warmth of the house, and leaned down to unlace her sneakers.

"They've started bombing," Eddie said.

His eyes were fixed on the television. When Rachel went to stand beside him, he reached up and squeezed her hand.

"It'll be over in a couple of days," he said.

Emily had called the day before to say that she and Matt were on their way to a demonstration in Boston against the impending war. Rachel had not repeated this news to Eddie, who would have been incensed, but she was secretly proud of her daughter.

She stood beside Eddie a moment longer before heading upstairs. As she was tugging the sweatshirt over her head, she heard a vehicle out on the road. She knew, without going to the window, that it was Nick. He often drove past on his way to the cove. She had silent conversations with the hum of the truck's engine. I'm sorry. I miss you. There's no other way.

A persistent shame dogged her, and the deep fear that even now they would be discovered. She could not deny that she had sought him out willingly, even eagerly. The person who had done this was not a woman wildly different from who she was now, though she might like to believe otherwise. She would live with this knowledge for the rest of her life.

Rachel peeled off her leggings. Downstairs, the TV broadcast droned on.

* * *

Alice turned the key in the lock and descended the porch steps with the order forms she had forgotten in her hand, certain she would find Brock up at the house where she had left him – in front of the television set, transfixed. He remembered the nightly broadcasts from Vietnam, he said, but this was different. They were watching a war start on television live.

She wished Nick had agreed to come for dinner that night, but he had begged off. Alice climbed the hill, feeling the loose stones give way beneath her feet. She should be content, she told herself, with the uneasy peace she sensed between her and Nick now. He had been contrite in recent weeks, more solicitous than usual. He had come to dinner more often.

Now that she was in her sixties, she knew the value of small things – a comfortable silence between two people, the fact of simply being present. She did not have time for grand emotions or grudges, for the frivolous waste of feeling in which she had once indulged. Her sense of what it meant to be alive was sharper and sweeter, as though the unfolding of each day were a marriage to which she had at last fully given her heart. She hoped her son would one day reach this place.

Alice crossed the road and headed up the hill. Through the window, she saw Brock seated on the couch, hands on his knees, leaning forward in anxious attention. She felt a surge of affection for him, for all the people sitting in front of television sets that night, frightened and unsure.

* * *

Nora gazed at the page of the book open in front of her. She could not concentrate on her reading tonight, even with a glass of wine beside the bed to lull her into a relaxed state. The voice of the radio announcer carried from the other room, where Isabelle remained seated at the kitchen table. Nora was glad they were on the island without a television. Hearing the news over the radio made it less hard to take.

The radio went still, and Isabelle came padding into the bedroom in her slippers.

"The war has officially started?" Nora said.

"Yes. The president said in his speech that this will not be another Vietnam."

"How reassuring."

"I guess the power's out all over Baghdad. The reporters are in the hotel. It sounds scary. "

Nora watched as Isabelle slipped off her pants. She had a bit of a belly, and her skin had gone slack in places, but the body she revealed as she stepped from underpants and bra, and wriggled into a nightgown, was not that changed from the body Nora had first loved so long ago.

Isabelle climbed beneath the covers beside Nora and reached for her own book. They remained like this, propped side by side on pillows, reading, their free hands linked together under the sheet.

* * *

George sat in his chair by the window. The television screen shone on the dresser across the room, but the rest of the room was dark. He tightened his grip on the armrests and peered into the mirror-like surface of the glass. Beyond the immediate curtain of black, he could make out the thin strip of the street along the dock behind the hotel, and farther out, the sweep of the water. He could not see the island, but he could feel it there, a speck of land nestled in the darkness.

The voice of one reporter after another came from the television with meager details about the bombing. He could not turn his head to watch. It was enough to listen, or half-listen, to their tones of hushed reverence.

His few possessions sat in cardboard boxes by the door. Only the TV and the last pieces of clothing were left. Nick and Alice would arrive in a few days to help him pack the final items and then drive him to the new place. Though he had been to visit the subsidized housing twice, he could not form a clear picture in his mind of the building or the room where he would live. When he closed his eyes, he saw the ferry approaching the dock on the island. He saw himself sitting on the bench in front of the store. He saw the children arriving in wet bathing suits, their feet covered in sand, to buy popsicles. Sometimes the children had stopped to speak to him.

It was winter now, not the time to be going to the island. He could feel the cold air seeping through the window frame. He crossed his arms, pulling his sweater over his chest. He would go to the island in the spring. The place would wait for him, as it always had.

* * *

Ruth wheeled her bike across the lawn. The geese let out a smattering of squawks and settled back down. A light shone in the downstairs window, but the truck was gone. When he called to tell her the bombing had begun, Nick had said the door would be open; she could just let herself in. He couldn't watch it, but she was free to make use of his television.

Ruth felt like she was doing something illicit as she reached for the remote lying on the coffee table inside. The image came up on the screen with a map of Baghdad, the TV already tuned to CNN. "There are tracer rounds going up into the sky in the direction of the presidential palace," the reporter said, his voice laced with static but still clear. "The city is deathly quiet."

After a moment, Ruth understood that these were the voices of the reporters live from Baghdad. They could not get a video feed out, but they had a telephone connection. From one of the upper floors of the hotel, they described the planes coming in and flashes filling the sky.

She sank back on the couch, filled with dismay at the thought that she was sitting here on Snow Island, in a warm house, following the coverage as though it were a made for TV special, and yet she was riveted by the shaky voices and their strange narration. The CNN reporters holed up in the hotel sounded almost giddy, like a bunch of teenage boys calling a football game.

That morning she had taken a photograph of a shell her aunt had left perched on a windowsill at the inn. The shell, carefully balanced on the thin lip of wood, appeared translucent in the light that fell through the glass. The whole island seemed to be held in its curved lines. Now it would have to contain the light of the bombs, too.

Unable to break away, Ruth stayed in front of the television for longer than she cared to admit, mesmerized and sick at the realization that she was mesmerized. She thought Nick might return, but he did not. In the weeks since Liza's visit, she had hired Nick to put a new roof on the inn. They were friends now, friends who maintained a careful distance. She had been too hasty in judging him, she told herself, and she supposed in the end, she had confused him as much as he confused her.

The reporters in Baghdad were cracking nervous jokes, telling each other not to get too close to the window, talking about how they had missed dinner in all the excitement. Ruth rose from the couch and switched off the TV. Back in New York, she knew, Liza would stay up all night, determined to be at least a witness, but she could not watch any more. She let herself out of the house, gave the sleeping geese a last glance, and rode off.

* * *

Nick sat in the truck at the edge of the road by the twin houses, which hovered in the dark, two shadows against the winter ground. His prediction, that they would have to tear down the walls of the Priscilla Alden around George, had almost come true. The construction would begin within days of George's leaving.

Nick opened the glove compartment and removed the bag of pot. He rolled a joint, lit it, and gazed up at the stars stabbing the wide expanse of sky. He supposed he was the only one on the island studying the stars that night. Everyone else was gathered around a television set.

He smoked the joint down to the end and stubbed it out in the ashtray. He could go by the hut, but he didn't expect to find anyone there. They were all over at Cliff's watching the coverage. In the notebook he would deliver to George when he went to help him move out of the Priscilla Alden, he noted the date and the time, and wrote in the margin, "Clear skies. No moon."

He did not turn on the tape player as he pulled away from the houses and steered the truck out to the main road. He listened to the crunch of the tires moving over the frozen ground and the whistle of the wind against the windows. When he came to the fork past his house, he took the road to the cove.

The lights at the Brovellis' were on, upstairs and down, a blaze of yellow making a stand against the cold. Nick drove on to the cove, where he shut off the engine and sat staring at the wind rippling the surface of the water like a hand trying to smooth cloth. He remembered the time when he was a teenager, and he had found a deer asleep in the marsh, curled into a bed of her own making, her legs tucked beneath her. Nothing in his life since then had seemed as perfect as that deer lost in an untroubled sleep. If he stepped from the truck and followed the path into the marsh, he imagined he would find her there still, waiting for him, but he was not about to plunge into that wild landscape, in the dark or the light. He started up the truck and went back the way he had come.

* * *

A warm front blew in after midnight, and with it, the thin mist of fog. The lighthouse beam swung in a slow, continuous circle, a ghostly finger cutting through the milky air. The wind went still, the surf quiet, and the island was muffled in silence. That silence stayed unbroken until morning, save for the mournful bleat of the foghorn that woke some of the islanders, who turned in their sleep, distantly aware of a change that troubled them, and aware, too, of what remained unchanged: the small circle of land surrounding them, and the water stretching beyond its shores.

Acknowledgments

I want to thank my agent, Deborah Schneider; my editor, Pat Walsh, and my publisher, David Poindexter; and the many people who provided encouragement and help with the manuscript, especially Ilya Kaminsky, Sandell Morse, James Vescovi, Merle and Pat Drown, Paul Nichols, Meryl Soto-Schwartz, Jim Sparrell, and the late Robert Dunn.